Help The Decent People

Tajai Calip

authorHOUSE

AuthorHouse™
1663 Liberty Drive
Bloomington, IN 47403
www.authorhouse.com
Phone: 833-262-8899

Published by AuthorHouse 04/02/2025

ISBN: 979-8-8230-4427-1 (sc)
ISBN: 979-8-8230-4426-4 (e)

Library of Congress Control Number: 2025903598

Print information available on the last page.

Any people depicted in stock imagery provided by Getty Images are models, and such images are being used for illustrative purposes only. Certain stock imagery © *Getty Images.*

This book is printed on acid-free paper.

CHAPTER 1

T HE VOTES WERE IN AND Elosie was infuriated their opponent was going to win. She started stuffing ballots in the ballot box for her best friend to win the election. The group of older women that came down together every year to the voting poll reported Elosie. Elosie was being carried away by volunteers who saw her stuffing the ballot boxes. Elosie best friend surprised by what she saw followed the volunteers to calm Elosie down.

"Lock all the doors and contact the police!" yelled one of the workers working at the election polls. The voters began yelling and screaming at one another about the votes being rigged. The voters supporting Alexis Worthington demanded a recount to make sure Elosie extra votes were not counted. The police arrived. An immediate silence felled. The voters waiting to see the hell unfold picked up some of the votes Elosie tried to stuff in the ballot and threw them in the trash.

The police handcuffed Elosie after searching her belongings. Elosie was being held in a corner of the building. Elosie squirmed to get out of the handcuffs resisting arrest claiming that she was innocent. The crowd booed Elosie throwing papers at her. The police dragged her out the building kicking and screaming. Elosie was placed in the back of the police car.

The locals clapped and danced in glory to the outrageous actions of Elosie glad that she was arrested. Elosie could be seen with extra ballots falling out of her backpack with police officers reaching for the backpack closing the police door.

"Did you see what was on instagram this morning Charley? Elosie was placed under arrests for being caught stuffing the ballots. The story is all over the internet!" Leilani scrolled through her iPhone.

Charley walked over to the television with a newspaper in his hand. He put down the newspaper immediately and pulled out his cell phone from his briefcase. The arrests were on every social network public platform.

"Terry how is Alexis? Elosie must've went crazy after I left the voting booth. I congratulated Alexis because if you saw all Alexis's supporters that showed up at the voting polls she had already won the election. She came to visit the people voting and was doing what she does best. Alexis was praising the people and telling the people to vote for her. She fought to the very last day of voting. Alexis visited most of the voting polls asking people to vote for her to receive the best representation for our county."

"Charley, Alexis is going to win. The votes are still being counted. The stunt Elosie pulled to help Alexis's opponent made Alexis a for sure win. You know the instigators cannot win fairly. The people that were at the voting poll when the incident took place are reporting that Elosie assaulted a police officer. The votes for Doris Vanguard will be investigated only at that voting poll location which will not take long to make sure that the votes stuffed for Doris are not valid. I will call you tomorrow for a meeting on what the next step should be for Alexis. Tell Alexis to call me. Doris did not have anything to do with Elosie's stunt. You know Doris adores Alexis."

"I will relay the message. Talk to you soon."

The day became engrossed with inquiries once Alexis stepped into her office. She was getting phone calls after phone calls about Elosie. The next few hours conducted of paperwork, reading, signing, and setting up appointments. Alexis had not even eaten lunch before Anthony Wentforth walked into her office with a huge pile of papers.

"Alexis this was at your front office door when I was coming up. I think Brad dropped this off to you about opening the new program for the kids at the new school. The teachers want you to be a part of the program and would like your staff to speak to the kids. The curriculum has not been fully completed. The school will be open in a few weeks. The school opening happened rapidly. The parents enrolled the kids in the new school at record pace. We may have to provide a waiting list to attend the new school."

"There is a waiting list already for the new school? How many parents have you spoken to about the new program Anthony?"

"None. I gave that assignment to Jason. Jason is going to see if there are enough teachers and staff to open a second school. Jason doesn't think that the new school will be able to enroll all of the students."

"Why am I just now hearing about this? I thought I told Jason to let me know last week. I did not receive any emails about any of this. I have fifteen minutes to speak with Douglas. He is off his marbles that Margaret is the City Council Director."

"Good luck with that. We might end up seeing more news reports if Douglas is not the City Council Director."

Alexis ran out the door frantically forgetting to grab her cell phone. Alexis reached her car and Anthony was on her heels throwing her cell phone to her.

"This is for you. It's urgent."

Alexis jumped in her front seat catching the phone.

"Hello."

"Alexis you won! You are the new mayor of this hectic county! We are going to need you to come to your new office right away. This position has needed to be filled for several months. There was a delay because.....well you know the reason."

"Are you serious?! I thought I wouldn't hear anything to the end of the week."

"Do not get too thrilled. You have a lot of work ahead of you. It is not as easy as you think. We have a full house of people outside the City Hall asking all kinds of questions and going off about what is being allowed in this city. You will be occupied for a couple of hours."

Alexis had a lot of great ideas and could care less about a couple of hours although her stomach was growling. Alexis pulled up to City Hall and was quite shocked at the mob in the middle of the building looking very discouraged. People were screaming, "Free Janice. Free Janice," with signs up that showed pictures of Janice's face on some of the signs. Alexis climbed up the steps to the City Hall and people started surrounding Alexis asking her what was she going to do about what happened to Janice Cowell.

"I will need time to gather my staff and set up a meeting with you guys to discuss the development. I hear that this is very consequential. I am going to need thirty minutes. The protesters can form a line by the meeting sector. I will open the door to the City Hall meeting room for the horde to come in after we have considered the pros and cons on a few things."

The natives moved to the side for the new mayor. Alexis gathered her staff confident this was going to be a better city for the people with her in office. One lady walked up to Alexis and thanked her for seeing the bothered taxpayers on short notice. Alexis shook her head approvingly to the woman and proceeded to her office to discuss a resolution.

Alexis sat down in her new office with numerous staff members joining in. The staff started reading to Alexis what happened to Janice Cowell while Alexis retrieved a pen to take notes. Alexis's assistant Heather was very thorough with what some of the staff evaluated in the Janice Cowell case. Janice Cowell was shot by a county sheriff at the local court after Janice's father was illegally arrested. Janice stated that the sheriff mishandled her elderly father. Janice stated that her father was innocent and he was being

4

arrested without bail. Janice rushed the sheriff with a comb and started swinging wildly to release her father. The sheriff had to shoot Janice to get her off of him. Janice continued after being shot to scratch at and hit the sheriff. Three other sheriffs rushed over to Janice to try to restrain her. After several minutes, Janice was finally taken away in an ambulance with handcuffs on her. The crowd wants Janice not charged for protecting her elderly father and Janice's father released for protecting his property."

"Why was Janice's father arrested?" Alexis conferred with her staff.

Heather researched her notes. Heather quickly reviewed what was told to her and answered Alexis question based on what was reported.

"Janice's father was accused of attacking a guy who he believed stole his money from his garage. Janice's father beat the guy unconscious with his thick cane. We are not sure if the money was stolen or if there is any evidence of the guy being the one who stole the money. The judge is holding Janice's father, Kevin Cowell in custody, until the judge can read the charges and look at the evidence." Heather placed her notes back in order and waited for Alexis to gather her thoughts.

Alexis was hushed. She studied all of the notes placed in front of her. Alexis wrote down a few more updates and grabbed her second notebook to jolt down notes that she needed to cross examine. The staff waited patiently looking over complaints as Alexis worked on what she was going to do for the angry people gathered outside of her office. By the time the thirty minutes was up, Alexis was prepared to make a statement.

"Open up the meeting room and allow the people to go inside so that I can make a statement. I think I have all of the information to formulate an apt retort. If there is anything else that you guys may have for me, email me. I will speak with the sheriff's office about the conditions of Janice Cowell and Kevin Cowell."

Alexis waited for the people to sit down and get settled in before speaking. The protesters tucked away their signs under their seats discussing concerns among themselves waiting for the mayor's response. Alexis sat down at the circled table facing the protesters in the meeting room with her colleagues and adjusted her papers in front of her.

"First, I would like to say thank you to all of you that are concerned. Mistreatment is not acceptable in our community. I received some documentation on the facts as I was approaching the building. I was unaware of Janice and Kevin Cowell's circumstances. I am on my way to the sheriff's office to speak with the sheriff who was involved in the escapade. I will also speak with the staff that schedules the court cases for people who are attending the local courts. You all are welcomed to follow me to the sheriff's office. If not, I can set up another meeting to resume this misunderstanding sometime next week. We will all work together to get this contretemps commenced. If Millie Wood is in the audience, can you please stand up?"

Millie stood up and raised her hand. Millie was a tall woman, middle aged, and relieved the mayor addressed her questions about the housing on her block. It was becoming a hazard and Millie was tired of waiting for someone to do something.

Millie expressed friendliness obliging the mayor before she traipsed out with one of the representatives to finally receive cooperation where Millie lived. The representative waltzed up to Millie shaking her hand and leading Millie out of the conference room.

"Whomever is coming along, follow me." Alexis trotted toward the exit of the City Hall building on her way to her car.

The crowd followed Alexis getting in their cars giving Alexis praises for taking her oath seriously. Alexis felt great doing what she loved for her community. Alexis had a full agenda that she wanted to share with the people of the community to raise funding and help families prosper. Alexis was using some of her own money to make sure that the projects were opened to the community to stop the scams and unjust crimes in the city. Alexis and numerous protesters got out of their cars at the local sheriff's office. The head of the sheriff department was waiting for the mayor and greeted Alexis.

"I apologize for what Janice and Kevin Cowell are facing Alexis. You know that I would do anything to help resolve this unfortunate mischief. I met with the sheriff. We have him on leave to get medical attention. Billy is not going to press charges on Janice. The sheriff clearly understands that Janice was protecting her elderly father. We cannot release Janice's father until his court date. The court has to find out what happened, look at all the facts, and make the best determination. I did contact the judge and asked if he will allow Janice's father to get released on house arrest because of his heart condition. Kevin Cowell will be monitored and confined with Janice and other home care supervision so that he gets the medical attention that he deserves. The man is strong as an ox. It does appear that the guy that Janice's father was fighting did steal a large amount of money from Mr. Cowell while the caretaker was in Mr. Cowell's care. Janice's father receives additional home care because Janice works two jobs. She has to hire other home care providers for her father when she is away at work. Janice's father will not obey the doctors or take any of his medication unless he has care providers to force him to do so."

Alexis hugged the head of the sheriff department Malcolm McCarrie. Alexis's team of good people in her community knew how to operate functionally to help the people.

"Janice will be pleased. We do not want the city to get out of control with this kind of nonsense. We have to nip these kinds of setbacks in the bud." Alexis turned toward the protesters.

The protesters thanked the sheriff. The protesters piled into their cars relieved that they could support Janice and her father. Most of the protesters knew Janice and how kind she was in the neighborhood. The protesters following the crowd knew Janice and Janice's father through other people and wanted to lend a hand.

CHAPTER 2

T HE SUN WAS BEAMING BRIGHTLY. The ethnic groups were out and about enjoying barbecues at picnics at the local parks. Charley drove by the community parks on his way to his office. Charley was looking forward to spending some time in the sun with his colleagues and his wife. Every other weekend the staff had a picnic or some type of gathering to encourage one another to keep up the good work. The gatherings only took place after everyone had accomplished their goals. Charley pulled up to his job eager to finish mailing off the last responses to families making an appearance for advanced programs. The coterie wanted to throw a block party at one of the locations by the City Hall. Charley had signed off on the event to encourage people to reap the benefits of a peaceful time. The day was getting better and better as Charley grabbed all of the other letters he had to mail off and headed to the gathering to meet his colleagues. On the way out of City Hall, Charley bumped into Leilani.

"Leilani, I thought you were already gone."

"I had to grab something from your office. I left my passport and my coat in your office. I will be headed out of the country on vacation. I was tearing up my house looking for my passport and coat. I remember I left both in your office. When I go on vacation, I have one week in Paris. I'm going to Hawaii for my second week of vacation. I will contact you via email for the block party project for Cancer awareness. Alexis told me to keep you posted."

Charley and Alexis exited out of the office together. Charley's wife approached him by his car after parking her vehicle. The two were going to the event together. Leilani had her high school sweetheart in the car waiting on her. They all droved out of the parking lot headed to the function. The lake was packed with people and all sorts of food captivating Leilani. Incomers were conversing, eating, and drinking beverages. Charley and his wife blended with the festive folks. Leilani jolted out her car to someone screaming. The onlookers rushed over to look at the stranger screaming. Someone had felled into the water and was trying to call out for help flapping their arms wildly. One of Charley's colleagues quickly jumped into the lake to pull the drowning young girl out of the water. She was panicking and her head kept going back down into the water. Danny rescued the young girl and everyone around the scene sprinted toward Danny patting him on the back and consoling the young victim. Camera crews pulled out their equipment following Danny and the young girl calling Danny a hero. Charley retrieved a towel from one of his co-workers to put over the young girl shivering body. Everyone stood glancing at Danny and the young girl. The camera crew wanted to know who the young girl was that was rescued out of the lake.

"Charley, who is that?" One of Charley's staff members Shelly asked.

'I'm not sure." Charley's wife walked over to Charley gently taking his hand for support. Charley's wife was concerned. The young girl fought to catch her breath."

Danny, Charley, and his wife circled back toward the food tables with the young stranger. The mayor's staff discovered the young girl lived near the lake and was taking a walk and felled into the lake by accident running after her dog. The dog was fine. The young girl lost her balance.

The spectators resulted back to their activities when they learned the girl was saved.

Charley's wife hugged a familiar face facing the big crowd. Charley and his wife planned family dinners with the Wither's. Kimberly filled the Wither's in on the tragedy. The Wither's listened with sympathy. After the Wither's spoke softly with the young girl and asked if she was okay, the Wither's sat down at their decorated spot. The young girl moved along with her dog. Charley and Kimberly joined the Wither's, Keith, and Pamela on the cool blanket.

"Kimberly, what are you and Charley going to bring to the Sunday dinner? I would love for you to whip up that bake spaghetti that you make. The spaghetti tasted delicious. The pan was so huge I had to take spaghetti to work. I cannot believe you and Charley do not have children. You guys cook so much food. You both are so thin. Where is all that food going?" Pamela teased.

Kimberly rubbed her tiny belly and shrugged her shoulders. Kimberly was very pretty and nicely groomed. She had a big family and was not thinking about having any children. Charley and Kimberly had been married for two years and were enjoying living alone in their big house with lots of space and two dogs.

"I jog all the time. I cannot hold any weight. I know once I'm older, I may end up gaining weight. Kimberly kissed her husband on the cheek. Charley winked at her and listened to the two women go on and on about everything women gossiped about.

Leilani and her boyfriend Evan joined the conversation. The two graduated from high school together. They were attending college. Leilani and Evan were planning to get married after college graduation. The three women left their men to their discussions and continued their own conversations about their next Sunday dinner. One of the representatives from another city walked up to the guys to ask about the next election.

10

"Henry, what are you doing in our neck of the woods? Are you eavesdropping to steal our ideas for your campaign?"

Henry laughed shaking his head no.

"Naw, nothing like that. I have a niece who lives a few blocks away. I was on my way back to my neck of the woods and remembered Leilani telling me about the social occasion. Leilani knows my wife. My wife teaches at the college Leilani attends. I don't require adversary knowledge to move the people in my county." Henry patted Charley on the back.

Henry joked with the men by the food stand. The guys piled up nice size plates. The fellas ate standing by the food table challenging a deep discussion about politics that led to who was the best debater.

"I work with the local newscast to take account on why the people in the media and the representatives are important. I am asking that the people in our state get behind given $3 a month to help fund the programs in their cities. We have to stay fair by maintaining programs that benefit the will of the people. If the representatives are paid fairly and the people are supplied with the necessities of life, we do not have to worry about misfeasance. I work with a few colleagues in other cities and states to de-escalate conflict." Charley paused to take a bite from his plate of food.

People born in this country do not have to have an address to work, get a bank account to save money, or have to live in a certain city or state to receive help as long as they were born in this country. People born in this country do not need an address on their ID to vote. People born in this country need to know the Universal basic English language for jobs, community functions, and other important benefits in this country. Most people do not care if people speak in their own languages among themselves. As long as at work, important functions, and businesses employees do not discriminate against English speakers.

"That sounds fair." Henry listened on taking in the conversation.

"The customers come first. We cannot force people that speak English to miss out on opportunities for people who speak more than one language.

11

Most people will not have to speak perfect English because their jobs doesn't require the employees to talk at work. The companies that require writing skills can pay for interpreters to translate. There can only be one Universal language in order for inclusion to exist. Cell phones have translations of every language if anyone cannot speak English. Otherwise there will be exclusion and a large ratio of inequality in our communities. All the different languages have divided the people. The different languages is why people think that certain communities are just for their race of people because of the language barriers. Research has proven that those actions mean that it is time to change the system to make the system work for everyone. Representatives are a big part of this great new system so that we are all supported to stay stable and functional. I implemented this into my new workload to encourage everyone in the country to get sparky. The representatives cannot expect people born in this country to have the necessities of life if greedy people are making that impossible. It would not make any sense to fault victims for something that victims cannot control by hateful hate groups in this country."

"Charley, that is remarkable and a sustainable way to help our country reap the benefits in every household. I would love to be a part of what you got going on. I love how you have the newscasts involved to get positive statistics out to teach the people in this country about the way politics should be operated. Politics 101 is an intelligent way to educate the people on how we can all help one another."

"The mayor's staff should know that it is important that we don't make people think that we are trying to control their money by asking Congress or the federal government to help enforce taxes. The taxes collected should reward our own country. The mayor's staff has representatives going out to teach fair trades with our local businesses to give fair trading suggestions to offset reducing prices for the people who are lacking in groceries, gas, clothing, etc. Fair trading is vital to the economy. Our communities have to learn to trade with one another in our own communities before we trade with everyone else outside our country reasonably. We cannot keep overcharging our own people. The president has a lot of other countries that are trading fairly with us. Our communities cannot use that fair trading from other countries to sell higher prices to our own people tripling profits. All this greed has caused homelessness and other gruesome crisis situations."

"Impressive my friend. I love the way you think Charley. I'm going to call up a few of my colleagues when I get back home. I would love to set up a meeting with you to talk further about trading and using taxes to help the communities with programs. My community is rallying around fair taxes and social media awareness. I think your ideas Charley has taken politics to a whole other perspective. I can see us making fortunes for this country. Our associates have to get the people engaged that are affected by all the negative actions going on in the communities. I am impressed with Alexis going out with the protesters in the community to get the job done immediately. You all are doing tremendously favorable duties. I think you guys are going to bring notable change to this country."

The men carried on with enthusiasm. The day was filled with games and jokes. A few hours passed. Families packed up and left the lake promising to meet up again. The function was a great success for Henry. Henry was glad that he had stopped by to get involved with Charley's proposal. Henry was looking forward to working with the projects that can put the country in the limelight to succeed.

Alexis was in her positive state of being handing out gifts as she walked to her office at City Hall. Alexis felt good to be showing her support to her staff for doing honest bargains in the community. The mayor had an important meeting to go over plans to address the crimes in the city. Alexis supported a group project to have volunteers reach out to anyone who needed guidance with drugs and violence. The outcome was wondrous. The crime rate in the city since Alexis became the mayor felled short. Alexis used to work under the old mayor everyday to late at night to help the people in the community with numerous problems. All the footwork put into Alexis's goals was how she won and was the current mayor. Observers seem to be happier and felt safer. Alexis was working nonstop on housing knocking out homelessness once she took on the task. Alexis partnered with CEO's and other companies to hire people in the community. A fulfilling day to give out presents and continue to encourage her fellow team was Alexis's mission. Their jobs were very important and Alexis's colleagues played a key role in her success. One of Alexis's colleagues and best friend entered her office and closed the door. The two worked diligently to make sure that everything that was on her agenda for the day was completed and addressed. Alexis invited volunteers to decide on programs and funding for the families inquiries.

"Alexis, nice to see you." One of the store owners in the community embraced her.

"How are you doing Marty? My God you are looking bewitching. Your business is keeping you in top shape."

"I'm doing big things from your help to clean up the homelessness around our businesses. The new buildings that were renovated to help the people off the streets have made our businesses back popular. My business partners and I are happy as sand boys for your regulations. I wanted to come to your office to thank you in person. I'm glad that I ran into you. Lunch is on me. Order whatever you want."

Alexis's colleague smiled and looked up from the menu at Alexis. Alexis gave her an eyebrows glance shaking her head. Alexis was very familiar with that gaze when her colleague found something or someone interesting.

"I will order anything that I want. I am Amy Freeton, nice to meet you."

"Nice to meet you Amy, you can order whatever you want too. Lunch is on me. I'm for all that you guys do in the community. If you guys have any problems with anything on the menu let me know. I would love to help out in any way that I can with your public resolutions. Oh and Alexis count on me to help you out with the financial literacy programs that we discussed. I am speaking with business owners about our discussion. The owners are more than happy to subsidize. We are throwing a fundraiser to help fund your project. Do not forget to come out and give your wonderful speech. Make sure you bring Amy." Marty showed interest at Amy.

"Will do." Alexis high fived Amy.

"Alexis, I like your friend. He is the kind of man that knows how to treat the ladies."

"Amy please your greedy behind ready to eat." Alexis signaled for the waiter. The waiter brought out chips, dip, and a bottle of champagne, compliments from Marty.

Amy ordered all the appetizers. The appetizers included lobster bites, stuffed mushrooms, and steak kabobs with squash and zucchini on a stick and spicy shrimp. Alexis accepted that Amy was pleasing herself and deserved the break.

Amy loved how Alexis treated her staff. She was a copper-bottom person to work with and tackled the job with precision. The people in the community loved her and set store by how Alexis always put their needs ahead of her own.

Alexis gave away two cars to families working more than one job at a local funding to keep the families going to both worksites. The car giveaway showed dedicated leadership. Amy was happy to be among a sweet woman who had her priorities intact.

CHAPTER 3

"I AM STUFFED. I CANNOT MOVE a muscle Alexis. I think my tummy is about to pop wide open."

"That's what you get Amy. You know that you are too petite to be eating all that food. It's time we walk this meal off. Let's go for a walk by the lake. You and I can discuss how we are going to get the people involved for our upcoming marathon. You need the exercise eating all that food."

"Alexis seriously despite everything we have done what are we going to do about the criminality emailed to us that is going on all throughout the city. Our staff has to want to have classes to stay in junction on how politics and people actually work. Times have changed. We have to adjust to the new changes in order to effectuate motivational prosperity. The representatives allow the work force to get into the field to have a title. Politics is not a "title" job. Our communities have families that pivot on our help. The representatives cannot keep on ignoring the downfalls and unconstitutional violations in their districts. I think that we should let Anthony handle the staff and the classes. The mayor's staff has to set good examples and not bad examples by not allowing harm to come to innocent families."

"Amy, I am concerned about how the local courts are operating. You and I have to find someone in that department to give us an update. I am hearing a lot of pessimistic reports about how the people are being mistreated. Families attend the local courts for public services. A lot of people are saying that they are not receiving the legal help from the self help centers that they deserve. We can't set a methodology that people are to receive more legal help from the self help centers based on race. Our office cannot condone that type of behavior and support that kind of negativity in our community. The representatives cannot place the deputies in that kind of situation because the deputies have an oath to protect and serve everyone. The deputies cannot condone civil rights violations and constitutional violations on either side. I have to mill over all the emails that were sent to me about the programs and the organizations that are not benefiting most people. You and I cannot send people in funded places to find out that the people are not being taken seriously. Our community of people may have to close the programs down or stop using the programs as a part of this community. Our volunteers can formulate a respectable curriculum to teach about projects that serve the public honesty and with integrity. The new programs can help stop the violence making the protesters discontinue hostility toward staff members. Our cities and states have millions of illegal immigrants and migrants that are not supportive being chosen over other races born in this country that works prudently with others. The representatives in our communities cannot discriminate on our own born citizens in that category and take away their opportunities and benefits."

"The uncovering of tort is not complicated to comprehend. The reality is to not hire complicated groups to work in positions if they do not want to help certain people. Once we get the right team in order, the mayor's staff can have this community maneuvering smoothly. There are a few representatives in different cities working to get a bill passed to prevent people from running for office if the nominees do not qualify. The community of people and representatives are learning that candidates are getting into office seeking to support jobbery and sharp practice that takes place in mostly every city and state."

"I think we should center the interest on our bills being passed. I want to make certain that the responsible parties who disregarded the families in civil and criminal court are held liable. I want an investigation into the police department on which police officers are harassing residents based on rumors and envy. There cannot be law enforcement, prosecutors, and local court staff with mental health problems taking their problems out on local families. I have reliable people who want to become police officers. It's only fair that they get the job if they want the job. Representatives cannot help men and women in uniform abusing their powers. The chief of police stated that he will call me about the reports investigated of abuse of power. Citizens love the hard work that good police officers commit to every day. The community of people rallied to place the good police officers in the media so that their lives are not placed in danger because of bad polices poor policing. The noncompliant prosecutors are going to be held liable. I am jammed with emails about the emergency need to act on the violations of citizen's rights. The lack of responses prior is downright disrespectful. The former mayor allowed crime to pile up not following up with the complaints. I have to get the disorders lodged. The mayor's office is going to have to pull long hours."

The two women discussed the lamentable impacts of defiance calling it a night around 11:00 p.m. The women were bone-weary when they left Alexis's office. Amy decided that she would stay over Alexis's house and get an early embark with the chief of police the next morning. The women results made a difference.

The alarm clock sounded off. Amy rubbed her eyes. Her eyes were shut for no more than ten minutes when she heard the loud alarm sound. At least that was how Amy felt. Amy looked up to the sun through the blinds. A few seconds later, Alexis came into the room with hot soothing tea and fresh croissants.

18

"Amy, we have a long day ahead of us. My husband asked me did I hear a freight horn last night. Nathan was teasing you and that snoring."

Amy snorted taking the hot tea and a fresh croissant from the tray Alexis placed on the table beside the bed Amy was sleeping in.

"Alexis, you and hubby have jokes this morning huh. Why are you up this early? It is only 6:00 a.m. I was going to catch up on the civil discourse and labor rights and make a few calls. I thought I would not see you to around 7:30 a.m."

"Amy, my husband is off to work at 5:00 a.m. Sometimes he is quiet and other times he is making a lot of noise making provisions for his court cases with litigants. He wants to do the do before he leaves on most mornings. I cannot go back to sleep."

"Alexis, you are too much. I love how you freely speak about your husband. You are always in dream land when you talk about him. The kind of love you two have is rare. I don't know how you guys make it work with two demanding jobs. It is difficult for me to meet someone. Let alone, get engaged, and get married. My work makes it hard for me to meet anyone special. My favorite café calling my name, I'm stopping by the café. I skip meals all the time. That's why I splurge when we go out to eat."

"I packed you a healthy lunch and talked to Marty. You guys are going out on a date. Let me know how it goes." Alexis left before Amy could realize what she said.

"Wait! What? When did you speak to Marty?" Amy yelled out after Alexis.

After we came in late last night, I checked my voice messages and read a few email concerns for marching for babies and emergency renter's assistance program. Marty left me a message for your phone number. He wants you to be at the event he is having this weekend. He would like to ask you out. I told him that you would love to go out with a brilliant and reliable man." Alexis stuck her head back in the doorway.

"You did what? What makes you think that I want to go out?" Amy responded smiling at Alexis.

"That smile you keep giving me every time I mention Marty's name. Take yesterday for instance, when we discussed his event on how to motivate the city businesses to get back to coexisting with the neighborhood. You lit up brighter than Christmas lights listening to every word I said to Marty."

Amy contentment was glued to her face when Alexis returned with two beautiful dresses that were exquisite. Alexis's diamond studded low cut dress in her right hand glittery. Alexis placed the dresses on the bed and went to the bathroom with her tooth brush in her mouth.

"The dresses are prodigious. Which one are you going to wear?"

Alexis returned back into the room fully dressed. Amy was turning the water on full blast to soak and was confused when she saw Alexis dressed not wearing one of the dresses she showed Amy.

"What are the dresses for and why are you fully dressed?"

"The dresses are for you Amy, for all the revivals and protest marches to show beyond doubt that you are a true loyalist. I know that the dresses cannot make up for all the sacrifice that you make. I wanted to thank you personally from the bottom of my heart. You are a strong suit to the team. I really prize all the accessibility you get to the public for me. I'm about to finish up my makeup. I will meet you in the kitchen."

Amy dolled herself up. Amy floated into the kitchen comparably close to a top model with flawless makeup.

"Wow. You should wear the other dress on your date with Marty. You have a nice figure. You may get a bridal proposal." Alexis complimented her best friend.

"Girl stop! You are just saying that because you are my bestie."

"You are remarkable Amy. I have a necklace that will make your dress look more stylish." Alexis left the kitchen to fetch the necklace.

Alexis came back with a gift wrap of expensive wrapping removing the wrapping paper for Amy. Alexis motioned for Amy to turn her back to her to put the necklace around Amy's neck.

"Alexis this is the kindest thing anyone has ever done for me. Words cannot express my emotions on the way you are looking out for me." Amy eyes swelled up in tears.

"Do not go soft on me and ruin your makeup. Amy, we have to head out of here to meet the chief of police. Then you and I are going to be working on getting the other district representatives to join forces with us to make this country successful." Alexis gave Amy a hug.

Alexis and Amy drove in separate cars to meet the chief of police. The chief of police was waiting for the women in his office.

"Hello ladies. Sit down and make yourselves comfortable. The new police officers are excited to succor and learn from other veteran police officers who have succeeded in doing a wonderful job for this community. I have a list of the new police officer's names in this packet for the both of you. If you have any questions I am available all day." The chief of police handed the ladies the envelopes.

Alexis and Amy scanned through the envelope before asking their questions. Amy sat her envelope to the side asking the chief of police how did he feel about the crime in the city. The chief stated that crime was down and the community was helping with volunteers to make sure that the crime stayed down. Alexis inquired about the rotation and how the police officers were going to tackle the tougher neighborhoods on their beat. Alexis suggested that there be two police officers in the patrol vehicles to the rough neighborhoods and two police cruisers rotating in rougher areas to cover their beats to keep crime down. Alexis suggested that police officers were trained on mental health citizens. Amy suggested officers were screened for mental health. Alexis and Amy left satisfied with the chief of police answers and went to handle their onsite projects.

"Amy let's stop by Marty's place of business to give him the flyer to print out for his business friends for this weekend. We can park your car at City Hall and take my car." Alexis offered.

Amy was okay with that arrangement as her stomach did cart wheels thinking about going to Marty's enterprise. Amy high quality appearance knew she would get Marty's eye. Amy also knew that Alexis was playing match maker and behaving like it was all about the project. Amy went along with Alexis love connection parking her car at the City Hall getting into the car with Alexis. The two drove off into the direction of Marty's business. Marty owned a luxurious hotel and breakfast nook. The building royalty stood out. The employees were well groomed and very professional when the ladies walked into the building to talk to Marty. Marty was talking to a woman that images created a rare perfection that was difficult not to stare. Marty saw the ladies coming toward him and excused himself.

"What a salubrious surprise. What brings you two my way? I was not expecting to see your pretty faces for a few more days." Marty inspected Amy up and down and blew out a whistle.

Amy blushed knowing that she looked just as exotic as the woman Marty was talking to and gave Marty a hug. Amy inhaled Marty scent. He smelled crisp in an expensive tailored suit.

"Marty, Amy and I wanted to leave this flyer with you to give to your other business friends. Amy and I are going to come early to set up. We have a few people that have equipment for the stage and chairs for us to sit to give the presentation.' Alexis handed Marty the flyer.

"I will make sure to get this to my associates. I will be ready when you guys show up with the equipment. I will have a few employees waiting by the door. Was my appetizers satisfactorily? I can have hors d' oeuvres before you ladies hit the road."

"We can spare a few minutes before we head out." Amy interjected.

Alexis pulled out her cell phone. She had to let her staff know to begin the meeting about the charity auctions, book donations, and recycling program that the team scheduled without her. Alexis wanted to add the blood drive to the discussion when she got back. Alexis and Amy had to go to the hospital and make a quick appearance to visit the sick children and the elderly. The ladies were going over to the new school to speak with the teachers about the teacher's plans. The ride over to the new school gave Alexis enough time to text her secretary to have Anthony take the staff to the conference room for open discussions on effective politics. Alexis and Anthony was launching a new way to tackle being representatives that successfully indulge the families essentials.

Marty took the ladies to an area in the hotel that had the ladies gasping in amazement. The posh hotel setting made Alexis and Amy melt at the sight. Marty flagged down one of his guys to take their order.

"Christoph, give us a variety of the best and bring a round of lemonade. Make it quick for me. The ladies have a laboring day. I wanted to give them a sample of the chef's skillful meals." The young man smiled brightly and left after greeting the ladies.

A few seconds later the CEO of a Fortune 500 Company advanced toward Marty. Marty stood up and introduced his associate.

"This is Philip Taylor. He will be attending the event. He wants to help fund building capital and insurance projects and donate to the families programs for low income. My business partners and I have spoken with a lot of people that will be attending the event. There are a lot of resources that can help make this county strive. Let us know what else you two desire. My associates do not expect anything in return. The events are encouraging and a pleasure to assist." Marty looked from Amy to Alexis. Marty's associates sat down at the table.

The male waiter and two other employees came back with an assortment of the best looking food Alexis and Amy had seen. It was not the usual appetizers Alexis and Amy ate. The waiter described all the food and what the food was cooked with. The ladies were very impressed. Alexis and Amy sampled the dishes complimenting the food with high praises.

After the quick lunch the ladies hugged Marty and went to take care of usual business.

The hospital upgrades and full trained staff attended to their patients. Alexis espoused the care that the patients were receiving. Amy read to an elderly woman brushing her hair as the nurses spoke with Alexis about the upgrades at the hospital. Amy and Alexis visited every wing in the hospital talking to a lot of patients championing all of the upgrades. The visit was extremely awe-inspiring with a lot of great advice and funding ideas to keep the hospital clean, safe, and suitable with excellent care for the patients. Alexis and Amy wrapped up their visit and headed to their next destination before ending the day. The ladies decided to go visit the local county jail and take a peek in to check how the facilities were being maintained. There were complaints of unsanitary conditions and the mayor wanted to make sure that the renovations was first priority.

The ladies arrived with greetings of friendly gestures from one of the head deputies in charge. He was willing to give the ladies a tour and show the women what was being accomplished in the local jail. The workers and the mayor's office were working together to show how work was supervised without having to battle or debate over how tax dollars were dispersed. The rumors that the representatives, law enforcement, courts, congress, etc. can do what they wanted to do was cleared thorough investigations. Alexis wanted to show and prove to the communities that that was not how things worked in the real World. Employees who did not do their jobs did not work long-term. The new interventions in place due to the people who spoke out about the concerns of lack of responses to serious concerns complaints were pushed through. Gossip of abusive law enforcement and other public officials that never got disciplined were brought to the front line for serious conversations and disciplinary actions. Troublemakers who attacked families seeking justice and put other countries first did not stay in office. The work to change the system over the years because of people who refused to get educated on how a country was operated was in effect. The selfishness had affected every city and state. Amy wanted to know why people sought after positions to upset families and not do what was expected of their duties on the job. Alexis had so many high position friends that knew how to put the right people in charge in all the cities and states to end the abuse of power.

The deputy explained every step that was being taken and how the inmates were being reformed as a part of the new transformation. The inmates were working hard on the rebuilding of self. The inmates received less sentencing for good behavior accepting being rehabilitated. The reentry programs helped get inmates released early to become productive citizens.

"You are doing a boundless job deputy. We felicitate you guys coming in and changing the system for the better. I know it is difficult with negative people that have to be arrested because the criminals refuse to behave and live in a society that helps families and not harm families. The laziness of the employees before you guys who allowed these kinds of crimes to go on for far too long that you guys workload is immoderately demanding. We should not ever cave in to violence and intimidation to not progress in our counties. We are not here to serve corruption and violence. We are here to represent people that understand what is best for their families. I have to tune out many troublemakers because I know their only job is to get me off my game."

"You are doing a noteworthy job mayor. You are smart, positive, and influence alacrity. I come to work and the inmates are getting more in tune with what they did wrong and how the inmates can make their wrongs right. I am glad that we are changing the system one day at a time. I never believed that we couldn't' do it. I never worked with this many people who were willing to put in the time." The deputy walked with the ladies out of the jail.

Amy admired what Alexis contributed over the years working with other representatives and climbing her way to the top. The county was starting to feel back like home. The day light was fading. The streets were already beginning to get dark by the time Alexis and Amy drove to City Hall. Alexis and citizens had passed a bill to end sanctuary states because of nonstop protests about the pain and suffering that people in the country were going through. It was an opportune time to be in politics.

CHAPTER 4

"A LEXIS, I AM GOING TO head home and get on all the assignments that we have to take care of. Do not forget that first thing in the morning, we have to go visit the shelters and the gas stations where the community is rallying to make sure the changes are enforced. The shelter received the funding a few days ago for fresh beds, towels, food, and other shelter supplies. The janitors and other employees are keeping the facilities up and running. Can you believe how far we have come? This country does not need to depend on other countries for oil any more. This country is in a great position to do some amazing things." Amy felt wonderful.

"I embrace all the hard work we have completed to get to this point. This office cannot slack off."

"Alexis, you have a presence that people feel. The people do not feel like you are a threat. I don't see people rushing you disrespectfully because you are already doing everything you need to do for them. Most of the people are content to receive what they should have received decades ago. People are cashing in their rewards."

Alexis and Amy departed from a long day. Both ladies got home, showered, and fell straight to sleep.

The next morning Alexis's husband mentioned the free speech

controversy streaming online. The protesters were fighting for a young man that was incarcerated for speaking against a gay couple that wanted special treatment. The guy was saying that he refused to call anyone something that they were not. He was combating with the couple when the police arrived. The gay couple claimed he was threatening them."

"Honey, we hear about this kind of protest all the time. The gay community has too many demands that cannot be rectified. People do not know a lot about the gay groups or why they should comply to demands that are hard to determine. Most people cannot tell a transgender or transsexual or knows who is gay. Except the gays that are flamboyant. I am going back to sleep for another hour." Alexis rolled over to her left side and closed her eyes.

Alexis's husband giggled and bent down to kiss his wife before leaving for work. He knew his wife was working steadily and needed to get her rest to be able to tackle such a demanding position.

Alexis's husband was a judge and knew how challenging it was to have to deal with opposition. Judge Nathan stole another glance at Alexis sleeping and left locking the door behind him. Alexis's husband was planning a big day for the two of them without Alexis knowing. Nathan was going to have to drag Alexis away for a couple of days whether she liked it or not. She had plenty of warriors on her team that could do the job without her for a few days.

Alexis turned the alarm clock off. Alexis stretched and climbed out of bed. She was touched that her husband left breakfast for her in the microwave. Alexis loved that man. Alexis placed her tea down and heated up the breakfast. Alexis enjoyed her breakfast in silence thinking about the protest in the gay community. The gay community acceptance had come a long way. The push to take over was weighing in heavy on Alexis nerves. No group had the right to go after people based on their personal feelings.

The news was covering the story about the new renovation improvements going on at the jails. The inmates being interviewed on how the new jails made them feel human accepted their wrongs and committed to doing right until their released dates. The deputies were standing to the side monitoring the inmates as the inmates worked. There were also professional workers hired to make sure everything was in code and in compliance. Alexis was buoyant to have the inmates owning up to their part for being incarcerated. Alexis left for work.

"Good Morning."

"Good Morning. I see you are ready for the day. I have to grab a few things off my desk. You can get in the car. I will be right back." Alexis headed up to her office to grab her official seals and records before her and Amy took off. The body guards were in their all black SUV. Amy pulled out her cell phone to let the shelter know that she was on her way. Alexis and Amy had five different shelters to visit before the end of the day. The ladies figured that they would visit three of the shelters that morning to make sure that things were going as planned then take a break and visit the last shelters on the list before the end of the day. Alexis made her way to the car and the ladies pulled off.

"Mrs. Hampton. What a pleasure. I am glad that we can meet today." Alexis met up with the shelter's director.

"It is always a pleasure. I wasn't going to turn down a visit from the mayor. I am grateful how things are going on now with you in office. You guys have really turned this system around. I'm very happy that you have kept the momentum going. We need people to follow the ones who do right and not follow the ones who do wrong. I will appreciate it if you take my card. I am holding an event in a few weeks to support low income affordable housing. I know that you guys are very busy. I would love it if you guys can stop by. If you cannot stop by, I understand." Mrs. Hampton handed the mayor the shelter deets.

The shelter was designed like a huge mansion. There were beautiful furniture and paintings hanging up all over the shelter. The beds were lined up in rows with colorful covers and nice pillow cases on the beds.

The shelter had greatly improved. The shelter paintings belonged in an art gallery.

"Mrs. Hampton, where did you get the exquisite decorations?" Amy wondered.

"Would you believe that the paintings are from people who sleep in the shelters? This is how much talent that is without a home. My office is working with other agencies to get the people placed so that we can help the families with their professions. It is sad to let citizens this talented go to waste. I have gotten almost four hundred and fifty seven people placed already in permanent homes in three months. My staff is finding permanent places pretty quickly with this new system. We are working with friendly people. This office and the other locations have tons of people volunteering to speak with people with properties to house the ones who are on the streets and in the shelters. Thanks to you mayor, there are not too many people without shelter. The shelters should be successful at not leaving anyone behind at the end of the year."

Alexis shook her head in agreement. She loved how Mrs. Hampton spoke so proudly of the homeless people and knew that the homeless people were very important people who deserved to be treated fairly and with respect. The shelter truly showed how many of the homeless people were productive people and had the ability to change their lives for the better.

"What are your plans for the new shelter Mrs. Hampton?" Amy used her notepad to write down Mrs. Hampton's answers.

"The other shelters are going to do the same thing that we do here. This shelter serves breakfast before the ones living here temporarily go to look for jobs. The staff gives the ones who are not already working transportation costs to look for jobs. The ones living here are to be in the shelter no later than 10:00 p.m. Some of the jobs are full time jobs with overtime. This shelter provides dinner. People have access to washing machines and dryers. The ones that are already working help out with serving the food. The homeless ones advanced to moving in their own place give suggestions on healthy meals and help the other ones to get a job."

"The scheduling is on point. You are doing an uplifting service. I'm indebted to you to come, visit, and evince a clean and home like facility that welcomes people and help the ones willing to get back on their feet. This is a major way to motivate people who are down on their luck." Amy spun around earnestly.

"The people living here temporarily and my staff are one big family. All of us clean up after ourselves, raise money, and keep the communication open. All races and ages from 18 on up is welcome. The ones that want to stay have to meet the curfew time. We have another facility for the minors. Our shelters work very closely with social services. The staff helps with homework or whatever school studies they can. Our staff talks to the teachers. We work together so that everyone is on the same page and doing whatever they can do to lend a helping hand to the children. The shelter staff does our best. This shelter comes across a few obstacles every now and again. There is not much that we cannot handle." Mrs. Hampton was very confident of the results and efforts that she put forth.

Alexis and Amy gave reviews on the shelters that they visited. The shelters left an indisputable mark on how shelters had changed. The new system was looking up to its standards. The funding was being used appropriately. The people with jobs were pitching in to give money to the shelters to keep the shelters well kept. Mrs. Hampton did not allow the locals to give no more than fifty dollars a week. The fifty dollars added up from all the people living in the shelters for additional necessities. Families were receiving the funding in the way the funding was to be used to help families to move forward.

Alexis and Amy got back to the office and went into Alexis's office. Both ladies adjusted to another productive day with a lot of work completed.

CHAPTER 5

T HE ENTIRE STAFF AT THE City Hall was on a fast pace to get things cleaned up in the county. Things were in full progress as Alexis and Amy passed by neighborhoods and businesses cleaned and without homelessness. The ladies were on their way to a meeting with the churches to provide feedback to the voters who was concerned about the high cost of homes in the area. The church protested the fair housing act wanting to amend some changes to enforce better regulations for buying homes in the communities. The congregation expressed racial profiling and other discriminatory practices when it came down to purchasing property. The church members was fed up with the hypocrisy coming from Organizations that served who they liked and the banks strict policies wasn't any better. The restrictions made it impossible to obtain property. The church had invited the mayor to say a few words to the congregation. The church members worked with the loan officers and Organizations in the area that helped with first time home buyers that wanted to take out a second mortgage loan on their mortgage for renovations. Alexis and Amy stepped up to the front of the church. The pastor introduced the mayor and gave the mayor the floor. The church members were hoping for relief.

"The Organizations that Amy is passing out to you all have worked with us with your concerns. The Organizations are willing to help pull some strings to make sure that all of your needs are met. Amy and I have worked tirelessly on making phone calls to get everyone on board. If you have any questions or concerns the numbers are available to call. The staff and their operators are willing to answer any questions that you guys may have to purchase what fits your budget. As you all may know many of the affordable properties are in farther away areas. I know some of you are already home owners. We have names and contacts for the ones who already own homes. We have asked our volunteers to make contact via emails, telephone, and through written letters to the federal government about the high interest rates. We are fighting to pass a bill to reduce the high interest rates based on the incomes of the people in this county and find other ways to supplement funding. If any of you are willing to participate, please give Amy your contact information and she will email you with the names and contacts." Alexis hugged the pastor.

The church members were very excited reaching into their bags to give Amy their contact hook up. Amy happily accepted their contact numbers. The church members wanted accountability for federal agents and a law amending the federal government from having too much power over the country. The abuse of power and the unknown members of the federal government didn't sit too well with the church members.

"Amy, make sure to call the pastor and remind him that we will be attending Sunday church services. The church member who asked for information to help setup for the building of the second new school found plenty of hands to get the school ready before the date of opening. I was emailed last week I forgot to get back to the woman in charge."

Amy jolted down the reminder getting into the passenger side of the car. The federal government rally was taking place that weekend. The protesters wanted answers to why the federal government was not regulated like every other agency so that no one was taken advantage of.

The place that they loved to frequent had customers lined up outside the door. The ladies approached the restaurant. Amy saw a tall male wearing a brown hoodie pull out a gun and start shooting toward a crowd full of men. Amy rushed Alexis back toward the car. The body guards rushed out of their SUV guns drawn. The shooter saw the body guards and started fleeing. People ducked screaming to call 911. One of the men was shot in the arm. The other guy was hit by fragments of the bullets fired. There were not any fatalities. The body guards rushed Alexis and Amy into their black SUV. The third body guard jumped in Alexis's car after grabbing Alexis's car keys from her hands and they pulled off. Alexis knew that that was the end of Alexis driving for a while without her body guards.

Alexis and Amy pulled up to their meeting at City Hall. The people were rallying about the update of Janice Cowell and Kevin Cowell. Alexis gave the update at the bottom steps of City Hall.

"Yesterday, the head of the sheriff department told me that Janice Cowell is feeling better. She will be released from the hospital. Kevin will be released from custody and into her care with other caretakers. You guys can send the Cowell's flowers. The contact information is on the website on the cards. You can all get a card on your way out." Alexis handed out a few cards in her hand.

Alexis slumped down at her desk. It was a blessing to have family in the security business that could be her body guards when she needed them. The job sometimes got hectic. Her cell phone rang causing her folder to slip from her grasp. Alexis picked up the folder recovering a contact number. Alexis answered the cell phone. Her husband Nathan face appeared. Alexis spoke to her husband briefly. Amy faced Alexis signaling her to tell Nathan hello. The women worked from Alexis's office for a while going over the Million Woman March and the World Wide March for Freedom. Freedom to petition and the fair job opportunities was the biggest fight going on around the city. Alexis wanted to help the petitioners understand what petitions should be for to maintain codification. Alexis did not want the citizens to start creating petitions for anything and copying what her office

34

was assisting in to change the system. The opposition had to be stopped from obstructing justice and causing unnecessary debates to prolong ethics.

"Amy, I think we should bring in Charley and Leilani. Our office is going to be reaching out to young people. Charley and Leilani have a lot of knowledge that could steer the young people in the right direction. The mayor's office is doing open mic to reach the younger folks. If we surround the public opening around schools and colleges there is a better chance for the young ones to show up at this function."

"Charley and Leilani will love to reach the young people Alexis. Leilani is one step ahead than most with her public speaking and since this is going to be about college enrollment and college fees, Leilani will be the best person to speak on the matter since she is in college. The college's deans are attending. Leilani can bring pamphlets for enrollment from her college. The petitions for lower cost of college fees and enrollment are circulating through Charley and his helpers."

"Douglas wanted to come out and fight for free education and better healthcare. He felt that there were ways that we could come up with to fund free education and better healthcare. I will add Douglas to the schedule. Public speaking is fashionable for the college students."

"The fight for "Aspiration for a better life", will give many of the college students an opportunity to work for long-lived companies and help with funding and passing the laws to aid young people. Peer pressure and on screen violence has shaken the young people badly. I defend the young people's rights to be active and voice their viewpoints." Amy advocated for young people.

"I am all for changing the system Amy. If the system has not been working for us, why keep all the barriers up and keep bumping our heads. The communities are supposed to get wiser with time and not stand still with new technology. I don't think people should continue to do things the hard way and argue against one another for change that benefits everyone."

"Arguing to argue is the problem. People want to change for themselves.

That is why we have to draw up the petitions. The voters are not getting involved enough to stay on changes that has violated citizen's values. There is more fighting among the voters than voting. Our office hears about what is not being done when a lot of the people complaining can help out. It takes everyone for the right change to come. Change does not happen without everyone not doing their part. Everyone wants to be rich. Everyone cannot be rich. Everyone can get what they need to survive by saving money from working. The rest of what the people do is up to them and their budgets. Our job at the mayor's office is not to make people wealthy. The mayor's office encourages the community of people by providing a foundation for the city finances, implementing policies, and appointing staff. We preside over city council meetings, attend public events, and speak with constituents at meetings. I am not for turning down constituents who are being harassed to not attend the meetings. Everyone is accepted to speak their minds in my district." Alexis got up to stretch.

"Leilani's boyfriend Evan is doing a free class on saving money during the meeting. He has a few friends who work for banks and know a lot about investments and how to grow your money. Evan is going to speak to the college students tomorrow. I suggested that Leilani and Charley get involved because Charley, Leilani, and Evan were all going to be there anyway."

"The body guards are not letting us out of their sights. I will see them all night tonight. I know the shooting has nothing to do with us. You know how the body guards get when things like this happen. Whatever we need we can have the body guards pick it up for us."

"I'll call Leilani and Charley. They do not need that much time to prepare. Charley and Leilani love talking to young people."

Alexis and Amy worked on the operations unite rally. They were doing an appearance in the local high schools. The "You Are Not Alone", rally was a fruitful event.

Alexis had invited the body guards to join them. Alexis respected how the body guards let her do things her way and never bothered her. The body guards were very professional. One of the body guards stated that they will be standing outside the door and will let Alexis and Amy know if anyone tried to come in. Alexis nodded surveying scheduled upcoming meetings. Mostly all tasks were taken care of earlier. The staff earned a festive atmosphere for putting in the long hours.

Alexis was multitasking. Alexis caught a glimpse of Amy blushing with her ear up to the phone. Alexis knew it had to be Marty. Alexis felt jubilation for her friend as she dialed the number to Janice Cowell's hospital room. Alexis was making sure Janice and her father was squared away.

"Alexis you are going to be beatific when I tell you what Marty did."

Alexis waited for Amy to explain the sunny smile plastered on her face.

"Marty has written a check to give to our favorite charity. I will let him tell you how much the amount is written out for when he sees you at the planned public occasion."

Alexis was super hyped. She ran over to Amy jumping up and down. The work day was turning out to be worth the trouble.

Alexis's staff arrived early to set up brochures that their team wanted to pass out to the college tutees. A crowded group in every parts of the campus hung around talking about social engagements. The assembly was going to be a major success Alexis thought as Charley and Leilani pulled up with their significant others. Douglas with Amy along side him with his outreach youth program dictations brought along his wife and daughter. The team worked in two paired groups getting out everything that they all brought for the event preparing their speeches.

Amy's likewise college student image with her jeans, blazer, and her hair pulled up in a neat ponytail pinned her hope on the student's goals being reached. Alexis's young facial features wore comfortable fitting slacks, a colorful beautiful blouse, with her hair up in a nice bun. The team was prepared for the important discussions enabling qualified feedback and factual data.

"I am going to begin with my speech I worked on last night." Douglas stepped up to introduce himself. Douglas pointed to each member on his team saying their names with pride. He was lucky to be in a position to advance people the way he was given the chance. Douglas sacrificed a lot to get to where he was and wanted others to reach their dreams.

'I would like for you guys to open up your leaflets and look through the information about free education and better healthcare. If you agree with free education and better healthcare, sign the petition to pass a law to help people that cannot afford college and people who need healthcare. These are two very important necessities in life. They are the most expensive things that families suffer from in debt trying to pay every month when we can afford to provide the necessities for the families in this county. There is funding going to wasteful programs when the funding should go to these causes. The community of tax payers has to use funding for what makes us stronger and not what divides us as a people. I would like for you to take the pamphlets with you if there is anyone you did not bring here with you today to sign the petition. The address to mail or take to the physical office for the petition is included. The mayor's office has set up an online petition to generate as many signatures as possible so that we can make this official as soon as possible." Douglas stepped to the side for Leilani. The attendees roared in enthusiasm.

Leilani gave an excellent expression of words on the fundamental classes that the colleges offer and what colleges were located in the areas that are filled with scholar professors.

Charley kept the torch lit mastering the financial impositions involving funding for college students education. Charley fortified college being a priority. The event encouraged the beholders. Charley brushed on the importance of what degrees students can receive based on their backgrounds.

Alexis and Amy sat in support with their team as their group devoted firm acclimations to college students. The students used the time wisely to ask questions that interests them. The college students submitted actuality that guided the new college students with better class choices. The team ended the large circle endorsing the free education and better healthcare vision.

"Amy, I think we succeeded with free education and better healthcare for all the people."

"Some people won't come out to get educated assuming that the programs are not going to work. If the ones skeptical come out and listen to some of the speeches about why it can work from Douglas and the rest of the speakers in the crowd they will be affected in a positive way. People will gain a contrasting perspective on the idea. The recognition is online. People created group chat apps for ways to make sure people are being informed." Amy was confident that the work that they were doing would work out for the best.

"I like the idea of Leilani letting the college students know that the some of the degrees will be for one semester and that there will be training courses for certification that does not require two or four years of college. The college tuitions are tremendously high. Free education to create jobs and put money back into the communities can reduce a lot of debt. There was also the advice of Charley stating that the ones with a record can be trained in construction and how to use power tools to build homes to lower the price of ownership costs. The college classes added to the college curriculum generates decent incomes for families. That was a plus. The ideas of trading school courses pretty much covered all of the concerns about people who cannot work in certain job fields due to a pass record." Alexis checked off her index.

"The people that showed up reflected a positive social group for the topic. I think the function was successful and useful. I know with all of us working together and making sure to stay focused and complete follow-ups, everything will suffice." Amy was certain.

The team touched basis with social change and climate change calling it a night. Everyone in the mayor's office looked forward to their next gathering at the lively lake to take advantage of all the hard work that the staff finalized. The purposeful, and formal discourse, motivated and rewarded the team to keep going on strong.

CHAPTER 6

HUGE SPARKLING PARTY LIGHTS, ATTRACTIVE decorations, and gussy up tables with creative accessories complimented the magnificent hotel that Marty offered to have the financial support achieving the community objective. The cause was to campaign around bribery, improper influence by public or private interest, and misappropriation of public funds. People came from many discrete businesses and a variety of specific fields to support the charity. There were famous people arriving in record numbers. Marty good looking and dressed in all black aimed to take the funding sky high.

Alexis and Amy both stunning in sexy dresses that complimented their natural beauty wooed the guests. The event was about to begin. Everyone sat in the seats available and prepared for the introduction to the fundraiser. Several people gave Marty huge donations before the event started.

"I would like to congratulate Alexis and Amy on doing a superb job in our county. These women and their teams have gone far and beyond their duties to help everyone possible. I am very proud of the mayor. Alexis has kept the energy flowing with a profound impact. Alexis worked with the last mayor tirelessly and effortlessly to bring needed changes in a system that has always placed a negative barrier on the people. We are very proud to lift those barriers and help this community thrive." Marty held up a champagne glass to make a toast. The crowd sizzled. Marty toasted to making the new system work for everyone without prejudice and racist actions. The old system of employees that created the broken system was being removed for forcing the families into corruption and deceitful behaviors.

"I would like to give you guys the website and information to follow where the money is being distributed to help the families. Our staff will be posting regularly so that everyone knows who and what is being supported in our county with our funded programs. Do not form individual hate groups and commit unlawful investigations on donors that support their love ones and significant others financially, people supporting their love ones financially and in other healthy ways. That is not the citizen's business or job. If a crime is reported, the specific crime is the only means for probable cause. Law enforcement has to know how the person reporting the crime obtained the information. The representatives cannot have people harassing families out of envy." Alexis paused at the sound of loud applause.

"The mayor's office aims to support the second new school that will be an added addition to the first new school. The first new school has already been filled." Amy announced the second new school's plans.

The donors gaily catered to the mayor relentless zeal provided for the people.

The women spoke on all of the projects introduced with jobs that will pander to the cause. The mayor layout on her power point showed the donors how the projects were being created. The power point displayed the next steps to make sure that funding was stretched out on a precise budget giving families a lot of options to choose from. The research conducted was a thorough and thought out plan. The abandoned buildings that were renovated to house the homeless in the downtown areas of the communities so that the local businesses would not be affected were disentangled. The shelters provided clean and stable environments for families that needed second chances. Alexis showed the results on her power point along with the college public affair that her team had the previous day. The donations rolled in heavily. The hotels/motels were being regulated for known prostitution and drug dealers. People from out of town were concerned with the way hotels/motels were run down and people's belongings were stolen. The police was on the watch.

"Alexis visited the hospitals and patients to make sure that the patients were receiving the best care. The mayor has been making this county the best county in a long time. This community is fortunate to have someone of Alexis's qualities around." Marty hugged Alexis.

The fundraiser raised millions of dollars in no time once Alexis took office as the mayor. Alexis was looking forward to calling the Organizations where funding could be utilized to get the Organizations to work on using the money wisely. The donors enjoyed good music, food, and conversation after the mayor's speech.

Amy enjoyed talking to Marty and getting suggestions on how to get people involved in upcoming resourceful endeavors.

Charley and Leilani talked to the younger business owners about golden opportunities. The development was economically a success.

"Marty, do you think that the free college for all can benefit the communities so that working families can receive better education to upgrade their incomes?" Amy was asking Marty.

"I think that will be a sagacious way to get families higher wages to help their families." Marty's friend responded introducing himself and shaking Amy's hand.

"You are intriguing. Marty is this you?" Marty's friend was clowning around pulling his chain.

"Amy and I are making plans nosy man." Marty punched his friend and excused himself from the table so that they could talk.

"Nice meeting you Amy."

"Nice meeting you Roger."

The men walked around the event exchanging greetings with other people and clowning around. The photographer was taking lots of pictures and asking people to pose for the camera. Alexis was sitting with Leilani and Charley browsing through the genocide protest, the right to live, and privacy segments for their impending commitment. They worked on ways to bring the rebuttals to the community for review.

The team filed into Alexis's office the following evening summing up the meeting about wasteful spending and unwanted programs. Alexis and Amy received a phone call from their local news station to answer questions about the shooting at Alexis's favorite cafe. Alexis disconcerted about what took place was glad that the shooter was off the streets. The two males that were shot were out of the hospital. Alexis was light hearted that there were not any fatalities.

"Alexis, we can head on over to the park and do a quick recap about the opening after all the work the volunteers did to get the park back opened. I wanted to stop off at the grocery store by the park and speak to the manager. The manager called me to invite us over for something that is going on outside of the grocery store. I believe it has something to do with the petitions." Amy showed Alexis the message that was left for the mayor.

Alexis read the message reminding herself that she and Amy had infrastructure and new businesses to pay a visit.

"Alexis, park right there, I want to walk over to the ATM before we foster the petitioners. I need to get money out the ATM to pay the cleaners for my clothes. I have been putting off picking up my clothes too long. We been working late the cleaners is closed by the time we are done." Alexis waited for Amy to handle her business.

Alexis and Amy met the manager outside of the grocery store. The manager was concerned about new graffiti and wanted to paint a mural to attract new customers like some of the other businesses was doing in the neighborhood.

Alexis wrote down the complaint. Amy suggested that the manager have a security officer outside the business, that was what Amy suggested to the other business owners that had graffiti on their buildings. The manager thought that deterrent would work best.

The petition was to feed people that donated to the grocery stores for the unfortunate at a low cost. Alexis and Amy liked the idea of promoting food drives. It was a standard way to keep the funding going for people who were no longer working or retired.

Amy informed people that donated food to take advantage of the drive where volunteers dropped off food to the people's churches in the community that signed up at the local churches. The grocery stores are allowing their employees to participate in the drive, a splendid opportunity for people to help others through the food drive to battle hunger.

CHAPTER 7

Henry operated in his county going door to door to collect censor bureau input about the family concerns to win the election. Henry's team videoed constituents comments to prove that Henry should be reelected for office. The families welcomed Henry with open arms. A lot of people loved Henry as their representative and felt like he cared about what was happening in their lives. Henry was a dedicated father and his own family was seen numerous times coming out with him to support other families.

"Henry, time to go." Henry's wife fondled her husband's shoulders.

Henry arrived to find families in sync to voice the importance of the letters, phone calls, and emails addressed to his offices about Million Man March, and Occupy Wall Street. Henry invited Charley to help out and give insight since Charley's county was well known for alluring the locals. Charley's county was succeeding in everything even accommodating the wealthy. Charley did not want to leave the rich out or place any unnecessary burdens on the rich by over taxing. Charley brought a local journalist from his county to record Henry's upcoming election.

"Can you bring the transmitter up for us to get a better angle? This is going live." The camera man adjusted the electrical device for Henry.

Henry modified the stage pressing buttons to test the appliances. Henry incentivized tenants eager to receive remembrance for their agony lined up. Henry introduced Charley and the journalist. Occupiers of the county wanted their stories to be heard on TV. The crowd welcomed Charley wholeheartedly.

"I love to begin my discussion with ethical bulletins." Charley began with the crowd listening to every word.

"We have managed to pass crucial laws this year. I know a lot of you may have already heard about the new laws. We will read the new laws that passed. Our offices have listened to your questions and Henry will follow up with the emails and voice messages you guys mentioned encircling the rallies."

The crowd was at attention with flags swinging to support Henry. Participants had on t-shirts in support of Henry. The lover's of the country had on baseball caps and outdoor chairs with Henry's name on the chairs.

"Businesses cannot discriminate or fire employees for illegal immigrants or migrants complaints without cause or abuse their powers without paying monetary damages." The natives hurray and pragmatic remarks led Charley on.

"The law to support judges that maintain the law and help people without counsel receive fair court proceedings has passed. As long as the judges are not taking sides and the court findings show proof of fair decisions according to the court rules of law judges can receive gifts from their supporters. We deserve hard working new system court staff to receive rewards for their honesty and ethical excellence. It does not matter if the gifts are from their friends and colleagues. If the court cases are not a part of the judge's personal life and rewards, it is not the citizen's rights or business. The community of people cannot assume that the new system court staff is committing crimes, unless a case is investigated and there is proof of someone losing their court case based on a judge's criminal actions involving bribery. The law states that a judge can be removed from the bench immediately if any evidence of criminal wrongdoing is found to be intentional." Charley turned the page to what he was reading.

"The community of people with representative's assistance has finally succeeded in holding attorneys accountable for providing services for illegal immigrants and migrants who are in the wrong. The attorneys are somehow getting judges to grant damages to people who are not supposed to receive large sums of compensation for certain cases. Other cases are being dismissed that have more proof. The rights of the litigants with more proof than their opposing sides are being harassed. The attorneys and the judges are being held liable for violating certain people's rights with similar cases as other litigants that won millions of dollars. A lot of the litigants being denied have more proof for compensation and their cases are not being represented by prejudice attorneys. Some of the migrants in court are being served and are troubled people who lie and get paid off for their horrible lies. The judges and attorneys in violation of the criminal misconduct will get charged." Charley's announcement moved the believers.

"The bar of association is weeding out all the reckless lawbreaking staff that protects bad attorneys who only represent bad people."

Charley heard stomping in appreciation. He had to raise his hand to quiet the crowd down.

"Congress along with the community of people petitions has passed the law to protect law enforcement to do their job when there is probable cause and if any state does not remove their sanctuary status, the ones breaking the law will be prosecuted. All states must comply with law enforcement against illegal entry in the country. The illegal immigrants can apply to enter legally once their work visas or other documents expire. The president, congress, and the community of people are sending back all illegal immigrants and any migrants who help illegal immigrants enter the country illegally will receive strict consequences. The president is sending soldiers to help countries with dictators and heinous abusers until families are safe and stable." The citizens spirits were raised with Charley's spiffing corroboration.

48

Henry was proud to be standing in front of strong Patriots to instill in the country reshuffling of power and to give the families the peace that they have been fighting for for a long time.

"This law on illegal immigration matters to me because we are having a difficult time keeping vital businesses operating properly due to illegal border crossing distractions. Congress passed a law targeting citizens known for opposition without cause to not be able to vote in order to hinder and violate all of the laws that were passed to protect families. The laws passed to stop opposition from causing so much violence and deaths will not be amended or removed from the constitution for the first time in history. The reason being is due to all of the families that were left behind and suffered greatly because of what took place with illegal immigration and migrants who caused so much grief deliberately. The hateful hate groups will no longer be able to win by voting opposite to violate innocent families out of envy. It does not matter how many voters try to do so. If the opposition tries to stop positive attributions in the communities, their votes will not count. Someone with more experience in the community will make the final decisions because of the investigations of what has been going wrong with voting."

Henry's family rushed into his arms taking in the victory. Henry could live in the moment forever after all of the drudgery that was set forth to eliminate the conquered renegades. Tons and tons of citizens stressed through noncompliance at the hands of traitors. It was awesome to see the back breaking work pay off rising the people up with aspiration. Henry tears glistened in his eyes laying bare the opposition defeat. The opposition had been known to copycat off of positive attributes to keep the country in conflict. Henry couldn't fathom why anyone would work with troubled instigators versus citizens that were fighting for the good of everyone that was not a part of the violations of privacy and other human rights. He shook Charley hand firmly taking a long pause before gathering his thoughts. The gain could not have come at a better time to end the opposition tit for tat menaced behavior.

"Today mark one of the most significant achievements against opposition rebellion in history. None of the laws will have passed without great Patriots like the ones standing before us. You all fought to transform this country into unlimited possibilities and continuous efforts of greater heights superseding all adversaries. The volunteers fought every antagonistic group with strength and agility conquering a thrash. All of us made the passed laws the bedrock to protect what is most important. You all should be proud accomplishing public service for the people to feel safe and comfortable in their own neighborhoods. Some of the representatives measures passed managed to get people off the streets long-term. My staff and I have monitored the donations to make sure that the families were receiving the funding. My staff and I have stayed in the fight to bring the necessary programs to our counties to make sure families that has been affected mentally and physically or receiving the help that they deserve." Henry wiped away a tear.

"My staff and I have received sponsorship for hardship during the antagonism on citizen's finances wiping debts clean." Someone shouted out "Yes Lord", and the crowd broke into cheers.

"You guys have received what you deserve by paying fair taxes and receiving jobs with better wages. The interest rates has went down from the law that was passed that it is a crime to place excessive interest rates and high taxes on families to prevent the families from being able to get out of poverty. The federal government rally will show and prove that no one is above the law. There will not be any excuses to attack people without any repercussions. My office will continue to monitor and follow-up to keep the reasonable interest rates in effect. If we back off we will have to battle more opposition. My office cannot afford to let that happen again because the last attack on families took a big toll on our economy. Our communities lost many of the greatest fighters in this long run of taking back the community. The unnecessary profiteering has made laws much easier to pass."

Henry stood in unanimity with the brave souls. The pounding of fists and body pumping from the Herculean troopers made Henry fierce.

"A system we can actually trust that works this time around." Someone yelled.

Henry answered questions from the visitors and allowed families to share their heart felt stories live on TV. Homeowners and renters tuned in with sympathy. The looks on many of the onlooker's faces revealed emotional caring and solitude. It was definitely an archive to remember and a reason to fight to reinstate the trust.

"I am grateful for this moment to witness without doubt all of you healing together and helping one another in a time of relevance. The community of people is showing that we can stay strong in the storm and work together to beat any storm that comes our way. As a community we can face our problems head on and come up with solutions that fit all of our lives. Commitment is the kind of leadership that stands solid." Henry heart was heavy listening to what the local natives had to face that could have been avoided. Henry was in the fight for the long run to keep the locals from having to relive any of the hardship that was forced upon them at the hands of their own people.

"Henry, the people here are very fond of you. I can tell that you take self pride in representing the people in this county. Thank you for inviting me and my wife. I am a phone call away. I have to confer with Anthony on his politics 101 class. My staff is preparing the new team to be more productive with rapid options. Your family is always welcome to stop by and give your pronouncement." Charley and Kimberly left giving Henry best wishes on his journey.

Charley and his wife formal engagement with Charley's colleagues to listen in on plans to enhance communication and legislation for the mayor's office was a sine qua non. The mayor executing the laws and ordinances passed by a municipal governing body was where Anthony student's studies ended in his book mark last class. The students were getting in profundity with overseeing city services that ensure public service departments were operating effectively. Charley and his wife entered the class nonplussed to observe many young faces in the class of politics 101. The young people were prepared with notebooks and laptops. Charley and his wife took a seat not disturbing Anthony.

"I researched the population in our county and multiplied that number by the donations for the programs that were selected by the community." One of the students was saying to Anthony.

The representatives have had three different districts give rewards for their dedication to regulating the new city programs and making sure that everyone is helped. Congress and the citizens have also managed to make the lunch free for the students in public schools with low incomes overriding the state employees because of the state employee's corruption. The mayor was allowed to act in position of the state until the state was forced to comply to the state laws. The state employees were the main employees involved with criminal actions in large numbers. The taken over of power was expected to keep the counties from fallen under. The state employees never worked with the people liked they should. The state took a lot of money from people and gave them faulty call back numbers when the people wanted to ask questions. A state of emergency was declared to act in the state employee's position until new staff can be caught up on the corruption and clean up the damages. The federal government was worse by abusing their authority and not doing anything about what the state employees created.

"The monthly $3 dollar donations come out of all incomes every month to fund the programs. We are aware not everyone populating the country has an income. We had to estimate how much funding would be collected a month minus people without any income. I think this plan is a big success." The student passed around her groundwork.

"The volunteers have created a new census bureau process to count the number of people living in the households in our districts. After the count, we calculated the number of concerns in our districts." One of Anthony's students was reading off her progress sheet.

"The community of people found that the number one concern was the time frame it took to arrest and prosecute the ones who have deliberately violated their oaths and attacked families. The representatives and the people of the communities have people on top of the findings to make sure that their justice is taken seriously. We cannot allow representatives, law enforcement, court staff, prosecutors, congress members, etc. that are paid to not help the people oppressed. The detection was based on reported facts with proof that described personal feelings, beliefs, and envy being the reason for negating their duties. Personal feelings, beliefs, and envy are a serious concern among the households that provided their facts without knowing the people committing the crimes against them. The wrong questions were asked to the innocent. The suspects were not asked the right questions on purpose. A lot of people suffered because of this jealousy to try to send messages of their will instead of send messages by following the law." A student reported.

"There are way too many people that are affected by the voting process because of illegal pressures to vote for corrupted candidates. The families are asking for qualified candidates to keep the new system intact." A student sitting in the front row provided statistics from citizens.

"I agree." Anthony stepped up in the front of the class. The main pointers from his student's investigations proved that people were not being taught the way the law worked and the way politics should work. The city, state, and the federal government were doing their own lawless and reckless enforcement instead of applying the passed laws to citizen's violating all of their rights. The families were being attacked for not knowing that politics was hurting their fate and politics was forced in cases to not help their love ones.

"We can do a follow-up with the families who filed the complaints. Charley, Leilani, Alexis, Amy, and other staff from our team can get the families concerns answered rallying toward justice. The community is working on getting a program up and running next to City Hall. Residents can rely on protection and legal counsel. Anthony shuffled through his papers. Charley and his wife felt the class had a lot of potential to get young people incorporated to stop all the unnecessary violence and intimidation haunting the city.

"I would like to introduce Charley and his wife Kimberly who has come to check out the class." Anthony asked Charley and his wife Kimberly to come to the front of the class.

"I know most of you guys know Charley. I want Charley to share with the class his expertise on politics. Charley's education is crucial to our class on what I am to accomplish in the next four weeks. The class will be three months long with hands on cognition to safe proof the county for progressive decisions. The locals who vote or do not vote volunteers are pushing to prosecute troublemakers that follow people, or spot candidates signs in lawns, apartments, and on other personal property and rip down their signs. The candidates that some of the citizen's support other citizens try to make them uncomfortable if it is not their pick in the communities. Mail in and online voting is a work in progress for error free ballots. The citizens who vote or do not vote will be working with new police officers that comply to monitoring illegal devices that unlawfully monitor families in their homes without probable cause intimidating people. Intimidation is not the kind of resolution we use to resolve any issues when working with families. The mayor's office calls that kind of violation a felony. Anyone participating in that kind of criminal misconduct that is caught will be prosecuted to the fullest extent of the law."

"Cities and states use cameras to prevent crimes and not to commit crimes. The properties in this county have cameras where the most crimes take place. Our office have made the families aware that if anyone is caught filming anyone in their personal homes without consent, the ones caught will be prosecuted. The program selected to catch the criminals violating privacy and protection laws are experts that are trained in that field. The voters and people who do not vote do not violate innocent families to keep chaos going and make people in their own country feel like prisoners. Families that are not committing serious crimes against anyone in the communities will be protected." Charley pulled out his calendar.

"The petitions to sign into law to deter offenders from committing this kind of criminal misconduct will be posted publicly. The mayor's office is fully aware that not everyone wants to be on camera or in the media sharing their private lifestyles with strangers that can cause a lot of trouble for their families." Charley closed his calendar book.

"The mayor's office is having a celebration this weekend and all of you are invited. Guests will sign petitions to enforce all of the laws that passed in a timely manner with new training for law enforcement so that the arrests will be easier. The community of people does not want any police officers engaging in any kind of unnecessary roughness. The police officers will be trained to place people who commit certain crimes in the back seat of the patrol cars and not engage in any further conversation to create any kind of unnecessary chaos from developing. The city has lost a lot of revenue from lack of training law enforcement correctly. The violations are becoming a way to prevent law enforcement from being trusted to do their jobs. The community has requested that police officers not escalate tension with the suspects." The students weighed in admitting the laws had to be enforced properly.

Anthony students sparked questions on emergency crisis in areas where representation and law enforcement was not present. Anthony gave suggestions and examples on how to iron out obstacles if the proper authority was not present. Anthony turned off the electrical outlet and collected his books. Charley and his wife Kimberly waited for Anthony. Kimberly wanted to know how to get her friend's son in the class. Kimberly's friend son was an intern for the senator. He loved engaging in politics.

CHAPTER 8

HENRY OVERWORKED VISION BLURRED HIS anxiety was getting the best of him like it always did when he was fighting to win an election. Henry's wife could sense the agitation that her husband was feeling. Henry felt that he had to do more for families to stay safe after hearing about all of the horrific accounts that were perpetrated. Henry was not in his best superior strength to parley with his associates. He knew the fundraiser lifted the donors psyche. Henry and Astelle event was adorned with bright lights and donors dressed in beautiful gowns and expensive suits speaking to one another in total glee filled the occasion. The guests spotted Henry and Astelle erupting into loud applauds parading toward the crème de la creme.

"You guys are pretending to be excited to see me." Henry called out putting his best game face on for his welcoming friends. Astelle wanted to get through the night and take her husband home for him to de-stress.

Astelle made sure to make her rounds by saying hello to all of the donors. Astelle gave special one on one attention to show how much Henry and Astelle appreciated the donor's financial support. The A-list seemed to be making whoopee.

Out of no where one of Henry's associate's wives loudly scowled her husband. Astelle closed her eyes temporarily knowing the couple's history. Astelle knew Henry's associate Matthew's wife Marg personally. Marg did not bite her tongue no matter where she was when she was pissed off. Matthew showed signs of embarrassment and being terrified all at once.

"Matthew, how dare you flirt with this woman in my damn face?! Do you not see me sitting here? This is why I don't go anywhere with you! You are always embarrassing me with your weak spot for women and loose tongue when you are drinking." Matthew's wife snatched the glass from her husband's hand and threw the drink in his face.

Matthew froze doing the utmost to untangle what went wrong. Matthew's wife pushed on by grabbing Matthew out of his seat and dragging him toward the exit of the event with both her hands. The security guard separated the two. Matthew's wife was not having that. She shoved the security guard and grabbed her husband by the front of his shirt and pushed him out of the front door of the entrance. Matthew lost his balance and slid out of the front door falling at the top of the steps.

"Get up Matthew! I am not dealing with you tonight. We will finish this discussion at home. You are not hurt." Matthew's wife half drugged and pulled her husband up from the ground. The valet attendant drove up with their car. The valet attendant extended her arms out to aid in Matthew's wife getting in the car. Matthew's wife shoved the valet attendant and snatched open the passenger door throwing Matthew in the passenger seat and slamming the door in a rage. The valet attendant was very concerned as the couple drove off with Matthew's wife burning rubber out of the parking lot. The donors had jumped out from their seats staring on in bewilderment. Astelle was not moved at all. Astelle knew that she would be receiving a phone call later on in the night from Matthew's wife. Marg was not the type that waited to after an event was over to check her husband when he acted up. The donors made headway back to their seats after Marg burned rubber out of the parking lot. The onlookers cocked their heads in unison among one another. The lady that

Matthew allegedly flirted with decided to leave. She was discombobulated that Matthew and his wife had a fight over her. She felt out of place and did not feel comfortable going back into the event knowing that all eyes would be on her although it was not her fault.

Henry awkwardly undertook the audience using charm to calm the donors down.

"I did not mean for this to happen. My best pal doesn't go out of his way to make anyone uncomfortable. He is having a hard time with his marriage. If we can get back to passing the donations to the front, the show can go on." Henry faced turned beet red with humiliation. His wife held in hilarity standing close by her husband. Henry regained the floor to offer a prosperous ending speech for his friends. Astelle knew Henry was not unfamiliar with the couple marital woes. Astelle told her husband prior that maybe it was best if he did not invite the couple. Henry decided not to listen. Astelle found it strenuous to feel commiseration for her husband.

"Guys we all have those moments in long relationships. I am sure we are all grown enough to understand struggles in our lives and correlations. Let's not allow mishaps to put the kibosh on our intended cornerstone right." Astelle tried pumping up the crowd. The words of truth worked. The donors sympathized with thoughtful sentiments.

"I totally understand." One wife stroked her husband. He nudged his wife not to bring him into it the friction. The benefactors burst into cachinnation. Astelle's unfeigned words broke the ice easing the people back together.

Henry relieved that his wife saved him threw an airy kiss her way. He knew that Astelle was enjoying seeing him sweat because she had warned him. Henry did not think that Marg would behave that crazily in front of a room filled with philanthropist. Most often Marg spoke a few words then she would leave the disagreement alone. Henry assumed that Marg was fed up with Matthew. Marg could not manage her emotions and reactions. Henry's wife mentioned to him that Matthew exhibit disrespect from Marg more and more latterly. Henry would have to invite the two over to intercept the failing of the marriage.

"Henry, can you come over here for a second? I need you to speak to Dan. Dan thinks that the building is not suitable for the kind of purpose we are offering. Dan thinks we should put our colleagues on the second floor of the Watton building because the second floor space fits public speaking impeccably. What do you think Henry?"

Henry was in complete thought of Matthew and Marg marriage. Henry's buddy had to nudge him and ask Henry again snapping Henry out of his thoughts.

"I think either space will work. My offices have flexible colleagues who are appreciative and work hard no matter what. I don't think either space would matter. Dan can ask Johnny if they want to work in the other building. The expansion is almost finished."

"Henry, we might as well have our colleagues work out of there. The building will be up and running in a few days. There will not be any controversy on any of the spaces available."

"Henry, I spoke to Arnold. He didn't say that he did not want to work at the building that is almost completed. Arnold did say that the Watton building space would be much better. I wanted to mention the facts to you coming straight from Arnold's mouth. Anyway, this is a nice event, I appreciate my wife and I being invited. I needed to get away from all the pressure I am under. My campaign is going well. I'm in first place. I hope to keep first place. I need you all to come out and support me. I know I live farthest away. I planned our flight to support this event as soon as Henry let me know the minutiae."

"You never snatch forty winks Wilfred."

"That is why I'm in first place. I am obligated to juggle opposition in our county. Our county has water lines burnt out, abandoned buildings that the constituents have asked to be repaired, and people are operating businesses in hazardous ways. I visit every site with workers to superintend the complaints every time someone contacts my office. My staff noticed weird things going on the last couple of days with overcharging and not applying the law. Our office doesn't let people get harassed by hate groups that disregard the privacy and protection laws in our county. I don't want the citizens thinking that I do not care." Wilfred wiped his eye brow.

"That is the best way to keep the residents in seventh heaven. Never ignore the constituents and treat the constituents with respect. You will learn that the community will always support you." Henry stated with confidence.

"I hear you Henry. Your turnout is massive. I am proud of you my friend. You are a pillar in the community. I would love to schedule a time with you to go over key pointers for my campaign before I fly back home." Wilfred looked at his scheduling pad.

"Absolutely Wilfred. You set up the time before you fly back. Pencil me in where I can be of most service to your campaign. I'm going to bring my wife that way your wife does not get bored with all of our horseplay."

"My secretary will contact you with the particulars." Wilfred tilted his hat to Henry and went back to the seat where his wife was talking to another woman her raspberry tea ice melting.

The event took a turn for the best at the end for Henry advertisements and incentives. Henry's moment of drama with his associate had his guest reflecting on how precious time was in a relationship. Henry was concerned about Matthew and made a mental note to check on him later on after he got home.

"Honey, come and dance with me and take a load off of your mind. You are supposed to be enjoying yourself and hosting this event. You look frazzled and devitalized. I know Marg. She is not going to hurt Matthew too badly. She gets like that because she thinks her husband is trying to make her jealous."

"I think Matthew has been trying to make Marg jealous. Marg is not the type of woman Matthew should be playing with like that. The woman knows martial arts and bench press more weights than he does. Matthew needs to calm down before he ends up in the hospital. I thought Marg was going to kill Matthew. The way she grabbed him like a ragged doll, I think Marg shook him up pretty badly this time."

Astelle had to release the laughter that she had been trying to hold in. She could not hold it in any longer. Henry relaxed and joined in the laughter releasing a lot of unwanted stress that built up inside of him. The two danced to a few more songs with not a care besides uplifting one another. The comforting significance did not last long enough for Henry. He had to end the fun.

Henry and Astelle went home to a quiet house kicking off their shoes. The couple made it to the couch and could not make it up to their master bedroom. Henry kicked up his feet on the couch feet stool and closed his eyes. Astelle turned the television on, her husband nodded off within minutes. Astelle watched her favorite show for a while retrieving a blanket for her and her husband.

CHAPTER 9

MARG WAS IN A RAGE going off on Matthew from the time that they pulled up to their luxury home until the time she barged in through the front door kicking off her shoes and telling Matthew to leave her alone. Matthew couldn't get a word in edgewise to explain to Marg how much he loved her. He knew that was the only way he was going to get through the night alive. Marg was not trying to hear a word coming out of Matthew's mouth. She was furious roaming in the kitchen coming back out with champagne and a glass. She poured the first glass and gulped the champagne down like lemonade before sitting down on the living room sofa.

"Matthew, I raised millions of dollars for your associates funding and you have the audacity to demean me in front of all of those people gaping at some woman!" Marg hollered.

"I did no such thing! You embarrassed me acting a fool like I touched the woman or something. All I said was hi. You are always feeding more into something that does not exist. That is what is wrong with you Marg. You are gorgeous, smart, successful, and supportive. What would make you think that I was flirting by saying hello to a guest sitting at our table?" Matthew sounded irritated and tired.

"The way your eyes looked her body up and down when you said hi Matthew. Do not test me Matthew. You know exactly what I am talking about. Our closest friends were there. They are going to have a field day talking about how you disrespected me."

"First of all, no one is going to be talking about you because of me! They are going to be talking about you because you cannot control your temper. You had no reason to put your hands on me. I am your man woman! You have got to check yourself! You are not that upset. I looked at the gown the woman had on because it looks like the one I bought you! If you were not so damn crazy you would have noticed the gown too!"

Marg cocked her head in the air trying to remember what the woman had on. Sure enough it was similar to the gown Matthew bought her with a dozen of roses and a gift bag. Marg pretended not to remember and hurried toward the kitchen. Her husband continued to go off on her. Marg knew she had messed up.

"Where are you going big mouth? Oh, you don't remember the gown and gifts. Amnesia Marg? You cannot remember anything huh? You think I'm stupid. You think that I can't tell that you do remember and acted up for nothing." Matthew threw his shirt on the couch getting angrier.

"You better be glad that I love you. I was almost ready to put hands on your crazy behind. You know I'm not flirting with women in your face. I am a business man. Some of my main clients are women. They all know you and adore you. Get back in here Marg!"

Marg crept up the stairs tucking herself into the bed pretending to be knocked out sleep and could not hear her husband. She knew this was a fight she better let go of or the night could end very badly for her. Marg threw the cover on top of her fake snoring. Marg could hear Matthew going on and on. Matthew barreled toward the kitchen to confront Marg, when he could not find her in the kitchen Matthew raced up the stairs into their huge bedroom.

"You are not sleep." Matthew rushed toward his wife.

Marg did not budge. She kept on with her snoring act.

"Marg we will revisit this discussion in the morning. You will make this up to me. I want breakfast at 6 a.m. I want everything that I like hot and tasty." Matthew stormed out of the bedroom to go and sleep on the couch.

Marg knew she better set her alarm clock and make Matthew's breakfast early. Her husband was not letting her get away with the scene she caused. Marg dialed Astelle's number after her husband foot steps could be heard going back down the stairs.

"Marg, are you alright. I was about to call you. You shouldn't get yourself so upset over the little things in your marriage. Men compliment women all the time. Your husband adores you Marg."

"Astelle I was wrong this time. Matthew is furious with me. I wanted to call you and let you and Henry know that we made it home safely. I have to make this up to Matthew." Marg whispered into the phone.

Astelle assumed Marg had not calmed down. Astelle thought Marg was calling to keep up the fuss. When Astelle heard her whispering, Astelle knew Matthew slept downstairs. The two fought like toddlers at times. Their love over the years became complicated and edgy.

"Marg, you get some rest. You make sure to do something really nice for Matthew tomorrow. You know that you were wrong. That woman was not tripping off of Matthew. She knows how much he loves you."

"Astelle, I feel badly enough. Matthew already explained to me why he was looking at the woman because of the gown."

"I thought you knew it was because of the similar gown that Matthew bought you when we all went out and he gave you all those gifts?"

"Really, Astelle? You have to remember everything don't you? Don't remember the gown and gifts when we meet in a few days. I have already pretended to forget. Matthew would love to hear you say that you remember the gown and gifts. He will have a field day giving me the blues. I crawled up in the bed after he reminded me and pretended to snore. This man is

64

furious. I have never seen him this upset with me. I really acted a fool. I guess it is because I do not spend enough time with my husband. I am going to cook dinner all this week. I'm wrapping up work early everyday, I feel terrible. Tell Henry that I apologize. I do not want to be that wife that ruins all the fun at parties."

"Astelle, we do not think that you do these things intentionally. We know you are a woman in love with your husband. If you would have come to me before assuming that Matthew was flirting, I would have told you that he could have been admiring the gown because the gown reminded him of the one he bought you."

"Thanks for being a friend Astelle. I need to get some sleep. My husband expects breakfast at 6 a.m. Matthew is not going to forgive me for that stunt I pulled at you and your husband fundraiser. I will call you later on in the week. Astelle do not bring up the gown. Lord knows Matthew is not going to let up on this one."

"I will make an effort not to Marg." Astelle burst out laughing hanging up the phone.

"What is all the laughing about?" Henry woke up out of his sleep to Astelle hanging up the phone.

"That was Marg. She woke me up. She wanted to let us know that her and Matthew was fine and not to worry. They resolved their little fight and Marg is making it up to Matthew. Marg told me to tell you that she apologizes for the way she acted at your fundraiser. She didn't mean to cause a scene. She didn't mean to appear out of control and have been working a lot lately."

Henry moved closer to his wife. Henry wrapped his arms around his wife's waist and snuggled his face against her back. The couple went back to sleep.

Matthew woke up to breakfast in bed with all the tasty trimmings and his wife in sexy lingerie. Matthew held it together not to make jokes of his wife guilt as he sat up eating the breakfast. Matthew vaunted to himself

Tajai Calip

at how he had his hot-headed wife finally under control, although it was temporarily. He was going to take full advantage of the fight. Matthew knew Marg would not last that long being nice to him. Matthew was certain Marg remembered the gown and gifts when he saw all the breakfast favorites, squeezed orange juice, and his favorite biscuits. Matthew smiled to himself making sure that his wife did not notice his enjoyment biting into another bite of his breakfast. He picked up his orange juice. It was the best home squeezed orange juice that Matthew ever tasted. Matthew loved when his wife gave him attention and did wifey things for him. Matthew hated when his wife was preoccupied and could not make time for him. He was the one that thought that Marg was cheating. He never acted the way Marg acted last night. Now Matthew knew that they were both wrong.

"Do you want anything else my love?" Marg asked her husband sweetly not wanting to remember how she behaved the other night.

Matthew moved the breakfast to the side of the big bed and pulled his wife into his arms. He experienced guilt yearning for forgiveness to smooth things over and get their marriage back in order. The two fondled into their lovemaking. It had been a while since either had time for foreplay just a peck on the lips.

"Matthew, I'm sorry. I have not been myself." Marg admitted once she and her husband finished three rounds of intense love making.

Matthew relaxed satisfied placing his head on his wife's shoulder. Matthew did not feel like moving or going anywhere. He had his secretary to hold all his calls. He had his conference calls paused. His last three meetings would all be made from home. Matthew lied down in oneness when Marg rescheduled her day and for the first time in years did not go to work. The couple enjoyed one another all day and got all of their business handled from home. Later on that night, Marg made a spectacular dinner. The two ate at the table with candles lit catching up on business concerning their careers. The lovers usually spoke shortly in spurts of time due to their immersed schedules.

66

"I could get used to this treatment." Marg goo goo eyed her husband.

"Me too sweetheart."

"People are depending on us in our professions. We could cut our hours and balance both worlds. I don't want our marriage turning into passing time in the bathroom. I'm coming to work with you tomorrow and on Thursday you are coming to work with me. Friday we have to meet Henry and Astelle at our favorite restaurant. The people that we work with will understand. Matthew, our lives cannot pass us by from being overworked."

Matthew savored his meal broad-minded that his wife understood how a household should operate between a man and a woman. The couple went to bed after a long session of passionate love making eager for the next day to come to embark on their journey all over again.

Marg rose up robotically utilizing their kitchen to cook for Matthew as she promised. Matthew woke up not too long thereupon. Marg witnessed exactly how thorough her husband was peeking at his schedule. Marg was deeply saddened for not acknowledging his perseverance. The fight made their marriage chemistry powerful. Matthew arrived at his office building with several employees talking a mile a minute to catch him up Matthew. It was only one day and Matthew's colleagues and his employees flung project updates and reports for his signature. Matthew's partners were parading around town for the upcoming assemblage. Marg perceived her husband's workload along with important colleagues and employees.

"Hello."

"Marg, can I count of you to make an appearance tomorrow? I want to take some photos of you to post for the show."

"Of course, I'm going to bring my husband." Marg chatted with a dear friend.

"My photographer will love to take pics of both of you. When you arrive the booth will be at the regular photo venue."

Marg resumed to being noiseless watching her husband work. Matthew, a well-built man, with a big heart had Marg deeply in love. Matthew back at doing what he loved with his associates and his employees felt at home.

Matthew trudged over to his wife landing his hands on her shoulders. Matthew plodded Marg out of the door and into a vehicle waiting on the curb outside his office building. The devotees were on their way to Matthew's next forum.

"Matthew, Terry is on the phone. He said to meet at the fourth street location because he does not have time to get to the location that you guys usually meet at."

Matthew instructed the driver and Marg snuggled with her husband feeling dominant by his side.

"Babe, you can go inside. I'm going to take the call on the Cancer foundation and the chromosome research. Martha has suggested creating a link to submit our research on a new platform. It is best I learn how to use the link for the research."

"I love you." Matthew lightly bit his wife on the lips before getting out of the car.

"I wanted to give my wife brownie points for her kindness and dedication to my conscientiousness. I'm glad she has taken time off to be with me to show her the things I do with you loyal people in front on me."

Matthew new meeting began on time. Marg went back to the back of the room sitting soundlessly after her phone call ended. Marg fascination to learn some of her husband's businesses kept her focused. Marg studied leaflets tuning in to multiple responsibilities.

Marg engaged in her follow-ups. Marg listened to her husband and his colleagues introduce reproductive standards for the chromosome project. The group remained logical about offsets and abnormalities. Marg was besotted with how well the group worked together.

Matthew last meeting for the day transmogrified into his business partners wearing disguises for his introduction to a new brand study. Matthew warned his wife the last encounter would be an eye full. Matthew and Marg spoke for a couple of minutes. Another new group was filling in the comfortable chairs in disguises. Matthew's associates passed out informative inscriptions. A skit was performed.

Matthew and Marg drained from the day opened the front door to an overflow of mail. Marg energy evaporated. Marg and her husband embraced one another not saying a word. The two frozen in place cozied up motionless. Matthew and Marg slumbered near the refrigerator for cold water. Marg met her husband at the kitchen table longing for a long laving.

"Matthew, your commitment to what you do everyday has me looking at you in a different light. Your job is demanding. Your group handles pressure like pros. One meeting, after another meeting, at a fast pace like that, is not what I expected. I know you are wiped out. I'm drained from all the multiple contrasts simulations you conduct for your studies. Tomorrow your day will be less demanding. My team is playful and uncalculating, a spontaneous bunch of staff without too much haphazard ideas to balance the office. I provide a lot of services for client's potential endeavors. My exertions enfold in depth top priority outturns."

Marg remained on the first floor cozying up to the heated bathroom too shagged out to climb up the stairs to the second floor bathroom. The couple slumbered in the guest bedroom once Marg put her night gown on.

The next morning Marg was flipping eggs faithfully. The streak was not over. His wife actually kept her word to cook for the entire week. Matthew unquestionably knew a day or two would be all he was getting out of Marg, Marg was stubborn and Matthew was secure in one's belief that Marg would result back to her old ways of ordering food. Or Marg would have company bring food on their way over. Other times Matthew and Marg picked up food for whichever one was coming home first after a lengthy day because Marg didn't trust another woman in the home to tend to the home. Marg allowed the house to be thoroughly cleaned twice a week and maintained the home in between like a responsible housewife. Marg refused to let a woman stay in her home because she did not like how

Matthew misbehaved around women. Matthew was not going to let any man stay in the home to do the cooking and cleaning. Matthew did not want his wife to stop the routine. Matthew dressed casual for a gripping day with his wife. Matthew well rested body set on meeting the new people that his wife encountered with everyday.

"You look debonair." Marg reached over and gave her husband a peck.

Matthew patted his wife behind smelling the French vanilla coffee, waffles, chicken, sausage, hash browns, and eggs.

"So do you. You are looking scrumptious." Matthew flirted.

It was time to drop in at Marg's place of business. The moment Matthew stepped inside the building. Lights. Camera. Action. People flooded his wife with cameras, taking snapshots asking Marg questions. Matthew thought to himself that his wife's place of business was incredible.

"Marg, how do you feel about the development in the next block over that may jeopardize a lot of local businesses?" Marg knew that she would have to take up for a friend who decided to open a business that was frowned upon in the area.

"I heard that the building was approved by a majority of the people that lived in the surrounding neighborhood. As long as the business generates revenue and give some of the proceedings back to the neighborhood, I suppose that most of the neighbors will be welcoming. I know we had a few people apprehensive. Nothing bad has happened so far. The community can wait and see."

"Well, I have heard that a few people do not want the business to get approval and permits. We are interviewing the ones concerned I will make inquiries into their reasonings." The news reporter stated.

Marg regressed back to taking pictures and signing autographs. Her husband looked on in astonishment at how poised and professional his wife was in the spotlight.

"Marg, can you and your husband take a few photos on this side?" Marg's friend held the camera in position while Marg walked over to her husband. Matthew smiled taking beauteous shots with his wife. Marg's friend approved the negatives clicking the camera a few more times before leaving the couple alone. Marg's friend sneaked pics without either knowing. Matthew wrapped up consultation. Marg interview with the news reporters in giggly fashion ended with air brush kisses. The photos came out first rate making Chanel session easy. Chanel hated polishing photos. The couple flawless poses did not need any brushing up.

Matthew cheered Marg on reading through thick pages for more clarity on Marg's business. The supportive team worked by her side complimenting his wife grind. Marg in full swing of duty style with her team recoiled back when one lady walked up to her insinuating that Marg was taking sides with the new business development owner. The business owner was Marg's friend. Marg barked out a warning ready to pounce. Marg pushed herself up from her desk. Matthew knew reaching his wife and getting the lady approaching his wife out of the building was paramount. Marg week had been blossoming. Matthew did not want anyone to see that other side of Marg after a blessed week.

"Excuse me Miss. I think it is time for you to leave. I don't want my wife upset. She is working. Her place of business is off limits." Matthew escorted the lady out of the door. Marg sprang back into action not missing a beat.

CHAPTER 10

H ENRY RUSHED UP THE STAIRS to grab Astelle from out of the bed. He was so ecstatic Henry almost fell. Henry had been fighting forcefully and on a regular basis to turn what prosecutors was calling complex to simplicity for the people in his county that had sent him so many emails. The emails and voice messages haunted Henry at night and Henry was not going to stop fighting for the people until people started being arrested for what the criminals were doing in his county.

"Henry, what are you doing?' Astelle rushed the covers back up to her chest to go back to sleep.

Henry tugged the covers completely off of Astelle causing his wife to jolt up with a major attitude. Astelle snatched the covers back up to her chin when Henry turned the news up and Astelle gaped on disbelievingly. The moment of truth and the history of what the two had been fighting to accomplish had finally arrived. Astelle wide-eyed stare stuck to the TV validating public officials departments workers being arrested. A sweep in every major city and state covered the news of the arrests. Judges were handcuffed along with law enforcement and top position personnel who continued to take advantage of their positions at the worksites. Astelle struck her palms together wildly jumping out of bed bouncing up and down. She jumped into Henry's arms. Henry kissed his wife passionately. The phone rang breaking up the passionate moment.

"Henry, turn on the news?!" Matthew yelled into the phone with a relieved voice.

"I'm celebrating with Astelle!"

"You and Marg should swing by. All of us can speak to the representatives that fought to make this memorable time happen. The representatives that pushed the bills earned proper recognition." Henry couldn't contain his excitement.

"Marg and I will be joining you all shortly."

Matthew hung up the phone to share the victory with Marg.

Marg was baffled at the misbehaved clique. Many locals on camera could be seen crying and praising the Lord that people were going to jail to reimpose order in their lives. Victims spilled their stories on how much money through online scams they lost and all the programs that made only certain people rich. Marg felt saddened by what she learned from people revealing the names of the abusers she thought was good people. Some of the suspects arrested became Marg's friend through acquaintances. Marg refused to support scandals that destroyed blameless families. Marg turned up the volume to hear a guy speaking on how he felt the narcissists tried to make citizens feel they were lucky.

"The deceptive judge told me and my wife that we should be lucky because there were people in other countries hungry and without a lot of resources. The comment on stealing our savings and illegally arresting me was supposed to make me feel better about other countries problems. I don't have anything to do with people with dual citizenship that play off of us and make us feel like we should be grateful that they do not steal more and commit more crimes against us." The man stated in an angered voice.

Marg was shaking her head in agreement. The downfalls in a crooked system of manipulation was galling, Marg felt the aggressors that caused the crimes should not be freed. Marg was offended.

73

Matthew pricked up one ear buttoning his shirt. One of the representatives that Matthew and Marg befriended spoke to the reporters stating that their office rallied around successfully to pass a law that gives term limits. People who supported the term limits came forward to prove why it was necessary to remove people after a certain amount of time in office. The representative shared clips of data for how much money was being misused to help people in their counties. There were specific names and locations of people who was meeting and using the money for their own agendas while families starved and suffered from homelessness. The list went on forever. Photos of new prisons highly trained guards and convicts assigned to harm convicted felons photos were taking receiving money and bribes. Matthew turned the television off. His wife led him out the front door to their car to meet their friends. Nausea feelings about what transpired muddled their minds. The arrests were overdue for repeated transgression. Law enforcement assigned heavy ammunition to make sure that there were not any riots to protect the families who had spoken out about all the corruption.

"Marg gazed upon the streets of people pacing in deep colloquy. Signs held up saying "term limits" circulated among the rabble. Dozens of flowers and picture frames of casualties decorated the middle and corner streets in the neighborhoods. Marg was pissed heading toward the freeway. The freeway was packed.

"Matthew citizens are out from every path of life outraged by the immoral behavior."

"I know we should have taken the streets to Astelle and Henry's home. I had no idea this many people would be traveling. Everyone seems to be blithe about this transparency forcing actual accountability. I bet we are going to hear more and more families speaking out now that people are being arrested. The ones arrested are not the usual suspects seen on the news. It is about time we start doing better and not disappointing the people. I made sure to send all of the donations that we received to all of the programs and charities that we mentioned. The families really need the support. My staff made sure to post online. One of our closest friends has been arrested in all of this the man has enough money to retire." Matthew shook his head.

"The ones least expected are the ones who commit the most dirty deeds. I don't understand how the culpable can come to all of our meetings and fundraisers knowing what they have done. It makes all of us appear to be untrustworthy." Marg was disappointed.

"I do not put anything past anyone nowadays. We do not know honey. We think we know people until they are thrown in with the wolves to get paid off. Most of the people are going to take the money. People have not had to go to jail. The norm has been to blame people who cannot defend themselves. Some of our own colleagues have blemished innocent people's lives. The families tricked recovered from relentless hardship. I wouldn't ever force anyone in a nemesis."

"Matthew, we work too hard to do something that inhumane. Our budget works for us so that we do not need to steal from anyone. People give to our causes out of the kindness of their hearts. They support our truth about keeping the community stable. I think most of the ones involved did not even need the money. It is a damn shame to take resources away from poor people knowing that you already have enough. To go further with the unethical damage by arresting the ones who survived the continuous attacks is mind boggling. You and I have covered the most crooked programs with complaints reported that the dwellers were never given anything when they were referred to the programs. Our staff sent different races to the programs furnishing the data of the races that benefited. It was not a mistake. The programs are dividing people based on their race when they qualify for benefits. My office sent in undercover agents to bust up programs that have been getting away with the kinds of crimes that make you want to yawp." Marg facial expression bothered.

"There has to be actions of reinforcement to stay on malefactors who keep thinking that they can become program directors or hold titles to steal. The ones robbing folks blind have gotten too bold. The invaders saw all the evidence against them. It is best to make sure prosecutors and law enforcement that are not corrupted make the arrests and prosecute. I think a lot of people who worked in the public departments were in on the scams. That is why it has taken so long to end this fudging. Most of the representatives and concerned victims all had to get undercover agents to catch the offenders."

"Our department's staff keeps the undercover agents low key to confront the people violating the families in the programs rights and privacy. The intimidation keeps the scams going. The victims, public departments, agencies, and local businesses cannot afford to let infamy get out of hand. The arrests will send a message to the ones thinking about getting into high position that they can be charged based on the laws."

"Awareness is the goal. My office assisted to send a message to the ones who has been causing stumbling blocks by taking advantage of low income families. We will get the money back every time someone is overcharged. The sanctions and fines will go to the people being targeted. The law stands firmly to enforce suffering the consequences by being held liable for their actions. The way that our staff can tell if any of our undercover agents are a part of the plights is when the agents do not want to prosecute the evidence obtained legally. Evidence does not take long to figure out who is guilty. When the community of people cross a road block with law enforcement and prosecutors that would whether arrest someone who is not doing too much of anything versus people with a lot of evidence against them in the Media, those are the government employees that should be removed. Term limits are a structural balance. Term limits are a necessary dedication to the citizens who lost loved ones due to all of the lies originated by imposters that were actually the guilty ones." Matthew culminated.

Marg exited off the freeway reducing her tauntness. The freeway traffic was getting heavier. Marg wasn't regale by the heavy traffic. It was mystifying to overcome the thought that her own friends had looked her right in the eyes and lied to her. The deceit nagged Marg. She struggled to keep her shrewdness. Marg reached their destination at Astelle's winsome property chuffed to have a distraction from all the madness.

"Astelle, this is a scandalized ordeal!" Marg bellowed. The distraction vanished. The front door ajar with a few people already inside considering the pros and cons of the odium broadcast.

"Can you believe the boldness of the accused? Can you fathom Mario playing a part in a tasteless negligence? He is damn near a billionaire. How dare Mario interconnect in an unfavorable scheme! The news asserts that Mario compos mentis of innumerable programs that was duplicitous. The charities fronts diverted the authority attention elsewhere." Astelle rushed Marg into the kitchen to catch the camouflage unveiled.

"Marg, you are going to need to sit down for what I am about to share with you. This uncovering can infuse acute myocardial infarction. I did some digging and the headlines may be true." Marg slowly sat not wanting to hear what was about to come out of Astelle's mouth.

"Ferria is ensnarled. Ferria cashed many checks that were supposed to be sent to the charities that she was raising money for. The checks were being deposited into an offshore account." Marg almost felled out of her seat. Ferria was one of Astelle and Marg's closet girlfriends. They all grew up together. Marg had not seen Ferria in a while. Marg heard that Ferria was doing decent for herself. Marg sat feebly. She could not find any words to say delineate with what Astelle shared with her. The alleged crimes were a big traumatism. Marg was having an involuted time accepting the validation.

Astelle ambled over to the table and offered Marg some cold water.

Astelle under went problematic palpitation detecting Marg silently thunderstruck not verbalizing a word. Astelle positioned her chair next to her friend biting into one of the small sandwiches to calm her racing heart beat.

Henry saw the two women sitting and knew that Marg learned of Ferria's ruination. The couples confounded and ashamed retracted their certainty. The group of worrisome friends associated with mostly all of the people jumbled in the swindle. The buzz made them feel out of place. Henry gave Marg a hug leaving the two women alone.

CHAPTER 11

"Astelle I was thrilled when the accusers that I did not know were handcuffed. Seeing our own friends arrested hit me kind of hard. These are people who are successful, intelligent, and do not have to commit any of the crimes announced. For instance, take Mario. Mario is one of the smartest people that we know. He knows how to make a legal profit off of anything. I cannot imagine why any of the ones we know would want to use their skills to get over on people. Has the money made Mario that arrogant and careless? I cannot understand why Ferria would do this to her children. Ferria's children are going to be heartsick. The arrests are going to cause a lot of heartbreaks."

"I totally understand Marg. Why would friends of ours involve themselves in fraudulent business transactions? I would not expect our friends that have children to ever do something like this. I can understand if they were broke. These are people who grew up spoiled. Excuses are unacceptable. I have to say it, the ones that committed the crimes all deserve jail time. Too many people are hurting from what took place. Did you see the faces of the families on the news spilling out their guts? I almost cried. I hate to see that kind of mischief happen to anyone, let alone by friends that we know."

"True Astelle. The ones close to us that we met through different friends all went too far. Jail time is exactly what should be given out. People of our status have to protect our love ones and make sure that our love ones do not engage in this kind of contradicting activity. I do not want to see another person I know in the news headlines associated with immature actions that can bring us all down. I have called a meeting at my place of business. My office is going over everything. I do not want any heat coming down on me."

"It is not our job to worry about what people do off work if it is not associated with the company. I am concerned about people violating our company. I'm going to make sure the books are all intact." Astelle drank water clutching her chest.

"I can talk to the head of our board. Some of my staff is related to judges and can visit the prisons to see how many people have been in jail without probable cause because of the cover ups. You know when this kind of exploitation takes place innocent people are set up for the fall. The community and representatives cannot let the lies go on any further." Astelle glanced at her nails.

"My money and resources are for justice for the people. The legal connections my office offers to fight against injustices instead of abusing power is one of my company's goal. I did not like how David was arrested after Calvin was shot. David and Calvin are best friends. The courts have separated the two men and want people to believe that there was some kind of beef between David and Calvin the night of the shooting. Calvin seemed dazed as if he was drugged. Unlawful misconduct happens to too many people who do not have legal connections and programs that help. The community cannot stand back and watch the innocent go to jail for no reason." Marg tone was authoritarian.

"This is unbelievable to say the least. Famed public figures were arrested at their homes in front of their children. Others renowned families were dragged away from the buildings in handcuffs. It was like a big drug deal gone wrong. What is about to happen next is our community of people that complained about their money being taken to support bad businesses and ideas are coming to the forefront." Astelle pushed her chair to the side to give Matthew more room.

"What about the injured parties who has been incarcerated for years and have not committed a crime? What are we going to do about that? My office prepared a public statement to give a voice for the people not being represented justly." Marg affirmed.

"I have a few friends in law enforcement." Matthew pulled out a chair.

All the fuss had the community in a counterblast. Henry and Astelle were determined to even the odds with Matthew and Marg and square up to the insanity.

"I told Havana to contact the person that committed that crime against me online. She said the woman hung up in her face accusing my office of committing more crimes." Matthew was livid.

"We face controversy and denial when nothing is done about prior dissension." Matthew tossed a few olives into his mouth.

"People always clap back to the past if they are asked about accountability to get out of being held liable. The community of people cannot allow that reaction. Besides representatives and public officials have to stick with facts and specific cases reported at the time. Strangers cannot bring up issues that do not have any connection to the original complaint dates." Marg supported her husband's point of view.

"I told Havana to draw up the paperwork and have the ones who committed the online crime served. My attorney found all of the liable people to serve them. I am not about to take a loss because of something that is on the news. I do not have anything to do with what occurred. If I did I would be arrested." Matthew did not like being thrown in the middle of unsettling quarrels.

The three cronies forced to justify their actions sulked. Matthew was oppressed by the impact the crimes had on his businesses. He formed personal relationships with defendants proclaimed on the news. The crimes that Matthew's associates were arrested for would be sorted out. Matthew was reassured there was nothing that he did to have anyone coming at him. Although that was all true, the unknown online cynical doubters came at him behaving surely that he was guilty.

Marg, Astelle, and Matthew entered the living room. More people had arrived.

"I guess we are all going to have to put our heads together to come up with something workable." Astelle enjoined her guests.

Old pals from years back exchanged tip-offs from gossip on the streets. Chums nervously anticipated adverse consequences. The day turned into an abomination for the group the more the news kept putting out information of the crimes that were being reported by law enforcement.

Henry went into the kitchen with a few more men to cater to the bunch by bringing out trays of finger foods that were delivered earlier that morning after the news caught his eye. The workers were sent home for Henry's privacy. Henry hoped to find answers to get their associates out of trouble. Henry's grateful attitude toward the gang to get to the bottom of the huge disaster showed. Henry was more grateful that none of the ones in the circle currently had fingers pointed toward them. Henry undergo of dejection for the love ones that he did witnessed broadcasts taunted him. Some of the assumptions were egregious. Homeowners in the areas wept in a frenzy to hold their love ones being hauled off to jail with the love ones hands behind their backs and heads down trying to avoid the cameras. The children squealing voices echoed with terror. The news reporters scrambled to cover the stories frantically unfolding flustered perversity. Spectator's bodies overflowing the boulevard on pins and needles observed an underworld of inferior discovery under their own noses. The arrests trembling the least expected because of their widely spread relations with the rich and famous. It was truly a sad sight.

"Henry, I have someone on my cell phone that would like to speak to you." One friend handed Henry his cell phone.

Henry startled hearkened to diffuse the unimagined destruction.

"Hello." Henry accepted the cell phone caller in curiosity of who was on the other end of the receiver. Henry did not think that he could dissect any more bad news.

"Henry, this is attorney Meek. I was wondering if we could schedule a time for us to talk. I have a few people down here at the county jail that asked me to contact you. A few of my clients claim that they work for you. My clients are refuting the alleged grievances in the scandal on the morning news."

Henry hesitated wanting to reject getting involved but accepted the fate of disloyalty if he failed his workers pleas. Henry's choices were limited if any of his employees mentioned his name to an attorney at the jail.

"How can I be of assistance Meek?"

"Well, if you can provide the days and times of employment for the alleged crimes involving your employees, that would be a secure alibi to get the cases thrown out. My clients are not on any surveillance cameras. No one has been able to identify my clients cashing the checks. All we need is their work schedules to show my clients at work when the checks were cashed. I would have to ask you to let me look into your backlog to toss out if there were any meetings with the ones who cashed the checks."

"Who are the defendants? What were the checks for Meek?" Henry hoped that it was not any of his loyal clients or donors. Henry did not want to get anyone into any trouble hoping that he did not need an attorney himself.

"I can email you the suspected persons in question. I can also provide you with the amounts of checks that were allegedly cashed by your employees."

Henry scratched his head in incredulity. How did someone get checks and accused his employees of cashing the checks. Henry guessed that if the arguments were true the evidence would have had to be transactions not connected to his company. Henry would have known if any of his employees were placing checks into any of his business accounts.

"I would access my records for the evidence. I have to tell you that I operate a licit business. If there are checks involved, the checks were not involved in any of my business accounts. I check my accounts regularly. I keep receipts for all clients that I accept checks from on a monthly basis. The arrangements would be outside of my business."

"If that is the case, your employees have nothing to fear. The dates and times will prove their innocence. The witnesses who are making the accusations stated that they met with your employees a few times. Your employees are stating that they do not know the accusers. I don't know who to believe. All I know is that the log in on your computer database will help your employees get released. I can get my clients out on bail the faster you send me the proof."

"I can gather the proof right away." Henry hung up the phone handing the cell phone back to its possessor. Henry examined the living room every devoted ally was at work writing down what part of the slander the ally would cover and who the ally would contact. Marg dialed her true blue entourage about the arrests charges of their cortege. She wanted to know how was the evidence obtained and who reported the crimes. Astelle was online responding in a conference about what actions to take. The arrests professed individual transactions outside of the workplace. Astelle was not accused of aiding her associates some of the proof was hearsay. Astelle's intuition told her the absurd hearsay was a waste of time on annoying troublemakers that did not know what to do with their purpose of usefulness.

Henry cleared his throat to get his friends attention. Their heads was down in cell phones and computers. The supportive partisans took heed to Henry's presence.

"I think that we are being set up and the sufferers who are being accused have not committed what was alleged. I received requests from my employee's attorney. The alleged checks my employees are accused of receiving have to be fake checks. The checks are not connected to my employees work accounts. My employees do not know the accusers. The checks have not been posted in any of my employee's accounts. The attorney is asking that my employees are released on bail and that the alleged checks are authenticated before trying to charge my employees.

"Unfortunately Henry, there is evidence of a couple of our friends that we know that I am on the computer researching. The checks were not only posted in their accounts with verifications, the checks were reoccurring every two months in large amounts of money. The lowest check deposited in Ferria, Mario, and a few others accounts were for one hundred and fifty thousand dollars." Matthew's friend stated handing Henry his cell phone of the evidence.

"Damn." The group uttered under their breaths.

Henry was hopeful that his findings of a setup would bolster up for the people that he knew who got arrested. The discovery Henry found for his employees promised relief. Henry was thankful that his employees were being released. Henry did not know what he was going to do about his friends that cashed the checks. His first thought was to make sure that the ones involved returned the money back before the court dates. Henry was not the expert on how much jail time his friends could get for the crime. Henry knew that if his friends could produce the money that will help a lot.

"Astelle, a word with you in private." Henry guided Astelle toward the kitchen. Astelle ended her communications on all her devices to have a word with her husband. Astelle and Henry fundraiser awareness for Social Security and Mental Heath Services included all of his allies for support to help disability people and people that suffered mentally from tragedies in their lives. Henry had an early engagement he couldn't afford to miss for reform and revised amendments. Henry juggled multitudinous forums on his plate. His time was divided enough without adequate rest.

"Astelle, I surmise all of the money that Ferria and Mario collected is sitting in accounts. We cannot determine from the telecast if the funds were to be donated to another source. There isn't any certainty that anyone committed a crime yet between the two. Let's divide up the group to go down and speak with someone in charge. It will take too long for an answer by phone. The prosecutors need time to go over the charges. Our group can get a better understanding if we hear the facts from the horse's mouth. You and I can ride over to the jail to meet Ferria and Mario's attorneys. The attorneys are at different locations. I asked one of our associates to meet Mario's attorney. We can check on Ferria. Ferria's children reputation is more important. I can bring Ferria's youngest daughter to court. The judge will observe that Ferria is a mom that has to be with her daughter."

Astelle obliged her husband following his orders. She was proud of Henry taking charge without losing control. The bad publicity triggering the public induced enough for anyone to feel swamped. Instead, Henry monopolized the rhetoric with confidence maintaining holding his composure. Astelle felled into her husband's gentle arms for buttress. The companion reentered the living room to discuss the disturbing developments with their friends.

"It is time to meet our donors for the programs on the brink of being slashed." Henry concluded the meeting.

Professional drivers arrived to abettance Henry and his friends. Henry point of convergence was fleetingly disrupted to make calls, speak to his friends, and send information to attorneys.

Henry spotted supportive friends waiting for him and Astelle at the fundraiser. Most of the friends making their appearances caught a glimpse of the news and was talking about the horrific scene displayed in front of millions of people. The guests gave a big hand greeting Henry openly. Henry was fed up. He rolled over all night prior taking in a few hours of sleep. Henry straight posture revealed no signs of the dreadful night of butterflies in his stomach.

"What an exigent evening for our community notorious reported findings. I know you all have heard the bad news. Let's try to put that behind us and linchpin on the prestige at hand. It is important that we keep moving forward to help the people in our communities. The families rely on us now more than ever." Claps and cheers exploded.

"We all know what this evening is to bring forth. We plan to make a great impression for the citizens who are counting on us. Our mission post is that this event concocts miracles for the ones worthy of assuage. My lovely wife is passing out booklets for you all to look over. It will be greatly appreciated if you all take out some time to read the booklets. I am sure that you will find something that will suit all of your ideology." Henry stepped away.

Matthew arose contending his efforts in his speech of mercy for natives not available. Matthew ideas to benefit the people in disarray relied on the kind hearts in attendance. The pitch for durability to sustain the harmed community resonated among the followers. Matthew rigorous exemplar as a scholar melted the familiar faces center. Henry reunited with Matthew enlightened by a powerful adage. Matthew seized the evening with dignify entitlement.

CHAPTER 12

ALEXIS AND AMY RELINQUISHED CONTROL to key speakers invited to City Hall to speak. Alexis sat next to Leilani and Charley. Amy was crossed-legged on the other side of Leilani and Charley speaking to one of the representatives in private. Leilani perfected her lecture with Charley. The team satisfied corollary from all the suggestions that were brought forward.

"Alexis, I think that that is about all I have for you guys. I will leave my contact information for any of the clients that you guys speak to in housing to call me. I am not available on Fridays. Any other day is fine from 8:00 a.m. to 6:00 p.m.

"My staff appreciates all the help you have done for the locals in the community. I do have a few people that asked for your contact. I will get their names emailed to you before the end of the day." Alexis's speaker's tips craved.

"If there is not anything else or any questions we can all reconvene tomorrow at 9:00 a.m. in the conference room." Alexis team edifying advancement for what staff members propounded to the families afflicted from housing quandaries.

"Charley, are you going back to the office? I need to grab my black folder off of your desk. I left you notes from last week meeting. I hope you did not throw the folder away."

"Leilani, you know I do not throw folders away. The folder is tucked in my top drawer. The office door is unlocked. Can you lock the door back for me once you grab the folder? Kimberly and I have a date night tonight. She bought tickets to a concert. We have plans after the concert."

"Enjoy your date night. "Leilani motioned Charley off. Leilani's phone was beeping repeatedly. Leilani made plans to meet her besties for dinner at their usual spot.

"I am on my way." Leilani responded without saying hello into her cell phone one of her best friend's number on display.

"We will see you when you get here."

Leilani hung up the phone and locked Charley's office door behind her. The restaurant was not far from City Hall.

Leilani reached her destination. The restaurant was packed with cars. The restaurant procured the best food, drinks, and music. She enjoyed meeting her friends up there after a long work day. Evan always ended up coming to pick Leilani up with a few of his buddies as protectors. The crew would enjoy themselves for a few hours before the next work day or weekend.

Leilani and her friends surveilled the dance section of the classy restaurant enjoying the hip music. The customers in the restaurant tested out new dance moves with hands carelessly in the air posing to take selfies. Leilani locked in the diversion forgetting the order of drinks. Leilani danced over to the table signaling her friends. Giggles broke out when more drinks arrived at Leilani's table. One of Leilani's best friends had ordered drinks for the social set. The patrons in the restaurant kept clowning around lifting up drinks dazzled by the hosts. The hosts fraternized with Leilani's group vibes linking together in the photos. Goofy faces captured on phones in the distance.

The next morning Charley woke up exhausted. He was pooped from the previous day staying in bed all day was his goal.'

"Why are you laying down? Don't tell me an one night outing has you whopped." Kimberly pulled back the blinds.

"I'm staying in to replenish. I know I should be getting ready but I'm going to pass this time. I don't feel like being around a lot of people, besides the social get together is not mandatory. Our office throws delightful appreciation days to socialize. A way of basically saying thanks for all the work that we do for others. The staff does not have to go if the staff does not want to go."

"Come on Charley. I wanted to mingle with friends and catch up with Alexis. We haven't been talking lately. My days are work, work, and more work. After I visit you guys at work back to work I go. I'm caught up with all my responsibilities I had to complement before the ending of our six month time limit."

"Kimberly, you can go without me. You do not need me to come with you. There are several people that you can call to pick you up or drive to the lake by yourself. Call Leilani. Leilani loves hanging out with you."

"Let me give Leilani a call before she gets to the lake so she doesn't have to turn around."

"Sounds great." Charley laid back down in the bed. He turned on the television setting the timer for his movie. The vibrating noise vibrated his pillow.

Henry absorbed in checking on friends arrested called Charley.

"If you haven't already heard Mario and Ferria was arrested."

"Mario and Ferria were arrested for what?"

"I'm not sure yet. I am here at the jail to speak with Mario's attorney to find out what I can do to get Mario out of jail. I know the attorney is working on releasing Mario. Astelle has gone to check on Ferria. Astelle and I are going to pick up Ferria's daughter if Ferria is not released."

"I was lying in the bed. Two judge's names flashed across my tube.

The police was handcuffing the judges. The judges are resisting arrests. The reporters are saying the judges were guilty. The public officials wake up call to stop all the corruption that is accepted and tolerated publicly is being reexamined. The public departments don't want to affect the employees mandatory reporting of violations in the workplace. The representatives have to make the people that we represent trust us enforcing the reevaluations." Charley shot up from bed.

"Four prosecutors are involved. A few City Hall council members being removed vowed to cooperate I cannot tell you how many going down forced to resign after the reports of the families that were ill-treated. The city, state, and federal employees play off the people unawareness. There are too many departments that are not helping and the community doesn't want the buildings occupied. The mayor is over the city and should be able to address everything going wrong in the city no matter the state and federal employees. We are not making any progress separating who should make sure enforcements are enforced right away."

"I heard that a couple of internal affairs agents removed from their positions rolled over on the police at fault. The internal affairs agents removed were not reprimanding polices that were involved in major crimes. It was either them or the officers. I was sleeping in. I might as well get up. Alexis is going to be devastated." Charley grabbed a shirt.

"Law enforcement should have arrested judges committing criminal misconduct in the courts every time the crime takes place. The clerks are guilty of serious crimes in the courts too. Judges didn't gag or place injunctions on police or prosecutors abusing their authority. The courts are the main ones igniting all the riff raff in the communities refusing to check one another. The congress members forced to resign concealing sexual harassment, abuse, campaign and election crimes for colleagues were listed in controlling the courts. The resignations are mandatory and wanted. The recipients being attacked should have never had to wait for law enforcement to pursue the aggressors. The representatives, public officials, and the community forming hate groups are unacceptable. A lot of us knew that the people complaining about the serious corruption in high positions were being harassed. We didn't provide any protection on the level of ending the devastation. A lot of us tried to look the other way when the departments and public officials involved should've wanted to get all the troubled ones out of office a long time ago." Henry despised the nonsense.

"Some of us have come up with a new plan for law enforcement agencies in our cities and states. The citizens cannot allow private law enforcement that work for specific people to be the final voice in citizen's arrests. We demand fair investigations when holding anyone in jail long-term based on the law and not what private parties want to do without following the laws. The jails cannot be private, house people born in this country unfairly, and unjust without serious consequences held against the criminals committing the crimes. The people deserve reliable policing and honest workers. The residents accepting private jails in our cities and states that are knowledgeable that the private institutions are crooked and corrupt are hindering the cause for change. That action is bringing more chaos in the places that chaos is being cleaned up. It will not make any sense to arrest all of the people being arrested on the news to allow private jails to fan the flames by violating the laws established." Charley insisted.

"I agree. No one should be able to make up their own laws if it takes away from the citizens well being and financial independence. The agencies in charge nonchalant attitudes toward reckless and lawless actions fueled this fire. The government disregarding what ruin lives must be challenged. Our office wants to assist victims that were denied justice by firing the liable parties. The government employees stalling on preventing the injustices are the contradiction. The community not involved in none of the conflicts is asking to prevent injustices and instigating." Henry had had enough.

"How can law enforcement agencies let people log onto social media making surviving worse with intentions to harm innocent families. The platforms that help the criminals stay illicit brings more work for us to do. In order for us to end violence and deaths we need public platforms that speak about non-violent issues, i.e. exercising, cooking, dancing, jobs, etc. How is there going to be an end to violence and deaths with troublemakers all over the internet talking about savagery in front of millions of other people. If celebrities have died already from madness due to misinformation and disinformation, there should have been some kind of injunction in place. What makes law enforcement think that more famous people or their families are not going to be affected if the attacks persist? A lot of the instigators are not smart enough to be on the public platforms. The instigators are making resolutions impossible by lying and posting fake photos next to victims or with victims in the photos." Charley preached.

"The second someone calls the troublemakers out on the lies, the habitual liars have the audacity to behave as if they are upset. Whomever thought that this kind of ignorance was a good idea has placed all of us in drama. Our communities nor the representatives can achieve safety or stability permitting the troublemakers on social media to give rise to blather right in our faces." Henry chimed in.

"I think the instigators that forces citizens who are minding their business to have to constantly defend themselves need some form of ramifications. Our communities of families have too many people forced to get on social media to defend their name and character that do not favor social media. We have scammers creating companies to steal important and private information from people and post fake profiles online destroying too many families. Why would law enforcement ever allow something this uncivilized to happen?" Charley chewed over.

"Families are witnessing more and more deaths in the media. Our office is vigilant of innocent kids being caught up in drive by shootings because the parents conduct themselves worse than bad mannered kids on social media. It is obvious that social media made the cities and states more dangerous. If a lot of people do not like to read and do not know how to control their own households that can affect everyone. We all know what damages the instigators do to other people's household." Henry ignored the other call on his phone.

"I say we shut them down. We can put all of our resources together and start shutting this outlandish menaced trend down. The ones on social media promoting all the crimes got too many lives incarcerated, harmed, and killed. The hateful hate groups facing charges are attacking the witnesses." Charley reached for his wallet.

"The troublemakers should definitely be charged." Henry ended the call with Charley to call back some of the associates calling him.

Charley could hear Kimberly singing and cleaning up getting ready to leave. Charley asked his wife to wait for him. Kimberly was happy that her husband decided to accompany her to the lake. Kimberly bearing changed when Charley shared with her the conversation with Henry.

"Are you serious?"

"Yes. The news is reporting that more arrests are to take place in public departments for money laundering among unnumbered charges. I could hardly contain my anger. Henry confirmed the truth."

"Wow. Do you think Alexis knows about this?" Kimberly wondered.

"I don't know. That is why I am going to the lake. I'm about to tell Alexis about this outrageousness."

"Maybe we should tell her after the get together. Alexis need time to unwind. She has been working nonstop."

I will try to wait to after the bash for the bad press release. If the news casts is at the lake, Alexis may already know." Charley parked the vehicle fast pacing toward the lake with accessories and blankets.

Sure enough police officers were parked at the lake. The news casts was there with cameras everywhere. Charley rushed over to his colleagues.

Kimberly ran along side of Charley wondering why so many police officers were at the lake.

"Charley!" Someone yelled to catch Charley's attention. Charley was running to find Alexis. Charley turned his head catching sight of Alexis speaking with a few police officers. Alexis agitated expression obvious.

Charley rushed over to Alexis, the police officers asking her questions about a few of her co-workers made Alexis irritable. Alexis was saying that she did not know where they were. Alexis wanted to know why the police wanted to speak to some of her staff.

"Charley, have you spoken to Henry?'

"Yes. Why?"

"The police stated that someone told them that some of Henry's employees were going to be here today to meet with our co-workers to collect checks for an Organization that is under investigation. There has been an investigation into a lot of money laundering going into accounts that was scamming donors." Alexis disclosed to Charley in frustration.

"Officers, I can assure you that none of Henry's employees come to any of our appreciation ceremonies to collect bad checks from anyone in attendance. That is false information. I spoke to Henry this morning. Henry is a representative from a different county and district. Henry has never brought any of his employees to any of our public acknowledgements. Officer you are being fed lies. Henry has attended a recent event when he was out here visiting family."

The police officer wrote down Charley's statement leaving Charley his card for any additional information. Charley in return gave the police officer his business card. The men exchanged a few more words before the police officers cleared out.

Alexis was relieved but shook up about the revelation she was hearing.

"Alexis, I can meet up with Henry to find out why the police think Henry's employee's has any connection with our social acknowledgements. I'm pretty sure Henry employees are innocent."

"This is frightening Charley. My first hunch was that someone had passed away at first when I arrived and saw so many police officers."

"Some folks feel invincible. You know that Alexis. When the suspects are caught they are surprised when the news spread like a wild fire. Most people that commit certain crimes think that their secrets are going to be kept forever. A lot of money was allegedly taken from people who were promised support in programs that pay for their bills, some of the charities that use the money to pay for bills was behind and struggling. We have to make sure that the accusers are not in our circle. Something this unjust will shatter all the hard work and sacrifices we have made to help the families in our counties."

"We have countless of good people who attend our functions that know we are honest. We do not want to lose their support." Alexis's voice was shaky.

"There is not any way that we can lose their support because we post all of our donations. Our donors know exactly how much revenue we receive and how much money goes to the people in the programs that the taxpayers want to support. There is not a penny spent elsewhere. Our commitment is air tight. There isn't any wrongdoing. Amy posted the last donations. The donors were pleased." Charley boast.

"We have to make sure to keep our office honest and open. We passed another bill that has supporters wanting to attend our fundraisers. We are going to have great entertainment. The fundraiser is going to be victorious. We always hold up our end of the bargain. We are definitely not involved with whatever the news is reporting Charley."

"Do not concern yourself with the outrageous canard Alexis. We are going to help Henry get through this. Henry will not diddle anyone, he is well off."

"The defendants are well off. There has to be a good explanation for the mix up."

Alexis couldn't think of one reason.

"You have a point there. I don't know what made Mario and Ferria decide to commit the inescapable. Committing cons can end their careers for sure if there is evidence of malfeasance. I can only imagine the discomfiture the bunco has done to their families." Charley rubbed his elbow.

"Let's enjoy the gain. We sacrificed family time to enjoy this earning. We need to relax for a couple of hours. We have a live band. A special guest is performing. Let's get back to this great bash. We can rehash the bane when we have to." Alexis revived.

"I didn't want to discuss this today any way."

Alexis and Charley blended bodies with their colleagues. Family members took full advantage of the day savoring every minute of the performances. Standing ovations and balloons flying in the air for people who had outdone themselves reminded the co-workers what a powerful team they made. Amy was looking absolutely stunning. Marty could not keep his eyes off Amy. Amy could not take her eyes off of Marty.

Alexis was in total happiness hugging onto her husband enjoying fresh fruit and whipped cream. The band took time off for a break.

"Alluring Alexis." Marty held a balloon in his hand.

"Alexis and I know how to throw a well done job for our peers. All of us took long shifts meeting our goals. I do not want to ramble out all the details. Families of this community are going to be proud with our incredibly amazing, and prestigious asseveration. We are introducing big changes on Monday."

"The delayed developments for years are up and going since Alexis came into office and stopped the delaying of the city's expansion. We are exhilarated to show and prove through trust that positive change will benefit the city with the new developments."

"I am certain that the savants before us acted in accordance with all of the barriers that the savants opened for us. Our team is opening more doors for the people. That is the way that we are supposed to do things."

"The reckless followers of frown upon trends committing the universal atrocities do not qualify. The violators augmented a lot of tumult. The mayor's office has been steady with upholding representatives to remove toxic kinds of government selectives. We cannot allow barriers to be reestablished by people who do not qualify. We have been over acknowledging that people do not know how to protest and what their rights are to protect themselves. We are dealing with deceptive groups that are harassing people and trying to control people. We do not vote on those kinds of issues. It is not the citizen's rights to get into other peoples business out of prejudice and envious means and violate them."

The band's special guest performed four top notch songs. Alexis was mesmerized by the artist's beauty and soulful voice. Charley, his wife, Leilani, and her boyfriend danced slowly to the music.

"Amy, do you think that it is too soon for you to move in with me?" Marty thought the time was right to speak up about what he deemed for the last couple of months.

"What do we have to lose? We are both adults Marty. We can handle the relationship either way it turns out."

"If we fail, which I doubt if we fail, we agree to maintain a professional friendship." Marty eyes filled with love.

"Let's go for it. Right now, all I want is you in my arms dancing to this lovely song. It might be our wedding song."

Marty and Amy squeezed each other tightly taking in unforgettable memories together.

Alexis diverted to the people that she had grown to love dearly. She decided to pull her husband to the dance floor. Nathan willingly took his wife's hands.

"Let's take this party to the next level." The special guest singer band changed the music for the dances to dance in sequence. As time passed, terpsichoreans created new dances out of the original line dances. The dances performed smoothly and professionally with family and friends.

The public awareness event imaged a concert filled with people who danced for the artist. The dance in sequence lasted a while bringing the natives back to their seats huffing and puffing. The music zestful momentum exercised the citizens into shape.

"Alexis you move with style and grace." Nathan tried to keep up with his wife.

"Not too bad papa." Alexis glowed.

"The groups are all lit with babes and studs. Amy and Marty are re-exploring back in the day over there behaving similar to adolescents. What is all the grinning and whispering about?" Leilani waltzed over to Amy and Marty lost in one another.

"We might as well spill the beans. No time than presently to share our stimulating communiqué with news reporters all around." Marty expressed tenderness.

Amy tugged Marty arm eyes locking wanting Marty to wait. Marty shook his head no, and told the crowd he had an announcement to make. Amy cheeks turned bright red. She held her head down. Amy not prepared to tell the world bit down on her bottom lip. She was not going to rain on Marty's parade pausing to let Marty take over. The music stopped playing. All eyes fixated on Marty and Amy.

Marty bent down on one knee. Amy did not know Marty was about to propose to her. Amy took Marty's extended hand. Marty asked Amy to marry him. The throngs whistled at Marty bent on one knee.

"Marty, I will be honored to marry you." Amy nudged Marty.

"You treat me like you are my wife. You are a compassionate woman. Any man will be a fool not to marry you taking you off the market."

Alexis's eyes filled with tears. Alexis was over the moon for her best friend. Alexis knew if anyone deserved the spotlight it was Amy.

Alexis kissed Amy on both cheeks. Marty lifted Alexis up spinning her around for introducing him to such a wonderful person. Marty owed all of his happiness to Alexis.

"Alexis, you have made me the happiest man in the World. I do not know how I am going to ever repay you."

"Marty, you treat my girl right. That is all the repayment I need." Alexis hugged Marty asking all and sundry to grab a glass for a toast.

"Amy, Marty know how to bolt from the blue." Alexis fanned her tears.

"I wasn't expecting Marty to ask me to marry him." Amy kneaded Marty's ring.

"Amy you and Marty are two of my best friends. I am at a lost for words." Alexis tears getting the best of her.

"Remember to always be there for one another. Do not allow anyone to tear you two apart."

"Baby that was great advice." Nathan's ice in his lemonade clinked. Alexis used her napkin to wipe her husband's hand. Alexis's husband didn't drink alcohol at social gatherings, his job as a judge was scheduled twenty-four hour on-call, night emergencies to sign off on specific cases for warrants was not unusual.

The precious moment lasted for infinity for Marty and Amy.

Charley wife Kimberly latched on to her husband making way to their vehicle. The caterers gathered their food trays packing up all of their utensils and expensive cooking silverware. Helpers took down the stage cleaning up thoroughly leaving the lake. Camera crews and police officers were parked in the parking lot when Alexis and her husband were leaving. Alexis's mind was stuck on how special the event turned out to be and not concerned with accusations of suspects.

CHAPTER 13

HENRY EMPLOYEES WERE RELEASED AND apologized to Henry for the misunderstanding. Henry's employee's case was dropped when Henry brought the dates and times that the employees was at work. The workers alibi at the time of the alleged crimes cleared all doubts for the prosecutors.

Mario case was much more serious. Mario was looking at a lot of time if he was convicted of his alleged crimes. The attorney defense had to prove doubt and flaws. Mario did not have an alibi. The attorney thought it would be wise to take a deal to turn over the person who was the main source. Mario refused to roll over on anyone. Mario was arguing with his attorney when Henry walked in the visiting room.

"I am not accepting jail time. I do not have a record. You are supposed to be the best. You can make this all go away." Mario was heated.

"Mario, you do not have a record that is true, but there is a lot of evidence against you. The way things are unfolding the prosecutor thinks you have been committing this crime for a long time. I cannot see you not doing any time."

"I can accept funding from my supporters. That is not a crime. I did spend some of the money. I reported the money on my taxes being given to charities. The district attorney cannot prove that the charities did not receive the money."

"Witnesses may testify against you. If we take this to trial and the witnesses show up this can get real ugly for you."

"I will make sure that no one shows up for court if that is what you are concerned about. The case will be dropped."

"Mario, you cannot threaten witnesses. The prosecutors can add more charges."

"Who said anything about threatening the witnesses? I said the witnessing is not going to show up for court." Mario eyeballed daggers at his attorney.

"Henry, my main man." Mario simpered.

Henry was on tenterhooks about the outcome of checks spent on unreported items instead of what the money was to be spent on. Henry was fretful the investigation will end Mario's career. Henry wanted Mario to stop prattling like he had power over the court. Mario was going to end up serving years behind bars. Henry was immersed in finding ways to dig Mario out of the ditch he was buried in.

"Mario, arguing with your attorney wasting valuable time can come back to haunt you if this case is not resolved asap. I don't know what we are up against if this is true. Probation or parole is not on the table for this kind of crime. You would have to serve time. My brother you are fucked."

"I have a lot of backup. I am not stupid. I did cover my ass. I have receipts, statements, and money to cover every allegation that makes the prosecution appear incompetent. I don't blow money. Business associates can vouch for the money that the prosecution is charging me for Henry. You should know me better than that."

"Mario, I knew you were not a fool." Henry blew out a slow breath.

"I don't know who dropped the dime on me. I will found out. Whatever was discussed the snitch did not know that I had my side covered. I handled your other worry."

"What other worry?' Henry looked at Mario confused.

"Ferria."

Henry relieved that Mario was able to extend support to Ferria awaited Mario's explanation. Henry's mind was on Ferria's daughter. The toll of bringing Ferria's daughter to another home weighed on Henry's conscious. Henry was struggling to figure out a way to explain to Ferria's daughter why Ferria was not going to be able to pick her up. The sadness was crowding his judgment.

"My mind was on Ferria's daughter. You saved me from worrying about what to tell Ferria's daughter. I was worried sick about how she would react when I tell her she was going to be living with us for a while until her mom could come pick her up."

"Henry I told you, I know how to cover my behind. I have the attorney's assistant releasing Ferria. Your wife is over at the jail picking Ferria up. Ferria's daughter will not miss any time with her mother if I can help it. My associates are providing the money in another account to prove that none of the money was taken out of the account for the programs."

Henry accepted Mario explanation with stern affirmation.

'We are waiting on the confirmation to donate the money. We have made a huge profit. We will be able to donate extra. I know that will put everyone involved at ease. Besides, we do not have any contracts with the programs. We are the ones donating the money. There is not any crime here. The snitches that pressed the allegations are being sued for everything that they own now that I can back up my case with adequate evidence. I will make sure the envious accusers never make a mistake of coming after me again." Mario turned to face his attorney. Mario attorney was listening with a huge smile emerging following closely to his client's wrangle.

"I knew you would not end your career in this way Mario. If you lounge an Organization stating that the specific reason for the Organization is to donate to charities and do other specific dealings for people unfortunate.

That is an oral contract Mario. Why did you wait to tell me the good news?"

"I know that. That's what I been doing. I wanted to let you sweat a bit. I pay you enough money on retainer. I don't get into any trouble. It was worth the money I pay you." Mario smacked his attorney shoulder.

"You smuck motherfucker, Mario you certainly almost gave me a heart attack. I cannot believe you had me going for so long." The attorney unloosed his tie. The attorney turned on his laptop and sent emails to his office secretary for paperwork to be drawn for the prosecutor.

Henry and the attorney gave Mario a stare of incredulity. Henry and Mario's attorney comprehended that Mario was smart. Neither knew Mario had evidence to get out of the charges according to what was being reported in the media. Mario was basically trying to get the publicity to sue the snitch and force the prosecutors to tell where the prosecutors received their evidence. It was a fabulous backfire blow to the prosecutors. Henry sat there thinking that Mario was more intelligent than his attorney.

"Okay Mario. I have drawn up the necessary paperwork to dismiss the case. You are released on bail. I will have it served to the prosecutor's office. Meanwhile, do not get into any trouble. I appreciate what you have done for me to straightened out the case. I definitely appreciate the money you pay me to do my job." The attorney scurried away to handle more client's cases waiting for him at his desk.

"Henry, where are we about to go celebrate? I am going to need a few minutes to contact my woman. She was mad at me and said I better get out of this shit or I was going to be in deeper trouble with her. That is when my mind instituted results working nonstop." Mario thought about the woman he loved and adored so much.

"I will call my wife and let her know where to meet us. I can have someone pick up your woman. Or do you want her to meet us at the restaurant.'

"She has her own car. I can give her the name of the restaurant and the address. She can meet us there. That way I do not need to be dropped off at my car."

Henry called his wife. Henry conversed for a while before hanging up. Astelle grilled Henry.

"Henry, make sure not to mention anything to my woman. I will do all of the talking. I'm in hot water. My woman did not know that I had all this money. I have made investment deals. The smart investments made me a lot of money. That is why I was not worried about the charges."

"Mario, maybe we can get into a couple of investments together. I have never been tired of making money."

"My investments are all legit Henry. I am not worried about anything that the people are saying about me online. I will be able to give every dollar that was promised to the people for the programs and more. I will make the announcements tomorrow Henry at your fundraiser if you invite me, that way people will know that you are not affiliated with anyone that is crooked. I earn my money by using my brain. I give a lot of money away to strangers. I will not have my name defamed by people who are jealous of what I have. I gave half a million to young adults that were abused in this community to get the young adults safe housing and counseling. I do not have to go out of my way to help people that I do not know. I do this because I care about the people."

"I know you are a wise man Mario. We cannot let what people say about us stop us from doing what we love. I am not going to stop helping my community because of what other people have to say. Instead the people gossiping should help and find resolutions instead of causing disorder."

"Exactly, I am about to go over to my sexy rose before we go in. I will meet you at the table. You see the evil eyes she is giving me."

"She looks mad as hell."

"I bet her father put all that craziness in her head about me when he saw the newsflash. That man has never liked me. Her father thinks that I am a thug. I have proved to her father I am a legit business man. That is his only daughter. He does not want her dating anyone. Pretty soon we are going to be forced to get married. He won't allow any children until a ring is on that finger."

"Mario, I will have to agree. She is a beautiful woman. Dudes has had eyes for Karen since she was in high school. You got yourself a winner. She tough though."

Mario chuckled marching toward Karen. He knew he had to come up with a good elucidation for going to jail.

"Mario, why are we at this restaurant? I wanted to talk to you alone. Is it not enough you scared me half to death when you went to jail on TV. I had people calling me yapping at me at my job. My father cursed all night talking about he told me not to date you. What have you gotten yourself into Mario? Why are people saying that you are going to be in jail for a long time?'

"Karen, why are you listening to people before you talk to me? They don't know what's going on. You know how people love to talk. If something is put in the news gossip travels fast and the truth becomes nonexistent. People are going to talk. You can't let that bother you." Mario touched Karen face pecking her lips.

"At least hug your man before you go off on me. I was the one who had to sleep on hard cement all night in a cold ass cell. I am the one who is agitated and my reputation is in shreds. I am the one who is going to have to clear this mess up."

Karen frown turned into a small smile as she listened to Mario explain what happened and what he was doing to get the charges dropped. After Karen realized that her man was not going to jail, Karen was very excited and was ready to go into the restaurant to get Mario something to eat after starving in the jail all night. Mario knew his ideas would calm Karen down. The dedicated couple strolled into the restaurant meeting Henry, Henry's wife, and Ferria.

"Mario, Karen!" Ferria jumped up from the table. Astelle stood up to hug the couple after Ferria. They sat back down to discuss what ensued softened that there would not be any jail sentence, probation, or parole.

"Ferria, you know I will not let you go down for this. I have you covered my beautiful sister. Tell that man of yours he needs to stop running away from me on the golf course. I play unbiased." Mario chiacked.

Ferria looked at Mario with confusion in her eyes. How was Mario going to help her with her case? Ferria did take some of the money due to her overspending. Ferria couldn't cover the money before the court date her new home that she purchased did not leave enough dividends to cover the overspending. Ferria was counting down the days to her destiny.

"Ferria, do you remember that five million dollar deal we managed to do a couple of years ago with Thomason?" Mario quizzed looking at Ferria.

Ferria definitely remembered the deal. Mario and Ferria were celebrating for a week straight after the deal. At first Mario and Ferria thought they wouldn't be able to close the deal wasting their time.

"I managed to take my cut and make a massive fortune in an investment with a few buddies of mines. I put the money away and never looked back. The money has grown into over seventy five million dollars. I will tell you all about that. Karen shot Mario a look, she could not breathe for a second sipping her water. Karen thought she misperceived the conversation.

"I added your name to the investment to surprise you for what you did for me last year. You helped me in that deal with the real estate company. We made fifteen million dollars. I told you to save some of your money. Do not buy expensive homes in every city or state you work in. You bought too many cars. The big purchases add up fast."

"I spoke to my attorney. My attorney placed your portion of the investment in an account. You have more than enough money to show the prosecutor and judge if need be that you did not take any money from the donors. You have more than enough dough to donate to a few other programs like you have been doing."

The look on Ferria's face was speechless. Ferria tried to hold back tears flowing from her eyes. She thought she was about to have to spend time in jail away from her children for years. Mario huge favor would not go unnoticed. Ferria would not forget what Mario did for her. Ferria silently promised to budget and get someone to help her keep her finances in order.

"Mario, Thank you!" Ferria shakily embraced Mario tears streaming down her heavenly face."

Karen listened in hero worship benumbed at the reality that Mario kept all this hidden from her. Karen had no idea her man was that wealthy, she did not know how to feel about the new discovery."

"My attorney has drawn up dismissal papers for both of us. I received the text. The money has been donated. We can add a few charities of your liking if you want. Ferria we cannot slip up ever again. This was too close to landing us in the slammer. Someone has tried to take us down. You know when you are big bosses we are going to have haters getting into our personal business. We are going to have to be careful. We cannot trust anyone. The unknown accusers are calling the law on us." Mario dished out the 411.

"To our haters, may our haters provide strength for our long and prosperous future." Mario downed blended fruit water enjoying consolation on the faces of his love ones. Mario knew Ferria was not a bad person and deserved a second chance. Mario sponsored Ferria holding in high regard that she helped people including him get his finances right. Ferria continued with her good work in the communities.

Ferria was enlightened respectfully calling her man. Ferria's man, Ryan gracious gratitude thanked Mario. Ryan had money tied up in long-term investments. Ferria knew that Ryan was being watched. She did not know how she would be able to get money from Ryan without being detected. The large amounts will be a red flag with penalties for cashing in early. Ferria and Mario worked together on most deals through a couple of the accounts. It was wise to use one of the accounts to post the transactions to cover the money alleged of being taken out for personal purchases. The transfer of legit investments consistently made the money appeared to never been taken out for Ferria's large purchases.

Henry motivation to stay legit in his community and finding out his enemies had people making up stories to investigate his allies gained recognition. Henry was super pumped about the fundraiser coming up to help clear Mario's name. Mario's decision to donate to more charities made Henry slack off lecturing Mario. Mario was a welcomed resource in the World. The people were accounted for the way families should be regarded by Mario. Mario saved one of the nicest women that Henry and his wife cherished. Ferria stuck her neck out for people who did not deserve it at times because they had children. It was good to watch Mario stepping up to show Ferria benevolence. The table was filled with sincere hearts easing the friends into comfort.

CHAPTER 14

ALEXIS WOKE UP HER HUSBAND with morning loving before Nathan headed off to work. Alexis was working later on in the day and had free time to please her husband.

"It smells good in here." Nathan prepared for work after showering.

Alexis left out with Nathan. She was going to get her nails, feet, and lashes touched up. The sun was bright penetrating down on her front door.

Alexis let her hair down letting the warm breeze blow throughout the car. The radio was playing a slow R&B jam. Alexis slowly rocked her head to the beat turning onto the freeway. After Alexis pampered herself she decided to check on Amy. Alexis missed spending time with Amy because of the new relationship Amy was in. Amy was preoccupied most of her free time. Amy did a tremendous job at work. Alexis noticed Amy seemed to fully concentrated when she came in to work since Marty been in her life.

"Hey Alexis." Marty answered Amy's phone sounding in love.

"Hi Marty, where is your woman?"

"She ran back in the café to grab her latte. You know she cannot function without her latte. She is on her way to the office. Do you want me to have her call you back or do you mind holding the line."

"I can hold that will give me time to catch up with you."

"Speaking of catching up, we have people at one of my conferences interesting in scheduling time to meet with you about one of the businesses you had on the flyers you passed out at the fundraiser. A couple people want to socially entertain. I thought you would be the perfect person to reach out to the contacts. There will be a sizable donation to your favorite charity for your input."

"That sounds propitious Marty. Let me know. I will be there. My schedule is spontaneous. I can always make time for you brother be that as it may. I appreciate how you have my best friend coming to work happy as ever. She is more focused than I have ever seen her. Whatever you are doing make sure you keep doing it. Amy is making a big impression on some pretty important people."

"I am glad to hear that. I will do my part to make sure that your girl stays happy. She is a fresh breathe of air to be around. Amy is a positive, supportive, and an influential woman. We are doing quite well with the new living arrangements. You have to bring your husband over so we can have a house warming, no gifts. Here goes Amy. Nice talking to you Alexis."

"What's wrong Alexis?"

"Everything is fine Amy. I was checking in with you. I decided to come in early. I know you can handle it on your own. I am going to give you a hand any way."

"Alexis, you are the best. You did not have to come in early. I have a lot of help. I do appreciate you thinking of me nevertheless. I know after today you are not going to be free for some time speaking on all the protests that the constituents has wrote you about. You should have spoiled yourself."

"I did." Alexis laughed into the phone admiring her growing nails and own long black eye lashes in the rear view mirror.

"That's my girl. Well in that case. I will see you in a minute. Is it okay if we bump up the meeting with Douglas? I can have him meet you in your office in thirty minutes."

"That will work. I can be ready in thirty minutes. I need to get back to Douglas on the position he wants to fill." Alexis hung up the phone prepared to get all her work completed to attend the next couple of fundraisers for the right to legal counsel, wrongful incarceration, self-evictions, and fighting oppression.

Alexis pulled into her parking spot. Douglas was pulling up when she arrived. The two spoke briefly in the parking lot agreeing to make room for another associate who wanted to attend the children's right and economic justice discussion.

"Alexis, I didn't like how I was passed up on a position that I am most qualified for." Douglas went straight to the facts.

"I do understand Douglas. How about we have you speak to Kadie. We can see if we can arrange a few things around so that you can transition into that position without there being an unnecessary scene. You are the most qualified Douglas. You have been really patience and you have shown dedication and loyalty to the team."

"Thank you Alexis, I knew that I could count on you. I know the job like the back of my hand. My children are all grown up. I have a lot of free time. My wife and I split up last year. We continue to be friends and get along. She is not into Politics. She hates the limelight. She cannot stand attending fundraisers and talking to a lot of people."

"I'm broken hearted to hear about that Douglas."

"Don't feel sorry for me Alexis. I am good. I have a lot of support at home. My ex-wife does not give me any trouble. We go out from time to time. She does not want to remarry. You never know. We may end up back together." Douglas took Alexis's hand. The meeting dissolved. Douglas did not want to misspend any of Alexis's time. Douglas knew Alexis was bustling.

"Douglas good for you. You guys may end up back together. You are a dyed in the wool kind of gentlemen."

Douglas left Alexis's office feeling much better and confident that he could handle the extra promotion and all the other work he was involved in like a champ. Douglas was an excellent organizer and managed his time pretty well.

Alexis was greeted by Amy and one other associate preparing for her meetings for the day. The three canvassed over important places that Alexis was scheduled to drop in on. Alexis would be out of town on some of the visits. Alexis hated when she had to leave her husband. Her husband always managed to find things to do when she had to go away, not complaining, and remaining nurturing. Alexis and her husband talked on the phone most nights before going to bed.

"Alexis, do you want me to pack your camcorder this time?" Alexis finally returned home. Her husband helped her pack for her out of town expedition. Alexis was grateful to have someone in her corner that did not give her a difficult time when she had to leave. Her husband was respectful, trusting, and never doubted Alexis. Alexis answered her husband about the camcorder cramming a few more things to compress in her suitcase.

Alexis flitted out of the shower preparing to rest for the rest of the night with her husband.

"I know how your time is on a compacted schedule Alexis. That is why I got home early today to fix dinner. I knew it was going to be a tough day for you. I hate when you have to leave. I love that you make conditions better for other people. I miss you a lot whenever you are away."

"Are you really going to miss me?"

"Woman, I miss you everyday at work. I am going to miss you so much since you are leaving for more than a few hours." Nathan handed Alexis the hot tray of steamed vegetables, fish, and mashed potatoes."

Alexis gobbled down the food talking in between bites. The food was flavorsome. Mr. and Mrs. cuddled dewy-eyed about Alexis's trip out of town. Nathan composed his thoughts and fears. He didn't want anything to retract the cozy romantic rendezvous. Alexis's husband buff arms were protecting and reassuring. Nathan cradled his wife soft body yearning for her succulent touch. Nathan peeled off each layer of lingerie licking down Alexis's entire body. Alexis moaned in ecstasy for her husband harden core. The married couple moved to one another's rhythm in harmony reaching a climax indescribable. Nathan collapsed inside of Alexis. The lovers breathing heavily in each other's embrace falling asleep.

Nathan roused out his sleep by a pleasant dream. He unobtrusively garnered Alexis's suitcases by the front door.

"I do not feel like going." Alexis sighed rolling over to an empty bed.

Alexis heard the water running in the bathroom and rolled out of bed to the bathroom.

Alexis's husband opened the front door for Alexis with all of her belongings. The gleeful unit left for the airport.

Alexis arrived at the airport overhearing Amy and Marty saying their goodbyes. Leilani embosomed her Evan. All three women joined together to get on the airport.

"We are going to have an unforgettable time despite all the work we have to do. I met with four of the representatives last night. We outlined the targeted areas. The essential resources need to be polished up for the meeting. I want the strategic framework to mirror the facts and relate with what we are projecting to our audience." Amy chronicled to Alexis and Leilani.

Alexis was faithful to her team. She secured reliance bearing in mind her and her staff breezed through these kinds of commissions. The unequivocal attitudes were strong as the women boarded the airplane and took their seats ready for take off. The plane landed all three women had taken a quick nap. The refreshed belles were ready for the bid at hand.

"Alexis!" Amy scanned the congested airport laying eyes on a tall man calling her name.

"Ladies have your bags checked out. We will meet at the pick up passengers parking.

"I love the newfangled here. When I visit new places I am enraptured by the scenery. The stylish landscape gives me options of where I am planning my man next birthday party. Leilani peered around the car window rating the outlook.

"Young people, you guys energy is through the roof. Leilani, you are juggling college, internship, a relationship, and an extra job. How do you manage to stay full of energy?" Alexis yawned.

"I am up early, working out, and drinking my protein shakes. Those protein shakes really boost my energy level. I take early morning classes to get out of class in enough time to attend both of my jobs. My beau Evans works with me at one of my jobs. He always picks me up at my second job. It's easy breezy Alexis."

"I know what you mean. We are all multitasking. Multitasking is jollity in a way. We get to experience different standpoints. I like spending a lot of time with Marty. He is jaunty to hang around when he is not at work. He has some of the best stimulating conversations. Marty puts it down in the bedroom. I understand why people get married."

"I am so exultant for you Amy. I thought that you would never open up to having someone in your life. You went head first into this relationship. I guess your bestie was right. I know what I am talking about.'

Amy welcomed with open arms her bestie embrace.

"You do know what you are talking about when it comes to relationships Alexis. I took all of your advice. I listen to Marty. I give him space. I compliment Marty's efforts. I trust him. I am going to take it one day at a time. We agreed what we would do if the relationship ever came to an end."

"It is always wise to discuss alternatives and stick to your agreements Amy. Sticking to committed accordance keeps the relationship and friendships strong. You guys do not have to go through immature shenanigans like a lot of couples."

"I stay away from the media negative posts. I hope that the instigators making people lives miserable by attacking them on social media are shut down. It has been disturbing to hear about the aggressors committing the crimes for million of viewers to judge people based on words that most often are not factual. I do not dwell on my relationship. I focus on a path to help my self-growth. Online studies cover recipes and classes that you can learn how to make smart investments to make extra money. Online studies added useful "Do It Yourself", videos to save money. I take advantage of the self-help videos in the media. I am done with all that gossip silliness. I watch family videos and read positive sayings posts. An online video had a mayor on social media with his constituents fired up about people born in the district not wanting people working in other cities and states. What would make people that live in a district think that people born in the country cannot work wherever they want? Illegal Immigrants are upset at people born in the country when they receive benefits that should go to people born here. The education on the topic is not reaching the people thinking that they can tell people born here where to work and live if they are not causing any trouble. Some of the inept ringleaders are used to tearing stuff up and causing the most trouble. They don't want things to change. I thought about you Alexis. I knew you would cringe if you seen the video. People cannot allow anyone to get into the field of representation and not know how to handle undereducated people in the community. We can't go around lying to people saying gas lighting and breaking laws is power." Amy divulged.

"Look at the foolishness surrounding the social network. The agitators that are not familiar with how to protest think they can protest about things that are not their right. Some of the representatives are making it appear it is okay to not educate the undereducated people who don't know about protests and what protest are for. They come up with complaints that are ridiculous. The multiple arrests enforced bringing crooked and corrupted people to their knees prove we live in an unbalanced world. Luckily, Henry's friends were released. There continue to be a lot of people sentenced that will not be released because of the crimes that they committed to come up in the political World. The less educated instigators will try to scam anyone and anything to come up. The representatives should not not rally about what is a correct way to protest and what people should protest about." Alexis enumerated.

"I heard that the guy who was caught with that briefcase of money was an ex-friend of my cousin. He is in big trouble. He had all the evidence on him when his door was kicked in. My cousin ex-friend will not be able to squirm his way out of all that evidence against him." Leilani sadly confessed.

"The district attorneys are sorting through it. There will be an update soon enough. You know people are calling reporters about the incidents everyday. I am making sure none of this happens in our county. We cannot afford to let this muckraking reach our county after all the work we contributed to the community." Amy didn't want people that were unfamiliar with the way politics worked to give their office a hard time.

When the three women met at the front entrance to get back into the vehicle to head to the meeting, they were all speaking on how thrilled the women were of their opulent rooms.

"It is our duty to tour the city when the meetings are over. We have a few days to explore. I want to traverse the flatlands. Evan might relish being in a place that attractions are filled with unique features, land marks, and historical significance."

"Leilani, you love to go out."

"Well our men are not here. We should spend our time wisely with one another, we are in durable relationships. We are with the men of our dreams lovey dovey most of the time."

"I think we should make the most of our valuable time together Leilani." Amy was interested in festivals, cultural experiences, and unique local shops.

"Natural wonders of climbing the mountains or frequenting the beaches is my temptations." Alexis pinned her hair up in a ponytail unbuttoning her dress jacket.

The meeting discussions ranged from how to implement a plan that everyone could benefit from to what are the most important programs that should be supported and funded. The associates were at their full height doing their part to make certain every program came together placidly. Alexis held in high estimation the welfare of the families that were to benefit from the programs. Alexis's appreciation for how supportive and respectful the staff behaved at the financial support committee briefing was noticed and noted.

"That went well. Intensified and challenging results will brand us as inspiring the next generation of political parties." Amy took off her coat from the warm heat. The women took an uber driver for suggestions on where they should junket first.

The uber driver was a lot of help. The uber driver showed the women the best parts of the city dropping the women by a waterfall. The city was filled with restaurants and shopping centers that had the women staring with their mouths wide open.

"I can come back here a couple of times for a getaway." Leilani placed her jacket in her small bag. The ladies eyes set on the shopping centers.

People were bowling, shooting pool, throwing darts, roller skating, and eating pizza. Alexis saw couples in picture booths taking pictures and many people on a big stage singing and performing.

"What should we do first?"

"I'm not that hungry. I do not want to spoil my appetite for dinner." Amy began.

"We have a lot of selections to choose from." Alexis looked around.

"Leilani pulled Amy, Amy tugged Alexis, and in a matter of minutes the women were seated ordering at a very cozy setup in front of another colorful waterfall.

"Nice choice." Amy hypnotized by the waterfall.

"The waterfalls catch my attention all the time." Leilani took in the exotic beauty.

The waiter was a personable young man with jet black hair, numerous tattoos, and deep dimples.

"I am married but damn!" Alexis grinned once the waiter took their order.

"He is fine." Leilani nictated at the waiter.

"Focus ladies, there's a lot of temptation that can lead us in a hot water." Amy acknowledged.

"I am on my best behavior. I can look. I'm not doing anything wrong by looking." Alexis moved comfortably in her seat.

"I have to say. There is a lot to admire. OMG! Do you see those three guys over there gawking at us?" Amy blushed and looked away.

"I saw the guys when we were being seated. I didn't want to say anything. I thought you guys would want to go somewhere else." Leilani smiled devilishly.

"I knew it was not the waterfalls!' Alexis threw a napkin at Leliani.

"What!" Leilani responded innocently.

The waiter came back with the drinks and placed cup holders down. A full bucket of ice chips to battle the warmth and straws.

"This is soooo good."

"I love going out of town." Leilani's chipper demeanor was contagious.

The waiter pointed at the three men sitting not too far from the ladies.

"The gentlemen seated over there asked that I put your orders on their tab."

Alexis shook her head no, while Amy and Leilani grinned and said okay.

The waiter spoke elegantly with hospitality.

"Do not mind her. Tell the gentlemen we accept their warm reception. My friend is bashful." Leilani legitimized Alexis's resistance.

The waiter left the table to get the women food.

"We cannot let random guys buy our food and drinks. They might think that we are single."

"Technically, we are single. They don't know our relationship status. I never turn down a free meal and drinks." Leilani felt no shame in her free meal.

"I am going to have to agree with Leilani Alexis. Why can we not be pampered? They did not ask for anything in return. They initiated a conversation in a friendly manner. The guys can smell fresh meat. We are not from here. Locals show their conviviality wherever we visit. Relax, we are always laboring. We earn times to be catered to." Amy reclined.

"I would love ice-cream." Leilani loved desserts.

"I'm at your service Ms. lady ice cream coming right up." One of the guys treating the ladies approached the table extending his courtesy with tickets to a show.

"I could not help but notice the beauty occupying my joint. I have lived in this city all my life. I have never seen you three bonny women around here before. You must be visiting."

Amy gave Alexis the, "I told you so," look and answered yes to the fine man.

"I want to welcome you beautiful ladies to the city. I would love to pay for your meals to show you how much I appreciate when beautiful women come out and enjoy themselves."

"That is very kind of you. What is your name?" Leilani extended her hand.

"Call me L. I am known around here as L. My real Name is Lebanron."

"I am Leilani. That is Alexis and this is Amy. We are out here on a business trip. We are getting in long overdue play time."

"I love women who handle their business." L looked at all three women with sultry eyes.

"We appreciate your generosity." Amy read the tickets.

My boys and I have to scope out a blueprint for property. We are the owners to this fine establishment you ladies are visiting. We come in to check out the place every now and then to make sure everything is going well for our customers. Thank you for coming to this acclaimed city. I hope to see you ladies again." L laid his business card on the table.

"Whatever you ladies want ask my host. Enjoy the rest of your time here ladies. I am sure you will find this city to be one of the best." L fluttered his eyelids at the women. His other two friends making sheep's eye at the ladies standing up to exit the eatery.

Leilani looked at the business card. The card had three names with three faces matching the guys who were leaving on the business cards.

"They are the owner's girlllls!" Leilani murmured watching the men leave.

"I knew they looked too good and are too overdressed to be having lunch." Amy liked the designs on the card.

"I like how they were so polite." Alexis placed the card in her purse.

"You were about to turn down the offer from businessmen that we can invite to some of our rallies for needed causes. They can give us pointers with the programs and funding."

"There you go. You are always thinking about work."

"I have a man, thanks to you. What else can I think about?" Amy chewed her roll after dipping it into the tasty sauce.

"We have found a new spot. Too bad none of us are single." Leilani thought about Evan.

The women chatted about the next excursion hoping to meet potential donors to support their worthy cause.

CHAPTER 15

MARIO WANTED TO MOVE ON to flipping his profits for top opportunities. Mario had a lot of propositions to think through and did not have time to waste making sure that his name was cleared.

"I will forgather with you at the fundraiser Henry." Mario hugged Henry, Astelle, and Ferria his woman at his side longing to get home. Once the couple was out of earshot of their friends, Karen chastised Mario with calm anger.

"Why did you not tell me you had invested in all that money Mario? You do not trust me. I thought we were honest with each other. You are starting to make me feel like I do not know you at all."

"It's not like that Karen. I did not want to tell you anything until I knew for sure that everything was going to work out. I had a few hurdles that made me think that the investments could go in the wrong direction. When I was for sure the investments were steadfast, I was arrested, and here we are. You know everything. You don't have to castigate me. I am not doing anything that would jeopardize what we have together."

"My dad is furious. He is threatening to sue you. My job and my mom think that I was dragged into something you did criminally. I told my dad to chill out. My job and my mom have no reason to believe that I did anything wrong. I have an alibi. I was at work and working overtime during the allegations. My dad never listens to me. I don't want to talk to him when he gets that steamed. You know how he gets worked up for nothing. He can make the simplest thing end up in a blown up fiasco before realizing that he was wrong. He is going to the fundraiser. He will apologize for all the allegations. He had no right to go completely insane before I had a chance to talk to you."

"Don't take it personal. Fathers are always going to fight for their daughters. You are his only daughter. I am not taking it personally because the news did put the arrests on thick. If it was my daughter, I would be upset too. He has every right to want to protect you. I will talk to him about it. It is a father's duty to make sure that his daughter is alright."

"Tomorrow, when he comes to the fundraiser, I am sure that the clear up is going to help him realize that you are a responsible guy. I want you two to get along. You two are the best people in my life, including my mom of course but I'm referring to positive and dependable men in my life consistently. My dad has not let up being there for me when I need him the most since I was born. You have been faithful to me since we been together taking good care of me." Karen treasured her dad and man.

Mario parked the car opening up the door for Karen. Mario welcomed his home with his presence filled with gratitude. He was not gone but one day and it felt like weeks. Mario realized how fortunate he was.

"I'm not going to take anything for granted. I am grateful that this did not blow up in our faces. I don't understand why someone will call the authorities on me. I give a lot to people that I don't know. It is sad to discover jealous people are out there who cannot wait to see me fall. Tomorrow, I am going to get with the attorney to see if he has come up with who is responsible for this tip to the police before the fundraiser.

"That was covetous and wrong. I know people know how much you do for many people that are not just in this community. People are never satisfied. All they want to do is watch people fail. The more you give people, the more they are going to say that they have never received anything. Do not waste good energy with that kind of hating. It is not good for your health. You are appreciated. You know what you have been doing. I have a big check for the children's food and clothes drive. Martha and I raised a lot of money. I could not let Joy feel alone when she was asking for donations. We all look after each other. Martha knows a lot of rich people and so does my dad."

"Why did you not ask me to donate to Joy Karen? I would have helped."

"Mario I wrote a check for you for Joy."

"Oh it's like that."

"I knew you would not mind. I collected all of the other donations for Joy and added our part. I will give the donations to Joy. She is going to be overjoyed. She has been working round the clock at her new business. She continues to find time to help out the children and their parents in the neighborhood. We have a saint on our side. Most people donate online nowadays whatever they can. A little goes a long way when the money is all totaled up. We have made sure to keep the funds accredited to the right cause. I know how people think that the programs are a come up for the employers. We do not take any of the money that we get from donors to pay for our own expenses. We pay for our own expenditure with our own earned money. I think that a lot of people think that if you look too good, you are stealing money from the programs. Some of us know how to budget."

"I know my suits, watches, designer sun glasses, and my cars look like I am doing something wrong maybe. People do not know how much I invest my own earnings. The ones assuming are not educated. The instigators do not care about saying craze stuff about people that are on top of their game." Mario yawned.

'It is true that people are stealing a lot of money and using their Organizations as a front. There are too many people trying to do what other people are skilled at doing and running game on people to take from them. Your case should be dismissed because of the way you budget your money and cover your behind. There will be cases that are not going to be dismissed. The people being investigated have stolen the money and funded themselves. It is not right. I have to agree that there should be serious consequences for the kinds of public crimes that take from the poor. What makes the ones committing the crimes think that they are not going to be reported? Why do people who take money because of what their families are forced to go through jailed but not the ones that are greedy and embezzle even more money without needing the money?

"I heard about the new undercover agents working in the alleged corrupted Organizations and programs funded to catch criminals. A lot of the people that filed complaints were qualified for certain programs and turned away. If people start reporting those kinds of actions it brings red flags to all Organizations and businesses by people the community feel are a front for the illegal stuff some of the Organizations and businesses do."

"I told Joe not to do that at the job he works for that give funding and help to women in need with children. He gets upset if he cannot talk to some of the women that sign up for certain programs where he works. Joe will not help the women if the women do not talk to him. He is a dog. I told that fool to get into another job field. The women are mothers who are doing what they have to do for their children. Mothers do not have time for that fool."

"You are right." Karen acknowledged.

"Joe gets on my nerves. I went over to visit him one time. This lady was saying that she could not give him her phone number because she was with someone in a relationship. Do you know this fool asked her for her dude information to see if he qualified? She was like, "He doesn't leave with me." Joe was like well then you can go out with me. He is about to be on the news for sexual harassment. I'm not going to help his ass either. He don't care if the women or pregnant. Joe doesn't care if the women have a lot of kids. He continues to try to get their number. That hound needs to go to sex addiction classes."

"If the women he chasing already have a lot of kids, Joe knows he is not going to want to help with the kids. Joe needs help for real. I don't know how you are friends with him."

"Friends! That embarrassing ninga is my blood cousin. I tell people we know each other from high school. I do not want anyone researching my blood line." Mario hoped no one ever questioned him about Joe.

"Joe is your blood cousin?"

"See, you didn't even know. I don't tell people anything about Joe messy behind. That man has been like that for years. Do you know he had to do a year for grabbing this lady breast? She called 911 on his ass. He claimed it was an accident until they saw him on camera."

"Damn."

"That is what I said when I went to speak with his attorney to see why Joe was arrested. This pervert was blocking the woman from leaving the store in the mall. She kept pushing him. He latched on to her breast feeling on the lady talking about you know you want me. I am telling you, Joe is a hot mess. Don't let him get some liquor in him. I don't go out with him any more. I think he is still on probation."

"That is foul. Joe needs to stop. One day one of the women is going to hurt Joe."

"Joe keeps thinking he can get away with anything. People nowadays are fighting like crazy. I know you heard about Tim's woman stabbing him. He landed in the hospital! He was caught cheating."

"Wait! Hold on! Tim's woman stabbed him."

"Like he was a piece of meat! She stayed right in the house until the police came too. She did not run or make up any excuse. She told the police Tim had a woman in their house. The police did not take her to jail. The police took him to jail after he was released out of the hospital."

"What!"

"Tim's woman knows a lot of law enforcement. She is a good and solid woman. She works well with the kids in the community. She goes to church. She is in good with all Tim's family. Tim did not have any support. All of Tim's family members and friends were on her side. Tim was mad as hell."

"Why was Tim cheating?"

"Tim doesn't like his woman independence. She is too young and focused. I think he like them feisty older women that want him to spend money on them even though they have their own too. Tim love drama. He love going out with his boys and acting up. Some of the older cats are getting crazier every birthday. My dad got caught with his mistress. My mom talking about she got a side piece. I am telling you the World has gone mad. I told my mom she doesn't have no goddamn side piece. She better get in that kitchen and cook and sit down somewhere."

"I know you did not say that to your mom without catching a beat down. She threw my dad's ashtray at my head. I ran out the back door. I haven't been back. I'm going to let her calm down. I am ready to drop. Let's go to bed." Mario was laughing out of control.

"It's been a long day. I'm glad you are alright Mario. Don't you scare me like that again."

"I will be there in a minute."

Mario tapped his phone the mentioned of his cousin's side pieces had Mario reading a text from one of his female friends. He's relation with Karen was all he needed. Mario was tired of the lying to other women. His businesses and investments were booming. He had loyal clients. Mario had everything he wanted. All he needed was a good woman to share it with. Karen was the woman that Mario wanted. Mario loved how Karen took no BS and was always there for him. He was not about to lose a good thing. Mario text his side piece back and told her it was not cool to contact him then turned off his phone.

"Henry what time are we going to meet Charley and Kimberly? I told him that we will swing by before the fundraiser." Astelle called upstairs to her husband.

"We can meet Charley and Kimberly whenever you get ready. I have to do a few errands before the fundraiser. I can rearrange my schedule and meet Charley and Kimberly first since they are on the way to one of my errands."

"Let s go. I will not be able to make it in the office. I'm going to help you with Mario and Ferria transition. I can't take any further unwanted broadcast."

I received an email asking me to contact a woman journalist about my employee's arrest. She wants to do an interview with me from their newscast. She said she was glad that my employee's names were cleared and wanted to know if I could clear the air for the people who was concerned about why all the arrests were happening all over the cities and states."

"That will be productive air time Henry. It can be good for your position. This interview can benefit Mario and Ferria. You can let the reporter know that Mario and Ferria were charged and grouped up in the scandal as innocent bystanders. The more publicity Mario and Ferria get to clear their names would help their reputations. I think this is a great opportunity to let the people know you are not affiliated with any shady dealings."

"We can do the interview right after we speak with Charley and Kimberly. I knew the update would lighten your load of unwanted stress. I read the email. I feel much better knowing that we have supporters on our side that are helping to end this squabble."

"I know we are going to find out how this all came about. That is going to be another quarrel to grapple. We are going to be watched for every rally and protest we attend. It is not going to bother me since we have been completely honest. We have to be on our staff. We are not going down for other people's greed. I have heard about some of the guys giving the women a hard time when the women are going to the public services to conduct their business. I think we are going to have to do some firing soon."

"I am with that. This disrespect has lasted for too many years with too many complaints unresolved. We will let go of staff if we find out that the staff are harassing women. We cannot have people being forced to talk to guys to receive help. We have heard the disturbing complaints by a lot of credible women." Charley and Kimberly wanted to discuss similar confrontations to the reckless actions.

"We can discuss anything that will help the victims. Our schedules are clear to do what we need to do the next couple of weeks. We were offered funding sponsors to go on the trip."

Charley and Kimberly were waiting for Henry and Astelle outside of their home. They entered the home and went into full operation on what they were going to put into motion. Charley and Kimberly had an engagement that required their immediate attention. A family situation that was personal. The couple was knee deep with obligations. Kimberly sat down with a thump exasperated.

"What is wrong Kimberly?" Astelle questioned.

"A family emergency, I have to go to one of my relative's house. I really do not have the time to go. The tragedy cannot wait. There is something going wrong with my older cousin."

"Oh." Astelle hugged Kimberly.

"Family emergencies can happen all of a sudden at the wrong time. Charley does not want to go. I am not going alone. My family can be a bit much if you know what I mean." Kimberly never talked much about her family.

"I understand. My family has a variety of personalities. I have to call my family myself. We all get wrapped up in our own secular interests we forget to take time out to see how everyone is surviving." Astelle missed her family.

"That is true. I was always working and with my husband. I would meet up with my girlfriends going out on stress free trips when my husband was overstretched. I have not seen my family in years." Kimberly knew it was time for a visit.

"Time passes by faster than lightning. My mom has been upset at me for not coming to see her. I don't like how far my mom moved away. My mom wanted more peace so she moved to the middle of no where. I tried to talk my mom out of the move. She insisted that it was best for her internal growth. I wish I could see my mom more often. I don't think I can convince my mom to come and stay with me." Astelle had enough room for her mom to live comfortably with her and Henry.

"My older cousin may be coming to move in with me. That is the family emergency. I think she has broken up with her husband or someone died. We never know what to expect. She is good-natured, quiet, and stays to herself. She is my favorite cousins. I would love to have my cousin live with me. I get lonely sometimes living in our big house with our dogs. It would do me some good to be around decent family." Kimberly was anxious to find out if her cousin was going to stay with her.

"I know what you mean. How are the projects you are working on?" Astelle and everyone she knew had responsibilities that took up a lot of their time.

"It is going worthwhile. I know Charley mention to you what took place with some of my staff. We are going to have to enforce no dating or sleeping with any staff at work. We do not want the employees to bring their problems to the workplace."

"Henry and I have our views on the big scandal in the news. Everyone in my companies has been cleaning up their act and paying more attention to the complaints that they have been receiving. People are mad about not getting responses in a timely manner. I have my staff working on being more effective and faster. We have numerous places of businesses and countless investments. We are going to have to cut ties with a few of our workloads. We have made more than enough money." Astelle profits were exceedingly nifty.

"Working diverse companies does become enervated, we lose perspective on what is truly important. I know it has been rough for me. I have a cousin that does not live too far from me. She wants to come down when my older cousin arrives and go out. I don't like partying that much. My two cousins are different from one another. One is a party Queen. The other cousin loves to read and take care of business. I would not be surprise if she ends up staying home. She is a chef at cooking and love to clean. Her husband is not going to be able to do much without her. He is always on the go. My cousin tends to the home."

"They might work the kinks out in their marriage. You know couples have their disagreements. That doesn't mean that they do not make up."

"I would love for her to come out for a while."

"How is Charley feeling about the rumors?"

"He is handling himself with mature patience getting a lot of support. I am cheering him on for what he has been accomplishing in his life."

The ladies husbands finished their queries. Once Henry and Charley achieved their rejoinders, Charley's associate that knows a few journalists, asked to interview Henry. It was like a rollercoaster ride. Henry was up and down with people asking about his employees that were arrested.

"Astelle I have a few interviews. I do not know why people thought that I was a part of the disgraceful behavior. I didn't have anything to do with the dishonest intentions."

"Henry it does not have to be you personally all people have to hear to start trouble is that the ones being questioned knew you. Some people do not have anything better to do. I bet we find out this is all coming from nosy people who probably knew you were not present or was no where near the faulty actions. Henry you will have mendacious nonsense cleared up in no time. Mario will help you. Ferria is definitely not going to let anyone blame you."

I'm going to call Mario. You drive Astelle. I want to let Mario know when we are going to do the interviews. We cannot let this deceitful narrative consume our lives. We should speak to as many public platforms as possible on this insincere fable while the people are listening. We cannot afford to let more people think that this manipulative display of unreasonable assumptions is connected to us."

"Where are we headed?"

Henry gave Astelle the directions talking on the phone with Mario. Mario was thrilled. Mario thanked Henry over the phone agreeing to get the word out that he and Henry was innocent. Karen in wonder of what the phone conversation was about waited for Mario to tell her.

"Karen, Henry has a few interviews he is setting up for us. We are going to face the viewers to end this malicious and untruthful scandal in my name. I need you by my side. I have a few friends to contact to make sure that they show up to prove how flourishing our investments are going."

"That is marvelous Mario. I have our clothes in the other room. I don't want you having a fit about how you do not like what I picked out for you to wear." Karen warned Mario.

"I trust your taste. I got to roll out Karen. I have to get all my investors, and my associates caught up on the latest break. My attorney wants more money." Mario was rushing out of the door.

"Be careful. I will see you in a little while." Karen closed the front door and went in their room to find her shoes.

Mario sped on the freeway and made sure to exit off at one of his friend's house first. Mario had to make sure that the money was deposited into his account before his attorney could speak with the district attorney. Mario knew that he was going to be grilled by his attorney if the money was not deposited. Mario had all the answers to the accusations and funds to help Ferria. He was not going to waste any time on the matter. Mario wanted everything to be over and done with so that he could get back to his life.

"Mario. I have been waiting on you. I have a few documents for you to sign. I can have the money in your account today. If you need anything else let me know. I'm going out of town tonight. I will be back later on tomorrow night. If you need anything before then, my assistant will accommodate you."

Mario signed the paperwork. The money would be verified by the attorney and the district attorney. Mario and Ferria names would be cleared. Mario left his associate's house feeling blessed. Mario parked at his attorney's office. Mario's attorney was waiting for him. The attorney had already spoken with the district attorney. The case was going to be dismissed. The district attorney had to confirm the business account. The funds Mario handed his attorney sealed his fate. The attorney nodded with relief looking over the paperwork.

"Alright, Mario, we are done here. I will handle the rest. Make sure you do not get into any trouble. You will be watched for a while because the district attorneys want to prosecute as many people as possible in this big scandal. No one will be getting their cases dismissed without confirmation. We have criminals using illegal devices to hack into people's accounts. They are making fake receipts to steal money from people since the COVID. The money from the donors confirmed the money was donated to the programs."

"I told you to trust me."

"I trust you. I have to make sure you are aware of the circumstances as your attorney. You need to know what can happen to you if you do not cover your ass. I see that you have been listening."

Mario shook hands with his attorney and left his attorney's office. Mario had to get ready for the fundraiser with Henry. Mario knew this will be the biggest challenge since he had to make a speech about his arrest. Mario hated speaking in public about dirt on the news. He could not get around the over hyped story. Mario was going to be flooded with questions by reporters since the charges were dropped. Mario prepared for the questions going over some of the questions he knew he would be asked. Mario pulled back up at the house ready to answer any questions the reporters threw his way. His attorney had text him that the charges were dropped.

"Karen! Mario yelled for his woman to share the results.

Karen ran from the patio into the living room agitated by why Mario was yelling. She hoped he was not in any more trouble.

"I am a free man. The district attorney dropped the charges. Ferria is off the hook." Mario picked up Karen swinging her around the room.

"We have to go out after this baby and celebrate. I am not all the way in the clear yet. I have a few questions to answer when I am interviewed about how the charges got dropped. You know people are going to think that I aided the district attorney."

"Let the people assuming think whatever they want to think. Mario, you do not owe the haters anything but the proof. People are always going to suspect something. The district attorneys did not look like they were your friends in the news. If people want to take it there let them. You were about to be prosecuted. No one can claim the arrest were fake."

"I know. I have to tell my associates. I do not want my associates thinking that they cannot trust me. I did one day in jail. My associates might think that I am a snitch."

"A snitch to what, what could you be telling on? Your associates were not arrested. You were arrested. The charges were dropped."

"This is how the game goes baby. It doesn't have to make any sense. Our fight is to force people to make sense when they come for us or suffer the consequences."

CHAPTER 16

MARIO AND KAREN WERE DRESSED sharp as two couples on a red carpet runway. The crowd was bursting with energy awaiting the event to hear what all the fuss was about in the news. Henry and Astelle were wearing their designer clothes looking like top executives from a TV show. Henry was feeling good in a rush to get the news out to his supporters. Henry walked onto the stage and signaled for the people to take their seats. Mario stood beside Henry boldly ready to get the show started.

"I know you are all concerned about the hearsay in the media. I want to clear all that up before we enjoy the fundraiser. I have brought my associate that was one of the guys who was arrested."

Mario took the microphone from Henry adjusting the mic to fit his comfort level.

"My name is Mario Vandam. I am a business man who has donated to the most rewarding programs in this community and gave donations in other cities and states that housed homeless people and helped families in struggling times with bills. I know many of you are very familiar with my name and not my face."

People whispered looking up at Mario.

"Oh that is Mario Vandam." Someone could be heard saying.

The locals looked on pleased to be a part of the action.

"I had a terrible run in with the prosecutors who was doing their jobs based on information that the prosecutors received. I am not upset at the prosecutors for doing their jobs. I am upset at the envy that was committed. I am very happy to be here and help fund the important events to keep our communities thriving to help working families and families that cannot work. I know there are a lot of people who cannot work due to unfortunate surgeries and disabilities. None of us can blame anyone else in our communities for their impairments. I will not leave out people in health conditions that forces the ones affected to need funding because other people do not like helping people with limited restrictions. I have passed out my dismissal notice in my case to ease the minds of those of you who are skeptical. I do not want any of you to think that Henry is in any kind of scams. Henry is a great guy. He does not mind posting on his website where all the money goes after he receives large donations." The crowd stood up clapping for Mario's response to the allegations.

"Now that we have cleared the allegations up, let's get to why we are here. We have programs that serve law enforcement. There are programs that we provide funding for that serve veterans and senior citizens. We have expanded our buildings to accommodate the people without in these trying times. We are supplying law enforcement that has spoken up for corruption with new vehicles, uniforms, and better pay. The senior citizen's building has expanded into the downtown area to aid in helping the seniors with food and transportation. Mario donated a large amount of money for the children center for kids with high-risk problems. We are going to give you the details on the website. All of you can follow us on our journey in keeping the community stable and in peace." People stood in solitary with awe excited to hear the glorious ground breaking clarifications.

"Astelle, can you please come up here for a second?" Henry pointed to his wife who was talking to a friend who was congratulating Astelle.

"My wife has opened up a huge building for arts, crafts, and activities that keep all ages in shape including a gym. It will be available real soon."

Astelle blew kisses with her hands making heart shapes to show appreciation. Astelle honored the new center that was being set up to help the community get together and stay in the fun of the city.

"We are also building a new center for people who need medical and counseling resources. The certitude will be provided as we continue to get responses from the community on their concerns."

"Are we going to be able to have shares in the new projects?" One of the donors asked.

"I can speak with you about that option privately. I do believe that that option will be one of the benefits for the high donors.

"Mario, are you going to have to do any time or pay any fees?" Another donor asked.

"No. I did not do anything wrong. In fact I am going to donate more funds to worthy causes because of the scandal." Mario gave the donors a thumb up.

Everyone spoke in low voices among each other as Henry, Mario, and Astelle walked through the crowd answering questions one on one offering support dedicated to pledges. The event was to fund the projects and get everyone on board to make positive changes to the neighborhoods that were suffering the most. Mario passed out his business cards to the donors who were interested in contacting him. Henry was proud to see Mario tranquil. The event had people coming from all over the cities and states to ballyhoo the changes. Henry was known for drawing huge crowds of supporters because of all the positive outcomes he could produce.

"Karen, you made it over?" Astelle walked over to Karen giving her a kiss on the cheek.

"I had to come to support you guys. I appreciate your husband boosting optimism for Mario. Mario needs a positive influence in his life. He is smart and an ingenious business man. He has some ratchet associates and family. I cannot say that I do not have a few in my own circle."

"We all do." Astelle agreed.

"We are going to get along fine and dandy with the new projects underway. I have some stalwart friends who would love to support your next event."

Matthew came over with Marg. Karen was given Astelle some information on what she had in the works.

"Marg! Hey girl! I would like for you to meet Karen. Karen is going to be attending some of the fundraisers. She is in the same field of work that we do for her community, family and friends."

"How are you Karen? It is a pleasure to meet you. This is my husband Matthew. Astelle throws the best fundraisers. We get to eat the best food." Marg teasingly bragged biting into a spicy kabob.

"I can tell. The crowd is very comforting, a lot of nice couples. Mario and I hold in high esteem gratitude to be a part of Astelle and Henry's social functions, many people have included Mario and I in the exertion."

"That is how we operate. Welcome newbie." Matthew said to Karen.

"If you beautiful ladies would excuse me, I need to go over and talk to Henry. The guys are going to be psyche up to know that I fadangled floor seats to one of our favorite sports teams." Matthew paced toward Henry.

Marg shook her head at her husband. Marg and Matthew had been getting along much better. Marg thought at one point that her marriage was going to end. Instead her marriage had blossomed into something stronger than before. Matthew was being respectful. Marg was more understanding. Although Matthew continued to look a little too long at beautiful women as far as Marg was concerned. Marg noticed he was not overly puttering around with women the way he used to in the past. Marg thought to herself that her man was finally worn out.

"You and Matthew are closer. You are jovial and refreshed." Astelle congratulated her friend on her good humor.

"Matthew is working really hard to keep me companionable. I know it is a big change for him being that he was known as a player. I admire all his efforts."

"Men with a lot of money are expected to have a lot of women and other materialistic things. I cannot deal with all that baggage." Karen offered her opinion.

"I have to agree those kinds of expectations are lame and juvenile. I don't know how that craziness stuck when it came to men and money. To say that men should be with anyone they want if they are rich is not sane. People are saying that women should close their legs. The guys legs are the ones opened to every thing moving." Astelle added in.

"Matthew is in his right mind about my concerns. I love my husband. I used to not care when he flirted with women. I ask that he respects my presence however."

"That sounds pretty fair. Women nowadays are not the same. Some women will cause all kinds of problems in your marriage if your man allows the disrespect. I have no kind of patience for messy women and disrespectful men. I refuse to have to have a conversation about all kinds of women in my relationship." Karen was not the one to deal with eruptive arguments.

"I know that in most cases the women are not aware. I feel like women that are lied to and lied on are just as upset as we are in the unfaithful relationships. I learned not to blame a woman for a man's bad deeds. Men love to see women fighting over them. I make sure I tell my man when he is the problem. My man tells me when I am the problem."

The women stayed in their circle for a while enjoying the company and conversation before another group of people pulled Astelle away to ask her about her Women League's program. Marg and Karen made their way around the room making small talk with the donors.

"Mario, I have been looking all over for you." Karen finally saw Mario with two other gentlemen and a gorgeous woman.

"I saw you over there in deep conversation with Astelle. I didn't want to interrupt." Mario nudged Karen in the side.

"We were in a deep discussion. You know how women are when we get together. We were being keen on one another conversation.

"In a minute baby we are going to have to leave. I have to get up real early and meet Ferria. We have a lot of documents to look over."

"Whenever you ready to leave let me know."

Henry wanted to know how Mario wanted to handle the donations. Mario, Karen, and Henry were at the end of the room implementing their goals. Mario agreed to let Henry do what was best. The three decided to go ahead with the new projects that were a definite for families rallying for freedom and jobs. Henry wanted to keep the ball rolling by keeping all the businesses flowing so that the community stayed active and substantial.

"The projects are a secure way to keep violence out of our neighborhoods. We have something for all ages to do when they want to get out of the house. We have money flowing from the other businesses to keep all the businesses effective.

"Henry, I am going to call it a night. I will be in touch. I have a few investments of my own that needs my observation. Ferria is going to meet me tomorrow to get our little mishaps squared away and signed. I will feel much better once Ferria is back on her feet. I like how Ferria was willing to take the fall without involving anyone. That says a lot about Ferria's character."

"I love my sister. She is one of the premier intellects Astelle and I know. I was hurt when I saw Ferria getting arrested. I knew it had to be something that could be fixed. Ferria will not make that mistake again."

"We are all going to have her back this time. Ferria will shine like Ferria always shine in her envisions. We can set Ferria up with our financial advisers and see which ones she would like to work with."

"The best adjudication for Ferria well being would be applied."

Mario and Karen stamped the seal of approval on all of their friends and new friends. Mario and Karen had their own little thing about who they let in their circle to not get in any unnecessary drama.

Mario could not wait to get home to undress Karen with Karen classy physique in her fancy clothes.

"Karen, your father and I have to talk. I saw him giving me the eye. I was going to say something but he kept talking to Henry and ignoring me. Your mom was looking younger than you."

"I know my dad can be difficult. My mom does look good. I avoided my parents the entire occasion. I don't want anyone to listen to us arguing. My parents were invited to hear you clear your name. I will give my parents a call. My dad has to understand how I feel. I refused to talk about the allegations to my parents at the event."

"The discomfort will minimize. I could tell your dad wanted to apologize to me. You know your dad doesn't enjoy admitting when he is wrong. I'm not going to press him. Your dad will come to his senses after he reevaluate the set of circumstances. Your mom talked to me for a long time. She knew a few people there and was mingling effortlessly."

"My mom knows people wherever she goes. I knew she would probably recognize a few people at the fundraiser. My mom gave me that quick hug and was out of sight working the room conversing with most of the people who attended. It's not a big thing to me. My mom has behaved sociably all her life in big crowds. She knows how to handle herself accordingly in big crowds. My dad needs to chill on me and give me breathing room."

"You said it your dad knows his wife knows how to handle herself. Your mom is experienced. Your dad is worried about you. You are his baby girl. He will trust you more the more you continue to make good decisions."

Mario pulled up to his huge home. Karen carried a big bag out of the back seat. Mario opened the door taking the big bag from Karen to sit the big bag on the floor. Before Karen could get the door shut, Mario was all over her with kisses and hand rubs.

"Mario, let me shut the door." Karen was crimson.

Mario and Karen in lust, Mario kissed her up and down her neck. The two went full dive into touching and kissing and rubbing. Mario could hear his cell phone vibrating. He knew he should not answer the cell phone. Karen snatched his cell phone and threw it on the couch pushing Mario down on the couch. The night ended with Mario and Karen naked on the couch.

CHAPTER 17

Alexis arrived home from her trip with a husband on top of
the World to see her. Nathan had flowers all over the living room
with pink and red rose petals leading up to the bedroom. Soft playing
instruments with a soulful voice serenaded the bedroom stereo system.

"There goes my sunshine."

The room was fancied up with a huge banner that read "Welcome
Home." Lingerie was spread across bed. Alexis was impressed and felt like
a Queen. Alexis showered before arriving. She quickly freshened up in
the bathroom joining her husband in the bedroom. Alexis and Nathan
fed one another without saying one word. The two caressed and kissed
leading to intimacy.

"Sweetheart, I heard that a few of your associates were arrested. Are you
involved in anything that you would like to share with me?" Nathan asked.

"Baby, that is true. It was cringing. I found out not too long ago myself.
I am not involved. I will not put you and I lives in that kind of spotlight
knowing that we are already scrutinized for being in important positions.
I don't know the ones involved personally. Some of my colleagues know
the men and women who were arrested. I was in dismay as you are when I
was at the lake. The police came up to the lake to ask me some questions."

"Oh my, I hate that you had to go through that. You were questioned. You should have called me."

"It was nothing like that. It was more of the police inquiring about other people and asking me if I knew anything that's all. I told the police no. Charley pulled up and cleared up the misunderstanding. I was candor and relieved. I'm going to talk to Charley at work. He told me he would speak with the people the police were asking about."

"Good. Let me know if you need me to have our attorney come to the job."

"Me and my staff are already provided legal counsel. I want to make sure no one at our office is doing anything illegal. I don't want to get caught up in any dishonorable affairs. I have my team going through all of our paperwork and checking with the donations to validate that everything is in order. We run a smooth office and reach out to all the people in our county with the services that we provide. I am not worried about me in any drama. I know that it is not my office."

"I love your answer." Nathan hugged Alexis romantically. They scooted back down in their cozy firm bed listening to the soft music in the background taken full advantage of the rest of their time before going back to work.

"I can stay like this forever. We needed this time together. We are always industrious." Alexis exhaled.

"I know Alexis. We are going to take vacation time and get back to what we love doing which is being in one another's existence."

"Have you thought about children?"

"I thought you didn't want any children."

"I hear all the children running around outside Nathan. I think I might want one or two little ones running around us."

"I thought those words would never come out of your mouth. I stopped thinking about children once we decided before we were married not to have any children."

"No pressure Nathan. I wanted to let you know."

Alexis was in heaven. She had a great time with her girls and now she was spending quality time with her husband. Things couldn't get any better.

"I have something for you." Nathan gave Alexis a wrapped gift.

"You did not tell me that we were exchanging gifts."

"We are not exchanging gifts. I bought this for you because I think you earned this. I have been waiting for the right time to give it to you. We don't see each other that much with careers that clash. This is not the kind of gift that you hand over on the way out the door when we are on our way to work."

Alexis was rejoiced when she thought the day could not get any better, Alexis sat up to open the gift. She was thinking highly of Nathan vow. Her husband watched her face as she opened up the gift.

"The rings are stunning." Alexis gently put her hands on the gorgeous wedding ring set gasping with jouissance.

"Try the rings on. I wanted to get you an upgrade a long time ago. I had my colleague's wife come to my rescue to choose the perfect rings, she loves being of service with surprises for our staff dearest."

"You didn't have to do this honey, my God."

"I knew you would approve. I want you to always remember how much I love you. You never give me any grief." Alexis melted in love the way her husband loved her. Alexis always wanted to be married. She was living out her dream she vision since she was a young girl. Alexis never wanted children until that night looking at how attentive her husband was towards her.

"I have one more gift then I am going to take you into our jacuzzi and give you the rub down of your life." Nathan loved spending time with Alexis.

Alexis expressed admiration to her husband for being so attentive. Nathan always made her feel loved and wanted. It was everything Alexis imagined a marriage would be like.

"Close your eyes." Alexis closed her eyes and felt something being placed around her neck. It was a diamond necklace with her initials in the center. It was breathtaking to say the least.

"What has gotten into you? Whatever has you this spellbind I adore the new you." Alexis touched her necklace walking to the mirror. The mirror accentuated the jewelry the necklace was sparkling. Alexis was floating on air receiving all the gifts she was fond of it was a magical tenderness coming from Nathan.

"I am charmed by that nice car you bought me. The extra space in our home you turned into my office was thoughtful of you. I can get a lot of my work done at home instead of sitting in my office when court is closed I had to reward you for all the compelling things you did for me."

"I do appreciate the gifts Nathan. I didn't buy you that new car to receive something in return. I bought you that new car to fit all your court cases in the trunk. You needed a bigger trunk. The new office space here at the house gives us more time to be together."

"I love you sweetheart. You sure know how to make a man feel special."

Alexis and Nathan slowly climbed in the jacuzzi.

"I have saved money every since my mom and dad gave me that big savings when I turned 25 years old." Alexis missed her parents.

"You have made rewarding decisions with your investments I think we can afford to have at least one child. We can make a child tonight." Alexis's husband made love to her gently in their jacuzzi.

The night air in the warm jacuzzi made the temperature ideal for the lovers. Alexis felt like she was in a fairy tale with her knight and shining armor. Nathan played the satisfying role of giving Alexis what she desired and more.

Alexis and Nathan hated to remove themselves from one another. The days passed by too quickly. The nights shortened when they were in each other's arms.

"Last night would play in my head like my favorite song on the radio." Nathan slowly got out of bed.

"I want to make sure you are not starving yourself hubby. I know you dislike going out to eat alone. Make sure you grab some of the snacks I bought you to get you through the day. I know it is hard for you to eat the lunches I packed for you. You keep leaving the lunches in the refrigerator."

"I have people that go out for lunch to pick up food on their lunch breaks. They bring me back something every now and then. I eat in my office while I'm looking through all my court cases. My responsibilities have been overflowing."

"We have lawsuits for just about everything going on in this county and other counties courts that keep the courts tied up. I hope you don't mind if I stop by today and bring you a late lunch hubby. I will be in your area around that time wrapping up ideas with friends on a case study we are all a part of."

"You can stop by my work place unannounced any time you want. I would love to see you. You know you don't have to ask."

"I will remember that." Alexis handed Nathan his clothes that he had sitting out to put on. Alexis packed fresh fruit with low calorie snacks in a bag to hold her husband's appetite until she brought him something to eat."

Alexis cleaned the kitchen after her husband left for work. She had a long day ahead of her. Alexis needed to manage her time with all the duties on her schedule. Her office duties were scattered everywhere. Alexis was unsurprising to find Amy at her desk with her head in a book underlining paragraphs. Amy's desk was filled with memo notes and papers posted on her vision board and computer.

"Good morning Amy. What a day we are going to have."

"I have to catch up on my commitments that out of town trip we took left me with a close deadline. I met with Ashley and Brian earlier to set up the conference room. Our guests will be arriving this afternoon. In the next three hours I am going to double check that we have covered the agenda. I hate when things get piled up." Amy stacked her pile of papers neatly.

"We didn't have a choice. We had to go out of town to prepare for the summit. We have to leave again in three weeks. Do not forget what Leilani emailed us about the hate crimes rally. We are going to be a big hit when we announce this next challenge to sway the people to exercise the rights to fight for all races in the country. The exclusion in any hate bill law passed to give certain races power has divided the country into a bloody division. I think Charley, Douglas, and the rest of the team are going to love engaging in making people born in this country top priority The prejudice and personal divisions has caused a lot of unwanted suffering."

"The team will love the improvements Alexis. We are taking precautions. I knew we could pull it off. Our progress is impressive in the amount of time we have had to work on all the goals. We have advanced technology in this office receiving huge compliments and donations. Well known headliners are getting involved clearing the way for continuance with this palmy process. We don't want to slack off and things go back to being in complete chaos. It took a lot of time to clean up this community. This office can finally reap a big difference with all the effort we put into this change. The laws are being enforced. We have staff members assisting with the enforcement. My husband contributions to families utilizing the court for compensation and mediations motivated a lot of his colleagues to stay mindful of what the citizens are going through in legal proceedings. The courts have new programs where people are receiving quality care for judicial proceedings one on one. There are mediations and resolution time set up for people in litigations. I think the programs for courts should have been designed to resolve quick resolutions years ago. Some cases should be mediated I don't understand how so many counties were able to neglect all of their important duties."

"What were the public officials committing all the crimes thinking?

More importantly, why were the ones caught harassing all of the people on our complaints not charged? The victims I have contacted clearly were not a threat?" Alexis read aloud complaints that were reckless and petty toward the victims.

"It does not appear complaints were being taken seriously from all the overflow of complaints that we were receiving without any follow-ups or resources dated back years ago."

"We have eased a lot of locals stress addressing most of the spiteful actions."

"This office and the agencies that received a lot of the complaints have had to remove a lot of employees from public buildings for harassment on single women, men, and children. Can you imagine how much the single women have had to go through with the kind of men we caught in positions not qualified being dishonest to the women on the complaints? The images make me sick to my stomach." Amy stretched her arms.

"As the mayor that oversees the city developments I was sickened by all the videos. The mistrust and abuse of power is a damn shame. To have that many people not take their jobs seriously is pitiful. Too many people in office think that they are not going to be caught and disciplined."

"You would think grown people would not have to be told to do right at their jobs. I guess we were wrong." Amy clamped her hair barrette back in place.

"The transitions are bringing more single moms together to receive the awareness that they deserve. The mother's should not be worried about illegal setups and threats being reported by bitter men and women. We know that the single moms and many of the women married are not doing anything that was reported by the aggressors. The violators are abusing their powers." Alexis sighed.

"Parents least concern should be to go through unnecessary deception when the parents already have so much on their plates."

"I will get together with you in a couple of hours. My presentation for the demo is coming along informatively."

"Okay." Amy took a swig of her water.

The ladies glued themselves in their separate offices. Alexis verified her illustrations. The test Alexis conducted to make sure the experiment would work passed.

Charley was in his office with staff members when Leilani stopped by Charley's office to discuss what Charley was going to do about the deliberation with the chief of police that Alexis asked him to follow up on.

"Come on in Leilani, I know why you are here. I asked Douglas to do the follow up with the chief of police. I contacted the school board director who left me numerous emails about educational studies at the high school. A few other parents wanted some representatives from the mayor's office to come to the school board meeting to discuss some of the parent's safety concerns."

"I emailed you who called me to tell me that they would attend the school board meeting. Did you receive the link?" Leilani asked.

"I have not had time to check anything Leilani. I'm free to confirm. I can talk to the school principal. I have to go soon. We have an upset citizen about a neglected complaint at one of the city's programs for disability. I will fill you in as soon as we resolve the objection."

"I will let you know how the meeting goes Charley. I can update you in the morning. Don't overburden yourself. You know how you can get when that phone buzzing off the hook Charley."

Charley departed from Leilani leaving his office to go handle an urgent review.

Leilani went back to work. Leilani's boyfriend, Evan, came into the office to hand Leilani another assignment from Alexis. Leilani was working incessantly getting all of the work polished off. Evan sat down in her office to help. He had cleared up his allegiance and was ready to take Leilani out.

"I think we would be concluding in one hour or so. We can leave to check out that new place that was just built. The new temptation has shopping boutiques with designer clothing and fabrics. The scavenger hunt and wellness or spa package caught my eye."

"I can use a spa treatment. My body is aching from all the jobs I have been doing. We need to hurry up." Leilani turned on her computer. Evan took her other assignment.

Alexis and Amy were putting the final power point demo together for the civil disobedience, strikes, riots, and marches. Leilani and her boyfriend compiled the "Save the Planet", and "Black History Month", project. Leilani gave Alexis and Amy the Human Rights and Illegal Medicine outline. Evan provided the Labor protest and fight for Democracy and Government responses.

"Amy, do you have that list for the meeting? I left mines in my office."

Amy searched through her papers coming up with the list.

"Here it goes." Amy handed Alexis the list.

The meeting was packed with people who were inquiring about the recent mayhem showing all kinds of photos of proof. Alexis was preoccupied. The county had a lot of drawbacks in the mist of being managed. One lady provided Alexis with a photo of a group of people trashing the new buildings with other mobs of angry people protesting flags and tear gas used on the streets to break up peaceful assemblies for Human rights.

"I will have to make sure that I have our staff look into this. Thanks for coming down and sharing your concerns with me. I was not informed of the graffiti. We do have a couple of business owners that want murals on their property. I came back from out of town addressing similar perturbation. Business owners have expressed apprehension about coming to work to find their buildings covered with unwanted graffiti." Alexis agreed graffiti made the businesses less attractive.

"Mayor, I am personally panicked about the trash all over my building when I arrive at work most mornings I find this kind of lifestyle on my property." A bearded man provided disturbing activities going on near city hall.

Alexis took the photos viewing in horror.

Amy took the photos from Alexis's and saw drug addicts bodies disfigured and maimed lying on thee owner's property.

"Inconceivable!" Amy muttered.

Alexis turned away from the crowd and spoke to Amy briefly. The two women turned back toward the crowd to angry faces blurting out more questions. Alexis answered all of the questions directed at her. Alexis and Amy rushed to observe the location.

"Can you believe this Amy? I did not see this coming."

"I am appalled by this protestation."

"We have to find out who are the individuals in the photo to get this matter under control before the press gets a hold of the revolt."

"The activity going on by city hall is unacceptable. I guess we have focused on complaint after complaint out of the office we did not notice."

"The press will have a field day with this kind of stomach turning offense."

The women drove in silence thinking about how this kind of information can ruin all of their hard work. Alexis was disappointed and did not understand how they did not know about none of the mishaps going wrong that was mentioned at the meeting.

Alexis dropped lunch off to her husband in a hurry. Nathan was smiling from ear to ear when Alexis kept her promise and stopped by. Amy feedback for Alexis on the suspects gave optimism. Alexis's close friend, friend, drug dealer will be off the street. Alexis was told that the new drug was homemade and could take out someone with very small dosage.

"I know the names of the suspects in the photos. I have people researching for us. We have another crisis I have to be straight forward with you. Amy looked at Alexis with saddened eyes.

CHAPTER 18

H ENRY LINED UP NEW PROJECTS. He barely had time to sleep. Henry grabbed a handful of grapes devouring the sweet taste in his mouth. He took a long gulp of his cold beverage. Astelle was ready to suppress the negative finding she stumbled upon jogging downstairs to leave with Henry.

"Astelle, I am going to be ready in a few minutes. I'm waiting for this email to confirm what we need to give to the investigative journalists."

"I need to make a call any way. I will be in the living room."

Henry received his email confirmation on his laptop five minutes later and responded to the sender. Henry had to meet with his legal experts to remove the staff from the commissioner on judicial performance building for the numerous criminal actions that took place. Henry was meeting law enforcement at the building to make the arrests. Astelle was meeting a special unit of law enforcement to remove the staff from the community police review board that was helping corrupted public officials target certain families in the community. The news reported every criminal offense in the headlines every couple of minutes. The news advertised dirty deeds putting people affected by the criminal misconduct on the tube to help enforce the sweeps. Astelle was honored to be a part of the cleanup.

"Let's get going. My colleagues spoke with a few judges that confirmed that there were judges spreading hatred against certain litigants causing the victims a lot of unnecessary pain and suffering when the families went to court. The families were being prevented from getting on their feet and going forward with their court cases because of the life term employment by corrupted judges. A lot of representatives are working to stop this disturbing behavior that has lasted for years. Our office has finally been able to get people to join in to remove the judges. There are thousands of people illegally incarcerated and have records because of the judges criminal misconduct."

"I have all of the documentation and the confessions. I can send a copy to the district attorney's office."

"I need to email my associate to make sure that she gets a copy of the judge's names and distribute this information to her boss."

"The information cannot wait. We have to expedite the documents. The building is already surrounded with law enforcement. Indictments and witnesses need to be protected. I am going to represent some of the constituents in this matter by voicing what was committed and give their complaints to law enforcement."

Henry and Astelle had multiple people counting on them to make sure that the ones who kept attacking the families in the community did not get away again. It was past overdue that the ones who was wronged received their compensation and justice.

"The police are already putting people in the paddy wagon." Astelle pulled up and Henry got out of the car to hand the paperwork to the head person in charge.

Astelle watched as Henry spoke with a few of the guys in uniform and explained what he was told by the victims. The men expressed gratitude for his support and continued with bringing people out of the building. Onlookers looked astonished. A few minutes later, Astelle saw camera crews unloading their equipment asking the men in uniforms several questions about the arrests.

"I feel better that my part is concluded." Henry got back in the car with Astelle. Astelle turned out of the parking lot to rescue more families who was convinced to come forward and recount what was having a negative impact in their community.

Astelle and Henry reached the citizens police review board staff being removed hiding themselves from view. The building was being seized. The camera crew was making an announcement that the building would be closed for a few weeks and reopened with new staff to take over the pass statue complaints that the staff failed to enforce.

"Hi, Astelle. Sampson Blake. I am the contact that you were to give the names and information to about the disservices. I have spoken to the officers. The officers have confirmed that your story is true. We wanted to thank you for your brave and honest commitment to make sure that the families in this community are liberated. We need the families that were unlawfully left behind to receive the fair and equal justice that many other families benefited from isolating certain families by not representing them."

"It is my honor and my duty to serve the families who was attacked Mr. Blake. I would love to keep in contact with your office. I have more walls coming down in the communities where people have setup shop and are using some of the buildings to commit illegal activity that kill innocent people. I can confirm the addresses that we are enforcing the law at and doing a sweep removing the guilty identified."

"I would love to cover the story Astelle." Mr. Blake kissed Astelle's hand. Astelle watched buildings being taped and closed down with a big smile on her beautiful face.

The couple had been turning the upheaval that was hunting their community to a complete halt. Henry phone vibrated. Mario name came up on his screen.

"Good job Henry. I am fascinated with how you are getting back at the initiators who are the real criminals. I have committed more time and more money than most of the outlaws who are getting away with this malfeasance for decades."

"Doing the right thing feels exceptionally beneficial."

"Henry, you are going to be fond of reading what Karen and I accomplished. The recent courses of action are on our side not to be judged by the instigators who pointed their fingers at us. They are subjecting worse crimes behind closed doors."

Henry checked his email to read the article. Henry pleased with Mario and Karen commitments to the people discontinued the email.

"Mario, I knew you would be on board to end this. We can only help people by changing what we do ourselves. I heard about several families being bought out by people who were raising the prices on property so that the sellers would only sell to the highest bidder. How did you get the owners to stop allowing the prices to be raised and stick with the original price offers?"

"I have people. The buyers are refusing to offer a high price to move in the properties to keep the prices from going up. Business owners are accepting a fair rental price and standing firm. My associates and I are building in areas that accommodate the rich. We are leaving the neighborhoods alone where families have been able to house and feed their children affordably. The greed has violated families causing too much homelessness. We are stopping a lot of homelessness by leaving the affordable properties in communities for incomes that deserve a decent place to live."

"Mario you are a billionaire I would think you would jump at the chance to buy up low cost property." Henry beholds a remarkable transformation in Mario.

"I am much smarter now and realized what my actions were doing to innocent families. I couldn't sleep well at night knowing that I am the one putting the families in these positions. Besides we have plenty of places that we can buy property that does not affect anyone. Why go around making problems for people. That is how my boy got caught up in a cross fire."

"What happened?"

"A few older guys caught David by himself at a popular place where David knows the owner and shot him up. David survived. He went through a lot of therapy and rehabilitation. The families are fed up with the rich people getting away with all the crimes. The people of this community are prepared to hold the law in the streets. There are numerous news clippings of families buying guns to protect their properties."

"I would have to agree that that would be my mentality if I kept being pushed by troublemakers. I'm glad you are not the enemy Mario. You are setting a great example."

"I am also going to bring good paying jobs into the community with some of my business partners. We are working on the plans."

"That's the spirit, Mario growing up and thinking about other people before himself. I never thought I would see the day." Henry chuckled.

"Me either man. Hug your beautiful wife for me. I appreciate you for being there for me and Karen. My business partners and I will be supporting some of your fundraisers. I have to get back to making money."

"My wife is sitting next to me. We left a couple of sweeps that were removing some of the staff from the buildings where all of the corruption has been taking place. I am about to get back to money moves myself. You are welcome to bring Karen and have Sunday dinner with us. We would love to see the both of you."

"I might do that Henry. I will let you know before Sunday."

Henry and Astelle reached Henry's office. A huge crowd was carrying signs in favor of Henry for his stance to stop corruption in the city. The crowd ran towards Henry and Astelle. The camera men pushed microphones toward the couple asking about the sweeps in certain public buildings.

"Henry is it true that you were the one who pushed for the arrests of judges and public officials that were not servicing families in the community?"

"It is true. I am very proud to say that we are shutting the buildings down that failed the people and their families who was being mistreated. We will reopen as quickly as possible with new staff that service the community and do not turn anyone away or mistreat qualified people. If we hear about any of this kind of behavior going on, we will act without delay." The crowd roared and chanted Henry and Astelle's names in front of the cameras.

"Now if you guys will excuse us, my husband and I have so much more work to do for the people of this community. We are going to have to get to his office to contact more families in need to see how we can help. We value you all for coming out." Astelle walked past the crowd with Henry reaching the building and closing the door.

"The turn outs are amazing. Astelle, you really do have a lot of people who support this kind of change. I am very pleased that you did not give up on me. I thought you would want to throw in the towel."

"The families have waited long enough for equality and entity. We have enough money to retire comfortably that does not mean that we quit on the people who have supported us all of these years. It feels right to give back."

Astelle leaned back in the chair feeling a little dizzy.

"Astelle?" Henry rushed by his wife side.

Astelle was unhappy about the sick motion all of a sudden. She was feeling normal hours ago.

"I guess it is all the work we have been doing. The tiredness will pass give me a minute." Henry looked at Astelle with concern and pulled out his office chair next to Astelle sitting down by his computer. Emails and messages on his phone kept popping up. Henry pressed keys on the computer. Astelle sitting still fanned her face. Astelle tried to get up. She quickly had to sit back down. Henry checked Astelle's temperature to feel if she was warm. It was not uncommon to come down with the 24 hour bug in up and down weather.

"Let me send the responses off about our next fundraiser then I am taking you to the hospital."

"Henry, I am not going to the hospital. I am fatigued."

"I do not think so Astelle. I think you may be pregnant."

"Pregnant! I am not pregnant Henry. I had my period." Astelle stopped talking thinking about when was the last time that she had had her period.

"Exactly. I might be a dad. I knew you were too young for me." Henry poked boraz at Astelle.

"I'm not that young. My late forties may seem similar to my late twenties. Women are getting pregnant in their fifties. I guess I am young enough to have a baby. Henry you know that would not be a bad thing. We don't have anyone in our lives when we get older to share our wealth with. I was thinking about adopting. If we are pregnant, I would be very grateful."

Henry was shocked and glad that his wife was not upset at the thought of having his child. Henry knew that Astelle did not want children because of all the commitment she had. A baby would probably make things better."

Henry carried Astelle to the car opening the door for her and pulling Astelle's seatbelt over her like a fragile child.

"Henry, I do not need you treating me like a child. I may be having a child. I am a grown woman."

"This is all new to me."

"We are both new at this. We don't even know if I'm pregnant Henry. Let's not get our hopes up too high."

"I accept either way. I know we are going to be dedicated to one another with or without children."

Henry drove to the hospital. His wife dabbed her eyes and Henry parked. They drove into the hospital the private entrance way. Henry's private doctor that was a part of the family made house calls. Henry could not wait. Astelle almost fainted.

"Hello Henry and Astelle. Good to see you of course not under these circumstances. Let's take a look at what is going on Astelle. Can you get undress from the waist down and put on this gown? I will be back shortly." The doctor gave the couple a gown and left the room with his chart.

Astelle undressed on the hospital bed and placed her feet in the stirrups looking at her husband.

"Henry, I know it is stress because of all the new stuff we have been dealing with lately with our friends." Astelle squeezed her husband's hand and closed her eyes again hoping that she was right.

Henry said a quick prayer under his breath and continued to hold his wife's hand. He was apprehensive. He could not help but fidget in the chair next to his wife.

"Astelle I am going to do a few tests and have the nurse draw some blood. I will call you as soon as the results are in and we will go from there." The doctor started the examination. A nurse came in during the examination and took blood from Astelle. Astelle put her clothes back on. The doctor came back in the room with reading materials to deal with fatigue and stress wishing them well. Henry and Astelle thanked the doctor and left the hospital.

"I am not going to feel right until after we receive the results Astelle. We are going to go home. I can work from the house until we find out what is up with you."

"Henry, do not be so dramatic. I am not going to sit in the house until the doctor contact us. I have work to do and so do you. I have to get to the office and check with my staff. I cannot miss a lot of days. I have too many programs operating."

"Astelle please do not argue with me on this one. You know I never ask you for much. I don't want anything to happen to you. You can call your staff to stay on top of your meetings. I will do the same thing."

Astelle was too tired to argue with her husband. Henry stopped off to pick up soup and crackers for his wife. They entered their home and Henry grabbed a warm blanket and wrapped it around Astelle. Henry flipped through the pages of a book he was reading. Astelle had been doing new workouts and was sore. Her body could have been adjusting to the new routine.

CHAPTER 19

A MY RELATED THE BAD TIDINGS to Alexis. Alexis was mortified. Alexis made calls after calls. Alexis drove off to the new business in the area to speak with the business owner.

The building was built in the way of a learning site for patients who were having medical problems. The building had diagrams of body parts labeled. Patient's ailments and injuries revealed on pamphlets. People were all over the first floor occupying chairs with magazines waiting to be seen.

"I would like to speak with the person whose in charge of this business." Alexis asked the receptionist politely.

"Can I tell Mr. Dallas who wants to see him?"

"Alexis."

The receptionists paged her boss and offered Alexis and Amy beverages. Amy accepted water. Alexis sat next to Amy grabbing a magazine.

The owner of the building entered the building greeting Alexis and Amy.

"How can I help you ladies?" The owner was a tall handsome man.

"My name is Alexis. This is Amy. Is there some where we can talk privately? I would like to discuss a serious matter with you that was brought to my attention."

"Follow me." The tall man pushed through double doors and down a hallway making a left at the first door and opening the door with his keys. He held open the door for Alexis and Amy and asked the women to have a seat. The man waited for Alexis to speak.

"What is your name?" Alexis curiosity justifiable.

"I am Marshawn Dallas."

"Do you know who the guys are in the photos?" Alexis showed Marshawn the photos.

"Yes. They work for me. Why is there a problem?"

"Yes, there is a big problem. The guys in the photos were reported to be running some kind of illegal substances out of this building. Fentanyl I believe."

Marshawn looked on in horror. He looked at the photos again and cleared his throat.

"Are you here to question the guys or are you here to question me?"

"Both. I do not want to contact the authorities until I know exactly what is going on. I usually do not handle this kind of criminal violation but since it was brought to my attention and the person that was concerned is a close friend, I took it upon myself to make sure that there was enough probable cause before alerting the authorities. Marshawn, we can do this in two ways. You can contact your employees and put them on notice. Or we can call the police and have the employees involved removed from the building. We cannot allow this kind of behavior in our community around injured patients."

"I will contact the guys right away Alexis. Can I ask you who told you that my employees were engaging in illegal activities?"

"That is confidential information. I am concerned because the person who was sold the drug has a very bad heart and cannot take certain drugs."

"Oh I see."

"Like I stated, I usually do not get involved in this kind of matter directly. We are talking about a life or death infringement. My friend had to take this person to the hospital the other day. This person almost died. The information that was given to my friend was that this building is the building that supplied the drug. What do you do here?"

"We provide health education and classes to people who have gone through rehabilitation. The clients are in a three to five week class to complete their medical clearance from their doctors."

"Do you guys give prescriptions to the clients?'

"We provide feedback from the clients rehab to give prescriptions to the clients doctors based on the results."

"No one in this building provides any kind of drugs for the clients?"

"No." Marshawn sat back in his chair staring at the photo once more scratching his head.

Alexis and Amy looked at Marshawn for clues to whether or not he was telling the truth. The poker face was annoying Alexis. She could not tell if Marshawn was lying or if he truly did not know if something illegal could be going on in his building. Alexis pulled out her business card and asked Marshawn to call her once he spoke with his employees. Marshawn took the business card. His hands trembling when he realized Alexis was the mayor, he was familiar with the name. He did not recognize Alexis's face. Marshawn promised to get on his employees right away.

"Alexis, Marshawn could actually be telling the truth. He did not lie like he didn't know the guys in the photo."

"How could Marshawn lie about the photo? All I would have had to do was check with other clients and employees in the building to verify the employees. I can't imagine a business owner not knowing about his employees."

"Marshawn was not in the office when the receptionist contacted him. Most often in this kind of place the owner is not there everyday."

"I never thought about that. I saw the photo and wanted to have a close up of the building with the information you gave me."

"I know Alexis. We have to be a little patience with this and hear back from Marshawn about his employees. We don't know the specifics yet."

"I know Amy. I was upset with what happened to my friend love one. I didn't mean to overreact. I know my irritation is because of all the work that we have been dealing with that some times catches me off guard."

"Understandable. I do know how you feel. I have those days at times. I reacted like you when I received the information. I wanted to take the law into my own hands many times. I have actually taken the law into my own hands. So far the outcome has been in my favor. You know people will forget about all the hard work we do and focus on one screw up. It is the worse kind of feeling when the people you constantly help always focus on one or two mistakes made instead of numerous good deeds you have done in the community. The ones you help the most are the ones that will set you up to fail."

"That is so true. I did not want this drug overdose to get out to the press. I can relax knowing that if the story did get to the press that we already addressed the matter. That way my team is covered. We work too hard to have to deal with negative publicity."

"Alexis, we know that people are going to have side hustles. As a matter of fact there are plenty of unhealthy side hustles going on in the community. It is a bit different when it is in a place of business that doctors and patients are involved. Especially if someone almost dies or die from the drug that the doctors or employees give to the patients I could not let that happen."

"I have seen a few prostitutes when we are driving by to our fundraisers and meetings. The women are out in the open. They do not care who sees them."

"Our office has discussed this matter many times with law enforcement."

"Law enforcement arrests the prostitutes on the streets. The women are released and go to another location. The women are not going to stop until they are ready. Our office asks that police post where the prostitutes are for days. The women get wind of the police on the corners and stay out of view. Once the police leave, the women are back on the corners. The human trafficking has been a hazard of an unhealthy cycle for a long time."

"I know it is hard for women who cannot get jobs because they were discriminated on their past history and unlawful records. We have to expose and remove the public officials who gave the women unlawful records. The public officials that committed the illegal actions could be a part of the human trafficking ring. We need to break that all up."

"Our office has programs for the women. The women refuse to get into the programs. One of the programs for human trafficking a lady reached her last step, the lady was offered help with a job and a place to stay. She quit the program."

"Why go through all that commitment to quit. That doesn't make any sense."

"Some women love to have their own freedom and not punch into a clock."

"I would punch a clock any time than to be with strange men that might kill me. The streets are filled with predators that have to be monitored. Women cannot trust every stranger they meet."

"I wouldn't trust strangers without asking someone I know about them either. I wouldn't want to not know what may happen every time I got in the cars of the strangers dressed the way the women dressed."

"The women are taken a big chance on the streets. Some of the women are on heavy drugs and alcohol. That means they are not always aware of their surroundings."

"That is what is unpredictable about that kind of profession. Men are not going to care about a woman who sleeps with stranger's everyday. These are crazy men that won't take ownership in their part of sleeping with different women. The men are used to getting away with the woman being the blame. Some of the men are already abusive to their significant others and wives. I don't want to think about what one of the men will do to a prostitute when he gets upset."

Alexis and Amy pulled up to city hall unloading the vehicle with tall stacks of collaboration from city councils and other stake holders.

Charley heard back from a few citizens at the conferences about illegal misconduct being committed around the city. Charley helped his colleagues get the matter under control and spoke to some of the people that he knew to get a fast resolution to the problem.

Alexis and Amy filed into her office setting down all the paperwork and falling in chairs in the office. The phone was ringing nonstop. The computer and fax was buzzing. Alexis knew it was going to be a long day after what she discovered. Alexis had most of the problems under control and had to make a few phone calls. Meanwhile, Amy decided to call a duo phone conference with the staff. The office updated one another on who could do what and what was working and not working.

"We have to be on one accord with what we need to take care of in the office. Charley and Leilani speaking with the journalists to keep two-way communication open while Anthony has been teaching the politics classes to help our office. Anthony's schedule is swamped everyday because of the fast-paced classes and new groups coming in every four weeks to five weeks. We can arrange to have a few colleagues sit in on the classes. We do need some of the staff to listen to what Anthony is teaching to get the staff better prepared. We are going to have a tough few weeks ahead of us with all that we have learned."

"Alexis I can assign the staff you want to attend the class."

The two women worked from the office for the rest of the day after the wild rally calling it a quits around 10:00 p.m. Alexis's husband ranged on her line.

"I know it's late. You must be exhausted. I left spaghetti and garlic bread in the refrigerator. I have to run over to my mom's house. It's my dad. He's at the hospital. I will let you know if it is serious. Right now my dad is at the hospital for observations due to early signs of dementia. I will call you from work tomorrow. I'm staying with my mom to drop her off at the hospital on the way to work. My mom has a ride later on tomorrow to drop her and my dad at the house."

"Are you sure you do not want me to meet you over there?"

"No there is not anything you can do babe. Besides, your hands are already full. I would not want to keep you up all night. Go ahead and get you some rest."

"Goodnight." Alexis took her husband's advice longing to close her eyes. Amy informed her man that she was going to crash at Alexis's house.

The house smelled of Nathan's seasoned spaghetti and garlic bread when Alexis opened the door. Alexis went straight to the refrigerator grabbing a bowl to warm up spaghetti. Amy filled her bowl up heating the garlic bread.

"The rally was rowdy Alexis. I understand people have their opinions about birth control. I didn't agree with voters wanting to stick their noses in the households of married and single women bodies. I wasn't expecting the protestors to throw pregnancy tests and birth control pills. Sometimes the rallies are not healthy for kids to come out. I don't want to witness children being exposed to the hostility from opposition." Alexis and Amy went to bed.

CHAPTER 20

H ENRY HAD INTRODUCED A NEW product to his employees that was to hit the market when a call came in from the doctor. Three days had passed and Henry had his wife on lock down waiting for the results. Henry hurriedly ended the meeting and answered the call.

"Henry all of the tests came back negative. It could have been the stressful jobs that made Astelle fatigue. I know you told me to tell you the results first to not upset your wife. Astelle is going to be fine. She needs to get more rest and drink healthy liquids. Astelle can go back to work. Astelle has to minimize her stress. Other than that, Astelle is in perfect health."

Henry praised the Higher Power making the cross across his chest. Astelle was drinking cold lemon water. Henry handed Astelle the phone. Astelle spoke with the doctor.

"Well that's a relief. I need to get to work first thing in the morning. My staff is going crazy without me."

"Remember the doctor said to take it easy. You have to take care of yourself. Relax. I know you have other people that you can have handling more of your workload Astelle.

"I will arrange head of my staff to pick people to take over for a while. I have been overdoing it. We had the scare with our friends in the news.

That will place anyone in an uncomfortable position. I was worried about Ferria's daughter coming to stay with us. I wasn't prepared for what Ferria was accused of."

"Me either."

"Now that I have you off of my back, I have to make a few calls. It will not take long. We are opening up so many establishments that my hiring team needs my green light on the applicants."

"I cannot wait to get the programs opened and running. My staff and I can let the new set of eyes on the team decisions give us the direction we should go in. After all that we have been going through I see things getting better and better with the kind of team we have in place."

"I know we can keep up with all the companies. We have a lot of new people eager to help out."

Astelle made her calls to change some of the policies in the contract. She spoke with her associates about the in-depth summary completion. There were a few glitches that were making Astelle annoyed. Her last phone call had her fussing. Astelle found out that she would have to go all the way to another city to get one of her business dealings finalized. The bosses all wanted to meet. Astelle did not want to go yet knew she had to attend. Astelle didn't want to hear Henry lecturing her about taking it easy.

"Astelle, can you bring down my black folder when you come back downstairs? I left my treatise on the kitchen table when the doctor called."

Astelle couldn't avoid going out to make new changes to her business plans. Henry was working from home. There wouldn't be a way to leave without her husband finding out. Astelle figured she would give the short notice to him getting straight to the point.

"I don't want to argue about this trip. I know you are worried about me. I love you for wanting to take care of me. Tomorrow I will be catching a flight out to finalize an once in a lifetime deal that is going to make us a lot of money and help a lot of people. I can also give a huge sum of money to your upcoming fundraiser. I have a few other people that have already agreed to fund your future goals." Astelle kissed Henry on the forehead and handed him his folder.

"I like how you threw in my fundraiser to shut me up, Astelle that's not going to work. I have enough money. If you are going out of town, I am going out of town with you until I know for sure that you are okay. I don't want to hear anything else about it Astelle."

"Henry, you don't have to come with me. You have a lot of business prospects already set in motion."

"All of my business dealings are taken care of Astelle. Do not argue to talk me out of this. I'm packing after I get through with my paperwork in this container."

Henry carried the container to the table taking out his sorted analysis. Astelle shook her head smiling at her husband. She knew she was not going to get out of going out of town alone. Astelle thought it would actually be good to have her husband tag along so that they could take advantage of some of the festivities. She packed her clothes and shoes. Henry's suitcase next to hers Astelle placed Henry's clothes neatly in his suitcase.

The news was covering events that were coming to the city for people to get out and enjoy themselves. The carnivals, food tasting, wine tasting, rock climbing, soft ball, many concerts, and comedy shows being set up to welcome the community to months of fun. Numerous cities and states were offering the kind of fun people needed after the alleged COVID and other breakouts that had forced people to distance themselves for a while.

The major announcement for one of Astelle's business came after the commercial break. Two days of business training and hiring people who needed a job were the basics of Astelle's advertisement being endorsed on television. Astelle had already found a couple of guys that was going to fill some of the positions. She was grateful that her advertisements were being displayed in a variety of ways to get people to attend the business training to work. Astelle loved having new people join in from their community to work. A few other communities of workers kept the neighborhoods safe and stable by working. The families were able to participate in fundraisers and contribute to food drives and other needed programs due to the fair wages that made families feel comfortable spending money. The more people patronizing the businesses, the closer the community came together for a lot of the events to keep the community thriving.

"Astelle are your suitcases organized?" Henry's wife face fixed on the TV.

"Yes why?"

"Can you read over my speech? I know that every time I read my speeches a couple of times I continue to miss out on something."

"Sure darling." Henry handed Astelle his speech rearranging the items into the suitcase that Astelle packed to inspect what kind of clothes she packed for him. Henry removed four of the clothing and replaced the clothing with other clothes that he preferred. Henry satisfied with his selection closed the suitcases and set the suitcases to the side.

Henry was pleased to find Astelle on a roll with advertisements for her new business. People loved Astelle. She was gifted and fair with employees. Astelle always thought of ways to reward her employees and was very flexible with working hours for employees that had a family. Henry enjoyed that about Astelle. She operated her businesses with pazazz and a lot of experience. Henry picked up the documents on the table next to Astelle side of the bed. The outlines and blueprint of the new business projects and property was a gold mine. Astelle had really done her research on this new project. The revenue would be through the roof. He glanced over at his wife with her pencil in her hand she hated using pens when she corrected Henry speeches. She had a few circled marks.

"Henry you nailed the coffin with this verbal expression. You know practice makes perfect. I think you hit the key points perfectly. I would love to hear you say the speech out loud. That always set the right tone. It is easier to correct the speech when you say the words out loud."

Henry took the papers back from Astelle and read the entire speech.

His passion and enthusiastic tone gave the speech the liveliness the speech earned to reach a crowd of people who like to fund the kinds of events Henry brought to the table. It was not even any wonder why Henry always kept a full house of people at the events. His delivery was flawless. Astelle palms smacked together approvingly after Henry consummated his avowal giving him the encouragement he needed which is why he loved going over his speeches with his wife. She was always supportive and honest. Henry yearned for Astelle, she aimed at being a kind and giving person who enjoyed making other people happy. She had dedicated a lot of her life to other people and in return so many people had supported her dreams. Henry missed his wife when she was saving lives.

"Thanks babe. I know I can always count on you to give me your honest opinion."

"I think you are a natural Henry. You were born to do this job. The people love the way you are so attentive to their needs and their cause in the community. It is a blessing to find people that listen to total strangers and give them exactly what they ask for without blinking an eye. I knew you were the one for me the second I saw you."

Henry hugged Astelle the fainting earlier shuddered his axon. Astelle held on to her husband, Henry's coolness evaporating when the fatigue tormented his wife. The cell phone jotted the couple out of their trance.

"Hello." Astelle answered her cell phone.

"Astelle I fueled the private jet." Astelle's husband assistant arranged the trip with his private jet.

"Heather my husband is going to fly down with me."

"I know Henry is not letting you out of the woods that fast." Heather abreast on the facts of Astelle's medical alarm consoled her.

"You are right Heather. He is not."

"Take it easy Astelle. We were all in prayer for you when Henry called in."

"I told my husband not to make the fatigue a big deal. You know how Henry is about my health. I was worried about a friend from all that nonsense that was coming out in the news."

"I know Astelle. You could never be too careful. I'm glad that your husband is taking care of you. We cannot afford to lose someone as wonderful as you are with all the ideas and businesses savvy to help people who cannot afford expensive attorneys. There are going to be a lot of successful families once the families are hired to work for you. You are a resolute boss."

"I know I am right." Astelle chuckled.

"I will see you tomorrow Astelle."

"I will see you tomorrow Heather."

Astelle hung up the phone as Henry was leaving the room to get something out of the car. Henry was going back and forth over a lot of his schedule to prepare for the out of town business with Astelle. Astelle could hear him on his cell phone speaking with an associate about taking care of some matters for him until he was back from going out of town. Henry had to run down to his car to get his other briefcase to give his associate the contact information. Astelle felt badly that Henry had to work even more helping her because of her little health scare. Astelle knew that there was not anything that she could do to change Henry's mind. Astelle sat down on the bed watching the TV. She had changed the channel to an interesting movie and decided to relax before her business trip.

"Astelle I have your briefs and proposals completed. I took care of my last minute negotiations that came up. I am all yours tomorrow."

Astelle's husband wouldn't let Astelle do anything stressful. Henry encouraged Astelle to allow him to assist with her accumulating closing tender offers.

Marg and Matthew were getting their marriage back in order.

Astelle and Henry decided that that was a great idea working more together not to end up where their friend's marriage derailed. Astelle thought about inviting Marg and Matthew to go out of town with them.

"Henry, how would you feel if I invited Marg and Matthew to go out of town with us? It's because of those two big fights with Marg and Matthew at one of your fundraisers that we started spending more time together to help the couple stay married."

"That is up to you. I would not mind hanging out with Matthew. You know that's my boy. It would actually be fun now that those two are getting along so well."

Astelle was dialing Marg number listening to Henry. She wanted to give the couple enough time to decide. It was earlier in the day and if Marg and Matthew decided to go it would be plenty of time to arrange for the trip. At least that is what Astelle hoped.

"Marg, are you and Matthew free tomorrow to take an out of town trip with Henry and I. I'm going out of town to sign some contracts and meet with some of my business partners on a project we have gotten involved in."

"Hey Astelle. Let me ask Matthew, hang on one second." Marg cheery mouthpiece sent Astelle an inspiriting mindset.

Marg returned back on the line dodging a bullet of entertaining Matthew's cousin acquaintances. Marg and Matthew with little fun in between commercial practice, trade practice, and corporate culture craved some down time. Marg was in need of human contact that didn't require business suits and skirts.

"We will meet you guys at the airport."

"I cannot wait to see you and Matthew. We all have been self-absorbed in business acquisitions gaining control over assess and operations. We haven't had any time to do anything else. I don't see how all of the businesses that we have had to merge with dishonest business partners were able to stay afloat. The value of the businesses and their financial advisers was off course. Henry and I have invested a lot of money into the merges. We only see one another at the fundraisers unless we meet up for dinner at our houses. I don't want us to get so busy that we stop seeing one another."

"I'm glad you called me Astelle. I was about to call you to see when you and Henry was available. Henry told Matthew about him taking you to the doctor. I am so glad it wasn't anything serious."

"Henry cannot keep his mouth closed about my fatigue. He is going with me out of town to make sure that that was all it was. I'm not going to stay in the hotel after the contracts are signed. I'm going out and my husband better not try to stop me."

Marg sensed Astelle was agitated when her husband treated her like a baby. Marq was certain that the fatigue was exactly why Henry was going out of town with Astelle. Henry was ultra careful of Astelle's well being. Marg thought the concern was very sweet. Astelle was a great wife and overworked business woman.

"I already know that's why Henry was unshakeable about going out of town with you."

"Well, the more the merrier. Since we always have fun together we can make this a fun trip and get out to party once I am done. My meeting is in the afternoon. We have the rest of the day after that."

"I'm about to pack a few things. I will see you guys tomorrow Astelle."

CHAPTER 21

AMY INSTITUTED HER YOGA SERENELY not to wake up Alexis. Amy wanted to know how Nathan's father was doing but decided not to pry last night. Amy knew that Alexis was tired so she mulled over the dialogue for Alexis building consensus to gain support for policy initiatives last night hoping Alexis rested. Amy did multiple stretches and bends and got on her knees to do a few more stretching moves when Alexis collate day to day operations for her staff to read coming in the room to give Amy the first carbon copy.

"I didn't know you were up. Did I wake you?" Amy noticed Alexis appeared sapped.

"I had a rough time trying to fall asleep last night. My husband and his father being taken to the hospital hunted me all night. I should have gone over to Nathan's parent's house any way. I knew that I wasn't going to be able to sleep."

"Alexis Nathan is not going to not inform you if his father is worse. Nathan knows how much you care about his parents. You don't want to think about the worse when it could be something minor."

"Nathan's father has been going through medical scares. His mother is in perfect health to be older. She does yoga like you very early in the morning."

"What! Nathan's mother does yoga?"

"I'm going to have to go get her. We are going to have to do yoga together."

"Why did you not invite me to get my yoga on this morning?"

"Alexis please. You hate yoga. You are an old school jogger."

"I will do any exercises that I can to stay in shape. You know we are always getting invited to eat somewhere. The stress of gaining too much weight has always been a concern for me. I want to live long."

"That is why I exercise. We are always eating on something. I can't get too heavy. I got a new man." Amy blushed.

"How is Marty and you getting along?" Alexis asked.

"You know Marty. He did not want me to stay out all night. He was hoping that I came home last night. I told him that I heard you on the phone with Nathan about his father. Marty is sympathetic to family matters. He told me to take all the time I needed to be there for you guys."

"That sounds like Marty. He has always been a solace friend to me. I could not picture Marty with another woman the way you two clicked. You stole his heart. You are so good to Marty. He will be thanking me for the rest of his life."

"I'm the lucky one Alexis. I'm going to be thanking you for the rest of my life. I did not know Marty was that good at what he does." Amy seductive tone describing Marty made Alexis reach for a pillow to throw at Amy.

"Too much information! Should I call my in-laws or wait for my husband to call me? I am so worried. I don't know what to think about my father-in-law in the hospital."

"It is totally up to you. I'm sure your husband would understand if you checked in on them. It is the right thing to do."

Alexis dialed her husband's cell number anxious to hear how things were going. Her husband answered after the first ring.

"Hey honey. You didn't have to get up early to call me. You know I wouldn't forget to let you know if something happened."

"I couldn't sleep too worried about you and your parents. Is everything okay?"

"My father will be getting released later on today. I'm staying over here to make sure my mom doesn't call someone else to take her to the hospital to pick up my dad."

"I could have taken care of that for you."

'I know. I didn't want to bother you. Besides I needed to see my parents. It has been a while with all the work I have to do."

"I'm glad that everything is fine. Tell your parents I said hello. If you want we can stop by their house this weekend. I could whip up a great dinner for you all."

"I will really appreciate it if you can do that for my parent's sweetheart. I would love to spend more time with them. My mom is stretching around here limber than a tree leaves. She was up before me doing her yoga. I had to stagger into the kitchen half asleep because I heard some noise. I saw her making breakfast. She was rolling up her yoga mat at 5:30 a.m."

Alexis thought about her conversation with Amy. Alexis had not forgotten how in shape her mother-in-law was and how she has stayed in shape. Nathan's mom was aging at a slow rate. Her face was the same way the day Alexis met her. Alexis loved Nathan's mom. The woman was full of life. Alexis loved spending time with her mother-in-law. Most times her in-laws were out of town visiting someone else or some place romantic. Alexis and Nathan had friends and family that wanted to see his parents. Alexis's in-laws hardly stayed at home. Nathan couldn't keep up with his parents. Nathan's parents traveled too much.

"I'm going to head on to the hospital and talk to the doctor. My dad's doctor is finishing up with the tests he has been running on my father to make sure that my father is okay. My mom is going to be thrilled to see you honey. Did you happen to see my business proposition on the kitchen table? Fred is late for a meeting and wanted to grab the papers for us. You know we are dibbing and dabbing in a few side moneymakers. Will you make sure he gets the papers for me?"

"I put your papers on your desk in your office. I can get them for Fred. Is he on his way now?"

"He should be there already. He told me he was running late." Alexis's doorbell ranged. Alexis let Nathan know Fred was there ending the call to grab the papers.

Alexis opened the door to Fred handing him the papers. Fred rushed Alexis a hug jogging back to his car after thanking her.

"I was about to drive you over there myself." Amy could feel the mental strain from Alexis's voice.

"It is a burden lifted off of the shoulders when someone that you love is alright. I was so worried that today was going to bring bad news to our family. Nathan's father was under observations for early dementia and to make sure his medication was working. He is reacting to the medication positively this morning. The tests are to keep up with my father-in-law condition so that his condition does not get worse. Other than that my in-laws stay peripatetic."

"I know Nathan is relieved. Our parents aging can take a lot out of us. The doctor visits are the hardest. When we do not know what to expect and have to wait on the test results we can be a nervous wreck. I would love to come with you guys this weekend with Marty to meet Nathan's parents. Nathan's parents sound down to earth."

"You and Marty are always welcome. My husband's parents love company. They will be happy to see some friendly faces."

"Then it is settled. I will cook up my famous vegetables sautéed with steamed rice. I know you are going to whip up your hearty meals. It will be a splendid weekend with the ones Marty and I love the most." Amy was looking forward to the outing.

"Amy, we haven't eaten yet."

Amy pointed to the tea and fruit Alexis brought her. Amy thought that was breakfast. Amy should have known better the way Alexis loved to cook.

"Child please. I whipped up french toast, with strawberries, whip cream, eggs, and sausage in the kitchen."

"When did you manage to do all of this? I thought I smelled cinnamon."

"Usually when I can't sleep it is because I have exercised or rested earlier. This time I could not sleep thinking about my husband."

Amy had freshly awoke micromanaging her time making sure their business plans key points were mission statements, online donation platforms, and donation tiers. Amy had the financial projections, legal compliance, and volunteer management at the top of the page. The events and galas were clearly printed. Amy didn't forget to outline the grant writing material and the transparency accountability for all participants. Amy rounded up the dishes on her guest room table and was about to mop the floor.

"I got the dishes Alexis. You go ahead and get your clothes together for work. I will iron my pants after the dishes are washed and dried. You know I'm about to make another plate."

Alexis liked when Amy was over her house. Amy was a big helper. Alexis sat her glass in the sink. Alexis shifted her curtains to peek out of her window because she heard loud voices and saw her neighbors in a heated feud outside her bedroom window. All of Alexis's neighbors were coming outside or peering out of their windows. A loud bang had Alexis and other neighbors looking in the direction of a thrown coffee mug. The neighbors in question husband dodged the injury of the coffee mug hitting him in the head. The shattered heavy mug knocked out the husband's car window. Alexis knew the fight was going to get down and dirty. Alexis heard police's sirens. Police sirens were not uncommon in a neighborhood Alexis lived in when a fallen out manifest itself. Alexis knew someone had called the police. The sirens did not stop the neighbor's wife from high jumping at her husband with impact causing both of them to fall onto the grass. The neighbor rolled over on top of her husband trying to grab his collar. The husband desperately tried pushing the wife away. The police pulled up and removed the neighbor's wife off of him. The tantrum of children life coming out of the wife was hideous. Alexis could only imagine what the wife was going to pull from her sleeves next. By this time Amy had ran up the stairs to Alexis's room to the action. A dozen or more people outside of their homes encouraged the wife to fight the husband for cheating on her.

"You guys need to go back into your homes." One of the police officer instructed the nosy neighbors. A second load of police safeguarded the neighbor's husband to one of the patrol's car.

"Sir, can you tell me what is going on here?" The police questioned the husband.

"My wife is going crazy! She was splenetic with me because I was about to give someone a ride to work. I told her that I have my own car. She has her own car. I can take anyone I want to work if I want to."

The wife could be heard by the other patrol car caterwauling at her husband. Her nails sharp and positioned to lash out. She was very hot-tempered about the way her husband was explaining the story.

"He doesn't get to do any of that. That is why he got what he deserved. I do not know why he thinks that he is going to be married to me and do what he wants." The wife was screaming. The police put his handcuffs back onto his side and listened to the distraught husband.

"My wife takes a lot of people in this neighborhood to run errands. No one asks me how I feel. My wife does whatever she wants in her car."

"Errands are not the same as taking women you are eyeing places!" The wife spat ready to hit her husband.

The officer placed his hand in front of the wife keeping the two apart.

"I help our neighbors that are older with their errands. They don't drive any more. My husband is trying to compare what I do to him riding around with specific women. Your old tired behind need to go in the house and clean up behind yourself!"

"I do not drive specific people. I help most of the neighbors that I know. They are not all women. I do have male friends that get in my car." The husband fired back.

"When did you start doing this neighboring brotherly love? Huh? When did you decide to drive other women around and not one specific woman because when I asked you to take the Taylor's to their doctor appointment, you said that is not what you do! You took the single woman to her job more than a few times. You thought I didn't know. You know I know everything. I don't say anything to see how long you are going to act up. Officer this man thinks that I am some kind of fool. He is going to stop disrespecting me!" The police listened as their heads turned back and forth between the couple.

"I did not say that Birdie. You are making up your own account. I didn't feel like waiting in any doctor's office. I was only dropping off the neighbor a few miles. If you want to wait for people go ahead. I do not have to do what you do."

"Ma'am what do you want us to do? Is either of you hurt? You two cannot be fighting in the public and causing all this commotion. We do not want to have to take either of you to jail." One of the police officers stepped in.

"If anyone is going to jail it's going to be my wife. She is the nutty one grabbing me by my collar in front of my neighbors." The husband yelled so his wife could hear him. The other police officer didn't know what to say.

"You should not have walked away from me when I told you that you were not dropping that woman off any where." The wife held her husband's car keys.

"You need to give me my keys Birdie."

"I am not giving you anything until you get in the house!" The police watched on not knowing how to diffuse the argument since the married couple was older and the wife had a good point as far as one of the officers could tell.

The husband decided to go back into the house with his wife trailing behind him with his car keys. The police stayed posted to their front door closed. The officers went by their patrol vehicles to talk. After ten or so minutes the police left. The two neighbors did not come back out.

"Did you see that Alexis?"

"Yes. I have never seen anything like that in this neighborhood in my life."

"You are never here Alexis. The neighbors probably fight all the time."

"She told him didn't she?"

"I think the only reason why he listened is because he didn't want to go to jail. I bet they are going to be at it again real soon the way the husband kept side eyeing her."

"Thank God I don't be home during the day that often."

Alexis and Amy arrived to work talking a mile a minute about the drama that they had witnessed.

"Your neighborhood is interesting! I thought it was boring and the people behaved all uppity. You have some drama Kings and Queens as neighbors. I'm going to have to visit on the weekend more often." Amy japed with Alexis.

"I will take boring any day. I definitely don't want to find out the neighbors have a license to carry guns. The way she carried on with her man."

"She was upset. I thought she was going to do some major damage to her husband. She broke his car window out. They are going to have to replace that car window with their own money."

"It was quiet when we left. The wife probably whopped his behind and knocked him out!" Alexis swung left to right.

"As loud as the wife was we would be able to hear if the fight continued in the house. I think the poor man was too tired to fight with her and decided to go in the house and not drive anywhere knowing how the wife was going to set it off if he tried."

"Alexis he couldn't go anywhere anyway. She took the keys." Amy swung her keys.

"Amy you are a mess. We need to stop talking about older people gripes that turn violent. It was becoming serious and concerning. Someone could have ended up injured."

"I put my money on the wife." Amy tried to hide her laugh.

"You are wrong Amy. Let's get back to work. You have had enough caffeine this morning." Alexis pushed Amy into the office hanging up her coat.

Amy goofed off a little longer before settling down to get to her work. The office was Amy's safety net when she wanted to escape the craziness of the World. Amy was feeling good. Amy didn't care about the backlash she was going to receive about the decision to the final spending order for her bestie Alexis. Amy was there to assist her friend as the mayor and make the best decisions for the city's proposed budgets.

"Alexis you have two messages from Marshawn Dallas about the guys in that photo."

Alexis listened to the messages. She was taken aback by how Marshawn voice sounded strange. It was almost as if he was warning Alexis.

"I don't like the way Marshawn sounds. This kind of message is from a man that was threatened. He sounds like he is afraid to tell you to come by."

"I will make sure we send the authorities over there Amy. I don't think that it is safe to stay involved in this matter, besides this is law enforcement area of expertise."

"Yeah, but we are already involved. Marshawn knows who we are. What should we do about this?"

"I don't think that we are in any danger, do you?"

"I don't know Alexis. I can't state with certainty what the guys in that photo are capable of if they find out we want to know if they are doing wrong. We should be aware and alert now that we have listened to this message. We are going to have to have security come with us to the events until everything cools down."

"He sounds that worried to you Amy?"

"You heard the message. What do you think?"

"Marshawn doesn't sound right. There is definitely something wrong. Maybe he didn't know what the guys were doing in the building. Or maybe he did and he is being threatened to handle the situation. Meaning what? To handle us?"

"We shouldn't speculate. We don't know Marshawn or the guys in that photo mentality. We can have the authorities check it out to ascertain what way we should proceed going forward."

Amy recourse back to her guidelines in heavy thought. It wasn't healthy to assume the worse. Amy was rattled by the message and wanted to make sure that they were safe. Amy didn't know whether to call Marshawn or leave him an email. Amy knew the only way to really get a feel for the truth was to look Marshawn straight in the eyes. Amy knew Alexis was going to be extremely upset if she went to meet Marshawn by herself. Yet, Amy was tempted to do just that.

"Alexis, do you have anything to do outside of the office?"

"Not really, why what's up?"

"I'm going to go pick up a few folders that I need for my workload. Do you need me to bring you anything while I am out?"

"No, I'm good on everything for now Amy. I'm caught up on the policies recommendations."

"If you need me text me or call me. I won't be that long." Amy grabbed her coat and purse leaving her desk to accost Marshawn.

Amy stopped off to grab a latte hoping Marshawn was in his office.

The receptionist saw Amy coming near her desk and the receptionist's eyes bulged informing Amy that Marshawn was not in the office.

"I'm going to need you to call Marshawn and tell him that I am here. I received his messages."

The receptionist picked up the front desk phone. The receptionist hung up after a few minutes. Amy was told by the receptionist that Marshawn was on his way. The woman got up from her chair to lead Amy to a room for meetings and conferences. The receptionist closed the door behind her.

Two tall well built guys entered the room matching the guys on the photo. One of the guys gave Amy the stank face conveying disapproval. The other guy locked the door behind him glowering at Amy in a mean way. Amy was immediately uncomfortable and got up to leave.

'Sit down. You are not going anywhere. Where is the other lady that was with you the other day?"

Amy reproached back at the two men not answering right away.

"Where is Marshawn?"

CHAPTER 22

Henry and Astelle arrived at their private jet to see Marg and Matthew cocooned in one another. Astelle looked at her friend Marq and her husband and knew that the trip was going to be awesome. Astelle got a charge out of being with friends that knew how to have a good time. Henry sucka punched Matthew mirthfully lifting Marg off her feet in a bear hug. Henry could tell his friends were in love.

'You guys are a perfect pair. I see you both prepared for take off. Matthew you have to dress like we going on a photo shoot."

"Henry you know how Matthew is when he is going out. He is always trying to catch people's eyes then claim he doesn't know why women are staring at him. You and Astelle are quite the diversion. Both of you will be distracting folks in those fancy originals." Marg complimented.

"Compliments would get you everywhere." Henry escorted Matthew and Marg to the entrance to board the jet.

"Astelle, I have something for you." Henry gave Astelle a twinkling box. Henry asked that his wife open the gift after the meeting. Astelle put the box in her purse.

"The private jet Henry." Matthew was always inspired by Henry's wealth.

"Matthew, stop all that. You been on the private jet numerous of times." Marq pushed Matthew toward the entrance.

"I'm kidding with Henry. I always tease him about being rich."

"Astelle, Matthew love to try to get a rise out of me. We've been going at it since our college days you know that."

"Most of the time I succeed." Matthew laid it on thick.

The couples boarded the jet. They avoided the alcohol drinking juice and water. Astelle wanted to wait until after the contracts were signed to get turned up.

The jet took off smoothly. Astelle closed her eyes to catch a nap while Matthew and Henry talked away about everything and anything. Marg flipped through a magazine writing down information to order some of the products at a later time.

"That was a nice fly." Matthew gathered his handover bag exiting the jet with Henry, Astelle, and Marg in front of him.

"It was quick. I thought the flight would be longer." Marg inquired.

"Jets are quick you guys know that." Astelle answered.

The morning air was crisp. The sky rainbow sunset from the peeking sun in the far distance was romantic.

"Marg I will meet you back down here in thirty. I want to freshen up and see how the room looks." Astelle and Henry took the elevator to their room.

The hotel was magnificent with large bold colors that grabbed the guest's attention. The hotel was a deep maze of eccentric colors. Astelle loved the way the colors coordinated with the carpet and the furniture. Everything was dust free shining from the check in desk to the open elevators. Astelle's room key was waiting for her. The bright lights and decorated chandeliers dangling so high in the ceilings gave off a ballroom flavor.

"No wonder my associates wanted me to come out here. It's mega. I had no idea it was this ritzy. I'm glad I came out."

"I'm glad that you came out. Maybe this is what you needed Astelle, a different scenery to uplift you out of all that stress. I know Ferria and Mario's case took a huge toll on you."

"I'm feeling more of myself Henry. I'm going to have a whale of a time going around this town finding things to do."

"I bet you are Astelle. You have always loved to shop, party, and eat. There isn't anything wrong with that the way you are always in motion with files from every office you possess."

"Henry your supporting me goes without saying. I will get some shopping in for sure. I haven't shopped at regular stores in a long time since the designers and online shopping. People have gotten adjusted to the new way."

"People are trying to dress differently from everyone else. At the malls everyone buys the hottest outfits and we have twins everywhere." Henry self-styled.

"That is why I prefer online shopping and designers to fit me for my clothes. I cannot look like one of the ones out here doing the most. You know there are cameras everywhere."

"Women are a bit different from men. I can care less. I have designer suits. I'm not too good for the mall no matter how many designer suits I have in my closet."

"I know Henry. You don't have to remind me." Astelle held her hands up.

Henry received the room key and headed for the elevators with Astelle

The elevators rode without any feeling of being in an elevator. The elevator stopped soundlessly reaching their hotel room. Henry read his wife knowing that she was thinking what he was thinking about the elevators.

"You don't have to say anything." Henry shhhh his wife. They stepped out of the elevator.

Henry approached the room door the room was huge with a gorgeous dining area and stove. Astelle had not been in a hotel out of town in a while. Henry and Astelle was always staying at a friend's house or one of their own places that they bought when they went out of town. Astelle loved the hotel. It brought back so many good memories of when Astelle and Henry was first dating.

"Baby do you remember how we would get a room and hide for a day or two days? Our friends would be blowing us up wondering where we were."

"I do remember. Those were the good times. We would stay inside for two days ordering up room service and being pampered like spoiled kids."

"I didn't ever want to cook after those experiences. We started frequenting all of the restaurants to see who had the best food. It was great."

"It was great. I enjoy a home cooked meal. I actually love eating and cooking."

"There isn't anything like a nice place to live with good food. We have come a long way haven't we?"

"Yes we have. We have worked through tough times. We have succeeded. It took a lot of time and dedication to get to where we are."

'I'm glad we kept at it fighting against all barriers. We had envious people that kept trying to discourage us. It's a good thing that we did not listen to the haters or I do not know where we would be."

"I knew we could make it with one another. We both stayed focused and dedicated to what was most important."

"We were most important. Our faith has paid off. I'm opening one of the biggest and demanding sites that will bring in revenue to counter balance the programs threatening to be closed. We don't even need donors. We can help the people in our numerous communities on our own if we wanted to do so."

"Yeah but you know the donors are not going to accept that. The donors are just as important and want to stay involved and help out too. We are very lucky to have such a great team that supports other people who help themselves."

"No one left behind after all the money we have seen funded elsewhere. I am so glad we decided to pick up the slack and get more involved. It was a lot of upsetting reality to see how badly so many people were being mistreated with disinformation."

"The thought of deceptive people making so much money off of people that truly needed that money is horrific. The ones who committed the crimes do not have any shame. The embezzlers are pretending they were helping when the embezzlers were doing more wrong than helping."

"The ones involved stole money to use the money in the most selfish ways and came up with every excuse to try to make the people that was suppose to receive the money appear like they did not deserve the money. If the ones wronged would have received the money, they would be in a better position to do more for their families and the community."

"I cannot respect the ones who are causing all the problems going around making light of what they have done. There isn't anything that should be taken lightly for a heavy load of public felonies that destroyed so many families."

"I'm glad that a lot of the people were arrested. I hope the ones who stole all that money has to pay back all that money and never get to get in a position that they collect any money that is supposed to go to other people."

"What about all the new Organizations being allowed to make money off the people exploiting innocent families? The founders are making up all kinds of receipts to collect money. The Organizations are continuing to discriminate, divide, and blame other Organizations for what the founders guilty are doing themselves."

"It takes a real special team and honest people to do this kind of work. That is why I decided to get involved. We have too many materialistic jerks that are too full of themselves."

"Let's get downstairs. Matthew and Marg are probably waiting for us."

Matthew and Marg were in the lobby. Matthew flagged down Henry and Astelle exiting the elevator. The two couples made their way through the exit of the hotel with a car waiting.

"I'm going to have to come back out here to see that new plaza that is being built. The advertisements are saying how gorgeous the new boutiques are and how much the community is looking forward to the opening for people to have places to go."

"There isn't anything better than new places that open up in your community and people get to visit for the first time. It's the most rewarding feeling. I love the smell of the new buildings, the touch, and all the new designs. I enjoy the people that visit from all over the place. The excitement of spending money to have the first new creations that come out is inexpressible. I have always loved shopping when I was younger with my parents." Marg smiled.

"Women love to shop and show off their new gear. I don't think that I will ever not feel that way. I told Henry that I wanted to shop at some point after business is taken care of."

"Definitely, Astelle. Shopping is one of my favorite pastimes. The men will find something to do while we shop around, I'm sure."

"We are going to shop with you guys." Henry buzzed in squeezing Astelle's hand.

"Marg knows I'm about to pick up a few outfits since we are staying a few more days. I'm not going to hang out in suits. I want some loose fitting comfortable clothing to wear. I brought clothes for the meeting and one night out." Matthew shopped more than the women.

"Henry my husband shops online more than I do. I find new packages at my door every couple of weeks. Matthew needs to stop all that shopping."

"I was thinking about buying some property in one of the cities Henry. I love to be able to go other places and get away from my main resident sometimes. I know so many people where I have lived for 25 years. I feel all brand new when I visit other cities and see how the people behave when they see new faces." Matthew smiled.

Matthew assessed financial readiness, pre-approved clients, and considered desirable locations at one of his business. Marq would assist with making a competitive offer, a thorough home inspection, and potential closing terms. Marq was an expert at finding reasonable locations that fit the client's budgets.

"I bet you do love new faces." Marg rolled her eyes.

"Come on baby. It is not even like that. You know I have been on my best behavior. You have not had any problems out of me in a very long time."

"That is true." Marg gave Matthew a kiss.

"Astelle how do you feel about this new big project you are getting into? You know that this is going to take up a lot of your time." Marg asked.

"Actually Marg I have a hiring team. The load will be light. We have already decided who was going to handle what part of the project. I believe I will be able to manage. You are welcome to bring your expertise to the table any time you like. You have always been welcome Marg. I love working with you and Matthew."

"Thanks Astelle. Matthew and I would love helping out from time to time. I hope you would do the same for us. I know you heard about what is going on with me."

"Marg, we are going to run into a few bumps along the way. You are creative and an exceptional team player. I'm glad we met." Astelle enjoyed Marg's company.

The men wanted to golf and watch some sports. Henry was telling Matthew about a new golf course not far from where he lived. Matthew wanted to check out the golf course to use his recently purchased golf clubs he received from Marg.

Astelle workflow improvements, budgeting improvements, and resource allocations had Astelle top ranked in the business. Astelle was awarded on her market analysis and trends. Astelle's competitive landscapes and new products developments kept her on top of the business game. The new partners were signing contracts to move forward with sales strategies, long-term business goals, and team building activities.

Marq wanted to help Astelle with performance feedback, training and development opportunities, and brain storming new ideas.

Henry and Matthew insisted that Astelle make sure the contracts supported her ideas before she signed.

Astelle and Henry spoke about Astelle's meeting to expand her platform and build in varies locations.

"I think we should all go to my meeting Marg. I will handle my paperwork and get with my team to work out a few details. We can hang out wherever afterwards. If you guys are up for it we can hang out an extra day and find something to do tomorrow. I'm not in any rush."

"I'm not in a rush either. I'm looking forward to having some jollification. Where are we going out tonight?"

"I heard that they have a lovely grown up club that will do justice to our love handles. The dance floor is huge to work off some of our group eating." Matthew patted his arms and mid section.

"Where did you hear this? Marg interrogated Matthew.

"Friends."

"What friends Matthew?"

"My single buddies Marg. You know the ones you don't let me hang out with any more." Matthew gave Marg a sad look.

"Don't try to look pitiful Matthew. You are not a youngsta any more running around all hours of the night with your friends."

"I'm not an old man either Marg. I like to enjoy myself with the homeboys. I know how to behave when I'm not with you."

"Sounds good, if only I could believe that." Marg didn't want to remember the old Matthew. He was a big headache that used to work her nerves every other week. Marg never thought they would get this far in their marriage without killing one another.

"We can repose in the area of the meeting and take us a walk before the meeting. The area has a beautiful walk trail with big trees."

CHAPTER 23

"THE LAST PERSON YOU SHOULD be worried about is Marshawn. You should be worried about yourself. Where do you and your friend get off coming up in here asking questions?" One of the guys from the photo defied Amy.

Amy looked at the guy with a similar dislike on her face. Amy was flustered that the guys had her held up in a room to intimidate her.

"Would you prefer that I sent the police the photos instead?" Amy asked with major attitude.

"We prefer you stay out of our business if you know what is best for you." The second guy squared up ready to take a jab at Amy.

"You do not have that kind of business here. I'm not going to let you get in my face and stay quiet when it is my business. I work for the people of this community. Any time someone's life is placed in peril from drugs that were reported to come out of this building it is my business." Amy's irritation was transparent.

The guys walked over to huddle and talk away from Amy. Amy looked on trying to hear what the guys were saying but she could barely make out the words. Amy was frustrated and upset that she did not listened to

196

Alexis. Alexis will be worried soon if Amy did not call her to let her know where she was.

"Here is how this is going to go." One of the guys fed up with Amy hissed through clenched teeth. He was ready to do something bad to Amy.

"How what is going to go?" Amy defiantly ready to pounce on the guy matching his animosity.

"You are going to call your friend and tell her to meet you here. You do not tell her that we are here. You tell her Marshawn is here and wants to see her."

"I will not lie to my friend. I will not call her and tell her no such thing." Amy retorted back.

"If you don't cooperate my friend here is going to work you over pretty rough lady. We're not kidding with you."

"Go right ahead. That threat is going to land you behind bars."

"We are not going to jail. No one even knows you are here besides the receptionist that we pay to keep her mouth shut."

"People will start to look for me. Very important people and you will be caught eventually. My friend is well aware of what is going on here. She knows this was the last place that we were inquiring about. I'm certain that she would put two and two together."

"I'm not going to tell you again. Call your friend and ask her to come down here or suffer the consequences."

"I'm only going to tell you one more time. That is not going to happen." Amy pronounced each word slowly.

The guy with the blue coat rushed toward Amy with the second guy in green pulling him back.

"Wait a minute. We can't do this in here. We have clients out there. The clients will hear us and one of the clients may call the police."

"She's not about to leave this building."

"I didn't say that she was going anywhere. We're going to have to handle this in another way."

The thugs manhandled Amy. Amy socked the guy in the blue coat in the jaw. The guy in the green coat caught Amy fist when she swung on him and placed both her hands behind her back while the guy in the blue coat held Amy's legs. Amy could not move. Amy was in a rage. Amy hands were tied up and her legs were tied from the guy in the blue coat. Amy had her cell phone tucked and needed to find a way to get to her phone to call the police. Amy tried squirming out of the tied knots. Amy huffed and puffed feeling nauseous and had to calm herself down.

"What are we going to do about this problem?" The guy in the blue coat panting questioned his friend once they locked Amy in the room alone.

"I'm not sure yet."

"We are already caught up or did you not hear what she said. She is threatening to call the police."

"I told you not to react. You made her feel like she had no choice, which means that we have no choice. We have to get rid of her."

"Let's do this. I have people waiting on me."

"We're not going to get her out of here right now."

"We are going to have to wait until we close for the day. Do you not see all the people in there? This could cost us a lot dude if any of those people see us carrying out a woman tied up."

"You handle her. I don't have time for this. I have a shipment in a few minutes. I don't want to be late. I have a lot of packages coming in. This was not in my plans."

"This was not in any of our plans. Marshawn does not even know what we are doing. I managed to convince him that the ladies were lying about what they heard. If he finds out the truth, that will be another person that we will have to get rid of. If people start disappearing we are definitely going to get caught."

"I'm not worried about Marshawn. Marshawn doesn't know anything. I'm going to keep it that way. I'm more concerned with the two ladies. We have to find out who is the connection. The mayor's side kick has someone that has told her that there were drugs given to someone from here. We have to find out who that person is before we get rid of her."

"You go ahead with what you need to do. I will meet you back here close to the end of business. We can handle her then."

The two guys unsure how to handle Amy worried if someone was going to come to the work site on her behalf hurriedly left to meet up with their cohorts at different places.

Alexis's big black and beige clock hanging on the wall reminded her that it had been two hours since she heard from Amy. It was not routine that Amy not check in if she was going to be out of the office for a couple of hours. Alexis checked her cell phone to see if she had missed any calls. There was not any missed call. Alexis dialed Amy's number. The phone rang three times before going to voice mail. Alexis left Amy a voicemail to call her back when Amy received the message.

Amy twisted and turned her wrists to unloose the ropes on her hands to answer her phone. She knew it was Alexis. Amy needed to let Alexis know where she was and to call the police. Amy scoped out the room for a way to get the ropes off of her hands. Amy could not find anything and started twisting and turning her hands and feet again. The ropes moved with every attempt and Amy felt the knots loosening the more she twisted and turned her hands inwards and outwards. Amy could hear voices outside the door. The faded voices sounding farther and farther away, it was clear that the guys from the photos had left Amy in the room. Amy was wondering what were the guys going to do with her. She knew it was not going to be good if she did not get untied.

"I can have you come to this room and wait for Mark." Amy could hear the receptionist talking to someone by the door.

Amy tried standing up but the ropes were too tight on her legs. Amy felled to the floor rolling to the door and kicking the door with her tied feet in an effort to get the receptionist to open the door. The receptionist could be heard closing the door and walking past the door Amy was kicking. The receptionist kept walking as if she did not hear anything. Amy knew it was going to be a struggle to get out of the building unharmed because the receptionist was in with the guys in the photos. Amy kicked toward the door one more time as hard as she could with her feet. A door opened and Amy could hear the voice of the woman that had been talking to the receptionist.

"Is anyone there?" The voice called out.

Amy kicked the door again with so much force that the woman came to the door. The woman heard a boom sound and went over to the door that Amy was kicking and unlocked the lock and turned the door handle. The woman looked inside the door and saw Amy lying on the floor tied up and gasped.

"Oh My God! What happened to you?" The woman bent down untying Amy and helped Amy up to her feet. Amy placed her hands on the woman's lips and told the woman to stay silent. Amy explained that she was being held against her will from guys that worked in the building. The woman's eyes turned saucer big. Amy instructed the woman to go back to the other room and close the door. Amy locked the door she was locked in and tiptoed out of the back door. Amy took off running like a track star to her car. Amy turned the ignition switch on and drove out the parking lot tires squeaking loudly as the tires smoked from Amy excelerating. Amy hands shook holding the steering wheel and her legs were wobbly. Amy reached City Hall and rapidly leaped out of the car in a haste to Alexis's office.

"Alexis I was kidnapped!"

Alexis slammed down her computer and rushed over to where Amy was standing.

"The guys from the photos came to Marshawn's building and took me in a room and tied my hands and feet up."

"WHAT!" Alexis yelled.

"I wanted to speak with Marshawn to determine by his facial expression if I could tell if he was lying about knowing what the guys in the photo had done to your friend's friend. It is clear that Marshawn was not involved. The receptionist helped the guys keep me in the room with the door locked. A patient heard me on the floor kicking the door and let me out. I need to call the police." Amy explained in a rushed voice taking out her cell phone. Amy called the police and gave the police the description and the location to where she was held against her will.

"Amy let me speak with dispatch."

Alexis reached for the phone to cancel the call.

"I am going to call the chief of police directly. If the guys are not there the receptionist will give the guys a heads up that the police was there looking for them. We may never be able to catch them. The guys could flee."

"Why did I not think of that?"

"Everything is happening so fast Amy. I know you want these guys arrested. We have to sneak up on them. We cannot let anyone know that we called the police. The guys are going to come looking for you when they realize that you are not in that room. Call Marty and give him the 411 so that he and his friends can be on the look out for anyone suspiciously coming around. We are going to have to apprehend the guys before anyone gets hurt."

Amy called Marty realizing now that there was more at stake than she thought possible. Marty was going to be on the war path. Amy did not know how she was going to explain to Marty without him blowing up. Amy handed Alexis the phone after Marty picked up his phone. Amy was too pumped up to speak.

"Marty I need you to get to my office as soon as you can. We have a serious showdown materialized. Alexis and I need all people on deck to straightening out a treacherous encounter."

"Are you okay? Where is Amy?' Marty sounded very concerned.

"We are both okay. I don't want to shake you up. I will let you know everything once you get here."

"I'm on my way."

"I didn't want to tell him what happened to you and he drive here too fast and get into a wreck on the way. Marty can become exceedingly agitated when someone messes with who he loves. Marty is going to want to go after the guys himself."

"I know Alexis this can turn into something real ugly. I shouldn't have gone over there."

"You shouldn't have gone over there alone. Although that doesn't give the guys the right to kidnap you and tie you up. They should have known that that was not a good idea."

"I wanted to confront Marshawn and let him off with a warning. My intentions were to have Marshawn fire the guys so that he did not get caught up. He seems like a good business man. Instead we are going to have to warn Marshawn that he could be in possible danger. The guys will clearly go after Marshawn when they find out that I got out of there and try to hurt him."

"Amy I should have called Marshawn first. I forgot about that. That is why we both need to relax, slow down, and think about everything that we need to do. There are too many people's lives at stake. What do you think about the receptionist?"

"The receptionist should be arrested. She heard me kicking the door and walked right past me. I heard her voice talking to the woman who helped me in the room next to where I was tied up. If that woman would not have opened the door for me and I would not have gotten those ropes untied in time, I would hate to even think what those guys would have done to me."

"Amy the receptionist is responsible for helping the suspects attack you. I emailed the chief of police and gave him the rundown. I told him that we have to get police officers on the matter right away because of the circumstances. I gave the chief the photos of the guys."

"Good."

"Everything is going to be alright Amy. We will get those guys before they hurt anyone else. Don't stress out. I need you on your "A" game. Tell me what did the guys say to you and how did this conversation result in you getting tied up."

"I asked about Marshawn. The guys grilled me about where you were and to call you. I wasn't about to call you to come to where two psychos were. One of the guys threatened to hurt me saying what he was going to do to me if I did not call you. I told him to go ahead. That is when I was tied up. The guys discussed what they were going to do to me not to get caught. They asked me twice to contact you. I refused both times because I knew if you were ambushed no one was going to find us in time. They wanted me to make it sound as if everything was fine and for you to meet me to discuss what happened with the drug incident."

"Amy, it's not right you had to go through that alone for going to help Marshawn to stay out of trouble. Those guys that work for him are nothing more than thugs who picked a fight with the wrong women. We are going to have them arrested and charged with every count we can think of so that they never do this to another woman. Amy I'm going to make a few phone calls. I need Marshawn to help us catch the suspects off guard."

Alexis dialed Marshawn's number and told Marshawn that he needed to come to her office. Marshawn listened with sympathy. Alexis was in full beast role planning how she was going to take the thugs down.

"Alexis....Amy!" Marty called out the top of his lungs. Marty embraced Alexis and Amy. Alexis told Marty what the guys from the photo did to Amy. At the end of the story Marty sprung up ready to kill.

"Marty, calm down, I know that this is hard for you to hear. I just got off the phone with the man who employed the guys. He's going to help us catch the thugs."

"He better or I'm going after them myself." Marty pounded his fist together breathing heavily.

"Marty, sit down please. You are making me nervous." Amy patted the seat next to her. She had never seen Marty mad before. He was always very kind and supportive. Amy felt badly that her actions brought all his anger.

"Amy I can't sit down. I need a minute baby. You could have been harmed or worse killed. Do you know how that makes me feel?! I don't know what I would do without you. You are my life."

Amy wished she could rewind back and start the day over. She would not have visited Marshawn's office if she knew all of this was going to happen.

"Marty, I feel terrible. I didn't know visiting Marshawn's office would lead to me being tied up. I wanted the owner of the building to get on his employees. I thought if I went by there and let Marshawn know that he was going to have to let the guys go or he would be involved as well this craziness would end. My idea took a turn for the worse. The guys are going to be looking for me. I'm going to have to carry my gun. I had no idea that things were going to get this out of control. The guys were not supposed to be there. I believe the receptionist called them after I asked for Marshawn. Whatever they are doing there the receptionist is definitely a part of it."

"Amy, promise me that you will never do anything that unsafe again."

"I did not know the guys were crazy. Marshawn does not appear to be a ruthless man to me. He was very cooperative with Alexis and I when we went to his office to question him."

"Marshawn is not the problem. The guys he hired are the problem. If you had of spoken to Marshawn maybe this would not have occurred. It's not your fault. You went down there with good intentions. It is those guys fault Amy. Don't take this out on yourself. You are doing your job in this community." Marty hugged Amy.

Alexis, the chief of police, and Marshawn closed the door to get the facts together to catch the guys that roughed up Amy.

"Pardon my employees inexcusable manners. I'm sorry this happened to you." Marshawn apologized to Amy.

"We will get the guys responsible. I have a few police officers on their way to be briefed. Can you tell me what happened when you went down there to speak to Marshawn?" The chief of police questioned.

"I asked to speak to Marshawn to warn him that he needed to get rid of the guys working for him so that he would not end up in any trouble. The receptionist was told not to help me by the suspects. The guys told me to call Alexis and make it appear that nothing was wrong and for Alexis to meet me there at Marshawn's office. I refused twice. My feet and hands were tied up. I was locked in a room from the outside. I heard the guys discussing that they had to get rid of me outside the door. I heard something about a location to pick up something. The voices began to fade away. I am not sure exactly what the guys were picking up. I heard something about the end of business day. The guys could be heard by their footsteps leaving and left me in the room. A woman who was waiting in another room for someone else heard me kicking at the door. She opened the door. She helped me get loose. I told her not to say anything. I ran to my car."

The chief of police and Marshawn listened without any interruptions.

"I can't imagine that the guys would think that they can get away with tying Amy up unless they planned on taking her with them. I hate to think to harm or kill her. This is out of character for my two employees. The employees have known me for years. I have never had a complaint about them before. I haven't ever had a problem with them before. I will make sure that they get what they deserve. I had no idea they were using my business address to do illegal dealings. No one has ever told me anything like this. I will make sure that the receptionist gets what she deserves Amy. Thank you for calling me Alexis. I could have been the next person the guys tied up if I would have ever caught them in the act unexpectedly."

"I was thinking that Marshawn. That is why I contacted you."

Marshawn called the guys on a three way conference call. Everyone sat quietly as Marshawn set up a time to meet. After the meeting was in place, Alexis smiled brightly. She was glad that the drama was going to be over soon.

"Marshawn, I will have my police officers dressed in plain clothes comparably like your patients. The guys will not know what hit them once they meet you. You can wear this wire." The chief of police handed Marshawn a wire.

"We are about to meet in twenty minutes. The guys claimed that something happened that needs my urgency. I was asked to come to the office."

"They must recently found out that Amy got out the room." Alexis was not happy Amy was attacked by the suspects.

"I was thinking this is perfect timing to get the guys off the streets before they can alert anyone else to help them."

Marshawn, the chief of police, and the police officers that the chief contacted left Alexis's office to go to Marshawn's office.

CHAPTER 24

ASTELLE GOT TO THE MEETING overjoyed to be among her pillars of the communities. Her business partners were all there happily discussing the new projects and what a success it was going to be for the communities. Papers were neatly stacked in rows for each business partner. Astelle made an entrance that stopped the small talk and fell upon her arrival.

"There goes the main attraction." One of Astelle's best friends and colleague boosted hugging Astelle and planting a kiss on her forehead and both cheeks.

"Thank you Steven." You are looking younger and rested nowadays."

"You look fabulous as always Astelle. I'm exhausted keeping up with you Ms. lady." Steven did a turn around showing off his hand-stitched suit he designed himself.

Hi everyone. I'm glad you guys showed up and on time. I see that everyone concur with the modifications and the new plans for the project. I cannot wait to start working with some of you. It is going to be a pleasure to work with many of you again. We have all been active in putting in hours for huge profits. This is going to be a splendid experience for all of us to give back to the people who stood by our side." Astelle looked out at her business partners and started signing her paperwork with the others.

All of the partners read and discussed certain pages going over controversial pages in the contracts. Astelle's attorney had met her there along with a few other attorneys. The attorneys were discussing the contracts questioning what did not fall under what their clients discussed. There were a few concerns in question. A couple of changes were adjusted. The contracts were reread and finalized. The teammates pulled a stunt on Astelle without her being told. Astelle was in for a big surprise. Steven reached into a huge black chest below the long table revealing gold glasses with Astelle's name on the shot glasses. The shot glasses were filled with vodka by Steven. Steven and Astelle's friends sang her name bringing out party gifts. One of Astelle's closest confidantes came from the other room with a huge cake and candles on the cake. Matthew and Marg looked on in amusement very excited for their friend.

"This is swell Henry." Matthew whispered eyeing Astelle's favorite cake.

"Yeah Astelle is making big moves." Henry watched his wife.

"I have to admit the surprise was an intimate form of deepest appreciation that Astelle will never forget. Astelle background is known for outdoing her normal day in the business. Astelle finds complex situations to indulge in to get strangers out of misfortunes without charging a penny. Astelle's volunteer work and pro bono attorneys has saved so many people from bankruptcy, homelessness, and job loss." Marg knew Astelle to be A1.

"The cake is a genuine touch. Astelle's business crew blew out the candles. We know this is your favorite cake. Your business partners went all out and beyond to get your favorite cake. They truly love you Astelle." Henry's sensitive side taking over his heart.

"I love them as well. It is not like I do not do the same thing for some of my business partners at times. We all do special little things for one another."

"Are you still going to be down to go out and hit the town up Astelle?" Marg did not travel all the way to another city to stay in her hotel room.

"I told you guys we can stay an extra night or two if you guys are up for it. I do not mind." Astelle wasn't in any rush to leave the city.

"I am all for new experiences. I know Matthew is all for it. I cannot get him to say no to going out on the town even when he is sick. He is always ready to have a good time. I like Matthew passion when it is mostly directed at me." Marg jealousy visible.

"I want to hit the new spots in this city. I heard the people out here love to have a good time. I am sure that we will find ourselves intermixing with the locals acceptably. I want to go to the room and change. I saw some of the outfits that some of the people are wearing. I have a nice outfit that I could wear to blend in." Matthew had a small bag. He wished he had brought a change of clothes for after the meeting with Astelle.

"We are not going back to the room for you to change Matthew. You look good. You do not have to blend in with anyone. You are always trying to outdo people. Enjoy yourself and stop comparing yourself to others."

"I'm not comparing myself to others Marg. I want to wear something different to party in. We had to dress formal for Astelle's meeting."

"Wear it tomorrow Matthew. We are already by some of the places that we are going to check out. I don't feel like going back to the hotel for you to change clothes."

"Okay Marg. No problem. I don't want you to have a fit. I will wear this if you insist. I do look good in whatever I might add." Matthew brushed his suit jacket with his lint roller.

Astelle and her friends rooftop view was hard to leave. Astelle was feeling high off life freedom to move about and meet people that wanted better lives for themselves. Astelle beneficial partners that helped her help other people placed a huge smile on her pretty face. Astelle ducked into the restroom. She knew Matthew was going to have a fit because she was changing into a sleek black fitting dress with stunning white heels, pearls, and a nice watch from one of her colleagues. Astelle did a once over and whistled at herself in the mirror. She looked gorgeous. Marg pushed the door opened to the huge bathroom to see what was taking her friend so long. The rest of the crew posted by the bathroom in position to find out what the city had to offer.

"You sneaky little rascal." Marg circled around Astelle.

"How do I look?" Astelle posed in front of the mirror.

"I think you know exactly how you look Ms. Thang. Fine as the finest wine. Where do you find the time to stay in that kind of shape? Age is truly just a number. All the irresistible qualities you have you will give young people a run for their money." Marg loved sharing Astelle's life accomplishments.

"Thank you girl." Astelle had a positive friend to uplift her.

"You know Matthew about to give you hell the moment you walk out the bathroom. I don't know how you are going to stop him from wanting to put on different clothing. I guess we are going to have to go to the mall. Matthew likes to wear those flashy clothes when he is in the club. He wants all eyes directed at his womanizing ego." Marg liked the way Astelle did her hair and the perfume had to be expensive and famous. The fragrance had Marg wanting to buy a new fragrance before going out. She would have to found out what fragrance Astelle was wearing.

Matthew tapped his feet impatiently on the floor. Marg came out of the bathroom with Astelle unidentifiable. Matthew grabbed Marg and tugged on her asking what took her so long completely oblivious to Astelle. Astelle cleared her throat. Matthew did a double look thrown off balance.

"I know you did not change in the bathroom after all the blah blah blah I received from you hussy about me changing my rags. Oh hell no. Astelle how dare you. Although, I must say, damn you fine woman. Lord have mercy on the men where we are going. You are definitely going to turn heads in that get up. You have been putting in work. Milk does a body

good. Squats does a body good and whatever else you been doing Astelle."
Matthew hovered over Astelle taking in her sweet fragrance.

"Thanks Matthew. I had to change. I had on my business woman
attire. I want to look a little more suited for a good time and not look all
stuffy and professional."

"You achieved that my Sista. You are blazing tonight. You are going
to be the talk of the time missy. I guarantee we are going to have the best
time of your life. Tonight is all you. Tomorrow night will be all me. I aim
to impress my Queen." Matthew took Astelle by the arm. Marg almost in
tears for Astelle's supremacy was proud of her best friend. It was becoming
one of the best nights of Marg's life. Henry was at a loss of words as he
pushed Matthew to the side hugging his wife.

"I know the night is very young. We were going to go spend some time
at the shopping centers. I say we dance the night away until the wee hours
of the morning. I am behind schedule to shake my buns." Marg stepped
into the comfy ride next to Matthew."

"I didn't think we were going to take that long. I had no idea a DJ
was going to be invited at the meeting. I wasn't aware of any kind of
celebration." Astelle wanted to get the contracts signed and leave.

"I hope the DJ at this night club is as live as that young fella. He played
all of our favorite songs. The songs took me way back in the day of how
much fun we used to have." Matthew missed his old self.

"The years flew by us. It is true time flies when you are having fun."
Marg peeked out the window.

"I say we stay close by that club you mentioned Matthew. That way
we don't get caught up in traffic and miss the party. After a certain time
the streets are jammed with people trying to reach their destinations. We
should have stayed at your celebration Astelle until the club opened." Marg
was fond of Astelle's friends at her business meeting.

"Marg, I work with my colleagues all the time. I don't want to stay any
longer than I have to. I need time to myself with the original gang. We

do have fun together during business hours. We also need a break from one another. Most of the time when my work buddies and I get together we are always thinking about more work to do for others. I don't want to think about any projects or contracts. I'm going to be extremely off the grid when I return back to my office. I am covered in supporting ideas, benefits, and ongoing fights against humanity. I don't know when I am going to be able to take time off again."

"I hear that." Matthew told the driver the address to the place that they would descend on.

Marg gave Matthew a questionable look then withdrew her demeanor not to ruin the night about how Matthew gets around. The group wanted to party and get a feel for the town and leave their names in the mouths of strangers for years to come. Astelle was known for having that kind of effect on people. She was easy to talk to and got along with people instantly. Her attitude was on point. Astelle's comportment made her in the seven figures. The driver reached the location and Matthew very eager to get out opened the door. Marg hated that look and whacked Matthew. Marg scooted out the car door clutching her purse.

"What was that for Marg?! Don't start acting crazily. We are here for a good time. You know you are just as excited as I am."

"I doubt that. I bet this place bring back memories for you huh."

"You are thinking the wrong things. I have not done anything wrong Marg. Now stop all that and let's seize this time out." Matthew held the door opened for Marg.

The city was congested with city folks. It appeared a lot of people was feeling like Matthew and wanted to bask in the night life. Couples were everywhere walking the streets hugged up and hand to hand. Younger people talking, singing, and rapping to their own beat grasp attention. It felt really good to be a part of the action. Marg instantly snapped back to her chirpy self in sync with Henry, Astelle, and Matthew infatuated by the scene. Astelle noticed the congressman. He came up to her extending his hand out with a nice looking woman next to him.

"Astelle, my, my, my. What do I owe this pleasure? Why you didn't tell me you were coming down with your hubby. I could have arranged something for you guys and your friends."

"Congressman what a pleasant surprise! We are here on a business trip. We decided at the last minute to stay a couple of days."

"Oh, I see. Well you should call me tomorrow so we can all meet up and catch up. I would love to take you guys to some of my favorite places while you are here."

The congressman handed Henry and Astelle his business card.

"You know I have your number." Henry took the card tucking the card in his pants pocket.

"This is a new line to reach me immediately. I will be waiting for your call. Where are you guys headed?"

'We are going over there when it opens up." Matthew pointed to a huge decked out space.

"Oh yes. It is quite a lovely place to visit. We were going to stop by there tonight. My buddy that I grew up with owns this great place. I do not go out much. I decided we will shock him and surprise him with a visit tonight. What a surprise for me to see you guys. If you don't mind maybe we can tag along. No time like now to catch up." The congressman introduced the woman by his side.

Everyone introduced themselves ready to use their time to tour all of the places in between until it was time to go to the night club. The congressman had great taste and selected a popular site. The selection satisfied the visitors.

CHAPTER 25

L EILANI WAS TAKING ADVANTAGE OF her vacation and living it up. The tall palm drinks and umbrellas drinks were giving Leilani and Evan a vacation to remember. Leilani jumped into the water swimming a few laps in her nice bikini. Evan jumped in the water keeping up with her longing for the vacation. A tall lady in the water swam by Leilani and Evan complimenting the beautiful blue water.

The sky was foreshadowing a beautiful light blue with twinkles of white lines indicating the day would turn out sunny and warm. The sand was smooth and clean. The air smelled of assorted baked foods. Leilani could not be more humble and radiant. After completing a few more swims around the exotic beach, Evan and Leilani decided to stay on the sand adoring the polished sand stones with huge umbrellas and beach chairs. Men and women were play fighting in the sand and having volleyball contests. Rainbow kites with younger teens running across the sand could be seen throughout the suitable island for all family types. A few dogs and their owners were playing near by with the owners throwing the balls for the dogs to fetch. Assorted food and a drink bar could be found near the front of the extravagant place.

"Paris was breathtaking. Hawaii is gorgeous. I can lie back in the sun and rub my fingers in the sand all day and night. I think we should sleep on the beach instead of sleeping in our room tonight." Leilani exhaled.

"We can make a nice camp fire in those bins over there as long as we clean up when we leave. The bins are tin and black. I have marshmallows, chocolate, and graham crackers for the best smores. I have some of the juicy lobsters from the food bar. I would love to hang out all night. We don't get to do this often enough." Evan explored the opportunities on the beach.

The food bars and the drink bars were separated. On one huge table was all the fruit advertised on the commercials. Some fruit guests had never tasted before and wanted to try was displayed on the table. Another huge table had seafood of every kind. The guests grabbed salmon kabobs with shrimp and oysters. The table to the left had a bartender making every drink imaginable. An island looking couple chose two assorted fruit and alcohol drinks with the cute umbrellas.

A nice guy with a beer in his hand was flying a kite with his other hand. Evan searched for seashells. A frisbee flew in his direction. A little boy rushed by Evan to retrieve the frisbee throwing the frisbee back to his dad. Leilani noticed a guy talking to Evan handing him some glittering sea pearls. Evan transfixed by the sea pearls expressed gratitude to the stranger.

"Who was that?" The guy seemed to know Evan.

"I don't know anyone here. Remember we are on vacation. We are among a lot of strangers. People will ask us if we need aid at times." Evan eyes darted over to the blue waters. People swam further out shore making Evan think it was best to swim within the parameters of the beach.

"This vacation is going to be in my head for the rest of my life a story I will tell my kids and grandkids." Leilani was going to make Hawaii a regular place to frequent.

"This is definitely a beautiful place to visit." Evan always wanted palm trees on his block.

Evan reached for his suntan lotion putting the suntan lotion on his chest and legs. Evan bent over Leilani rubbing suntan lotion on Leilani before sitting back down to let the sun give him an overall tan color.

The beach was starting to fill up with people. Evan aimed up at the beautiful sky putting his sunglasses on his face. There was not any other place Evan would whether be than with Leilani enjoying the beach. He was weary from work and earned merits for his time consuming labor. Evan could feel his eyes growing heavy and decided he better sit up or he was going to doze off. Evan looked over to see Leilani's eyes closed.

"I am not sleep." Leilani could feel Evan looking at her.

"I will not say anything if you were asleep. This is a place of total relaxation and pampering. I almost dozed off myself. The weather is just right. The water is fantastic. The food is the best. I can't find one complaint."

"I told you we were going to have a great time here."

"I had a great time in Paris. Paris was filled with good people welcoming us with open arms. I won't ever forget Stew the guy we met at the gallery. I love the painting I bought for us. Paris has some cool art. I am going to have to take my mom to Paris. She loves paintings."

"Your mom will love Paris. Paris has so much artistic beauty that your mom adores. You two should go to Paris next year. Your mom said she was taking a vacation then. It would be nice to surprise her."

"I will do that. I know my mom will be ready to go to a place like Paris without any hesitation." Evan's mom loved to travel and send post cards to her family and friends. His mom spoke of Paris a lot.

A band set up shiny and expensive instruments on the beach. The melodies playing softly in Evan's ears made Evan slow down from over stimulating fascination. Evan knew the change of scenario might take him straight into a deep snore. Evan hadn't slept in what felt like days. It was like a dream. Evan didn't want to leave. Evan, Leilani, and their friends were always around music, food, and good people.

Couples danced and swayed in the sand as men put huge tropical

216

flowers in the women's hair with sparkling hair pins. Evan got up to get a flower and hair pin for Leilani. The flower and hair pin made Evan feel like a part of a dazzling culture. Leilani loved the flower and hair pin.

"I have always wanted to put a flower like this on the side of my hair. It looks so cute." Leilani touched the hair pin.

"The flowers and hair pins are unique and exquisite. You guys look so pretty." Evan looked around at the women with the flowers and hair pins on the side of their hair.

Ladies gathered in the middle of the beach with flowing beach skirts and bikini tops performing a dance with the instruments playing effortless in the background. The belly dances and hulu hoop dances were hypnotic. Families participated and joined in on the sidelines to imitate the great dancers joyfully.

The men came out of nowhere with fire jumping through the hulu hoops and spitting fire out of their mouths. The performances became more professionally advanced with tricks with animals and cannon balls setting the crowd off in astonishment. The crowd roared beating their chests wildly begging for more. The performers gave more and more satiated entertainment.

Evan and Leilani blended in with the performers in the rave. The couple swung one another around breaking off into a belly dance then some slow dance moves. Evan worked up an appetite craving something sweet pulling Leilani to the dessert bar.

German chocolate cake, velvet cake, boston cream cake, chocolate cake, and many other cakes had Evan standing at the dessert bar not knowing which dessert to choose. Leilani tasted a piece of the velvet cake and added ice cream to her plate. Leilani wanted to hurry up and get back out in the sand and dance some more. Evan could feel the urgency and chose a piece of german chocolate cake. The couple ate a small piece of cake with one scoop of ice cream and got back to the sand celebration.

Some of the performers were placing colored beads around the necks of the guests at the beach. Leilani dashed over with Evan to get some beads. Another performer began a line dance. The guests danced in a line. The back line acolytes threw themselves down in beach chairs and in the sand needing a second wind before rejoining the festivities. The laughter could be heard echoing all over the beach.

"That was refreshing Evan!" Leilani felled down in the beach chair.

"I thought I was going to pass out from all the moving around." Evan admitted breathlessly.

"You hung in there."

"Let's sleep on the beach tomorrow. I want to scrub in hot water, get in the comfortable bed, and watch a movie tonight."

"I knew you were going to say that." Leilani threw a grape at Evan.

Evan caught the grape with his mouth.

The performers were going strong in the sand with guests participating in every song, dance, and act. Evan and Leilani watched for a while in their beach chairs before packing it in and hitting the hay.

Evan did not make it to the shower before he was out for the count when Leilani came out of the closet with a set of clean clothes in her hands. Leilani tee-heed quietly not to wake Evan and closed the bathroom door. Leilani bathe and changed into her night gown turning down the volume on the remote to watch a hair-raising movie.

Evan woke up early the next day wondering how he slept for so long. Leilani had already gotten spruced up and was swimming at the beach with two women she met on her way to the beach. The women were splashing water and having a great time by the time Evan got to the beach.

"Ladies this is my beau Evan. As you can see he cannot hang." Leilani splashed the water toward Evan.

Evan jumped into the water splashing the water back on Leilani ignoring her taunts. Evan swan some feet away from Leilani rising up to take a breath.

"This place is calmative. I felled asleep. The room was very peaceful and quiet. I can't ever remember sleeping that long back at home."

"You missed the movie. It was a drama filled thriller movie." Leilani exaggerated knowing she felled asleep and did not see the whole movie.

"You watched the whole movie." Evan splashed more water on Leilani.

"Yep. It was an eye opener."

"Tell me the ending." Evan picked Leilani up and dunked her in the water.

Leilani laughed shaking off the water and wiping her face.

"I watched most of the movie."

"That's what I thought."

"At least I stayed up longer and was back up before you getting a swim before the crowd."

"I enjoyed every minute of sleep. No work and no interruptions. I'm ready to stay out on the beach tonight and toast the smores."

"Can we meet up with you guys tonight? My Mark is at work helping to build a pantry for a local family. We would love to toast smores by the fire with you two." One of the women asked Leilani floating on her back.

"If you like, Evan and I do not mind. It's not our beach." Leilani went underwater.

The women went underwater with Leilani popping back up throwing their hair out of their faces. The water temperature was cool and not too cold. Evan floated in the water for a while. Leilani tugged Evan to go to the beach chairs to sit down. The two women told Leilani that they would be back later and left.

"You met friends already."

"Out here I am bound to come across a few women swimming. The water feels amazing." Leilani squeezed water from her hair with her hands.

"The water has reduced all my stress levels in my entire body. I love swimming."

"I know Evan. You stay in the swimming pool at home when we are not at work."

"I concentrate better and my body is less tensed or stressed from a long day after a good swim too. Swimming is a good form of exercise. Swimming builds up my tight frame, but swimming makes me hungry." Leilani high tailed it to the food bar.

Swimmers stood along the side of the food bar making light conversation.

Evan was taking pleasure in biting into his croissant filled with cheese and steak when he heard screaming from a distance. Leilani eyes followed the screams. Evan looked up to see two bodies rolling around in the sand ripping one another apart. Evan and a few other people ran toward the rumble to break up the fight. The fighters would not let go of one another. Evan and a few other guys had to literally pull the guys apart. Once the dudes were pulled apart, the bigger individual stormed away leaving the smaller guy with Evan and the other gentlemen.

"Are you okay?" One of the fellas that stopped the fight asked.

"I'm fine. What a jerk!" The guy stalked off face reddened from the tussling.

Evan and the other guys gave one another the "I don't know what that was about look", shoulders shrugged in uncertainty. They did not have a clue what the fight was about and walked back to where they were before the fight started.

"What was that all about?" Leilani didn't want to cast aspersions on the mean faced guy.

"I'm not exactly an expert to say. Both guys seem to not want to discuss the fight. The two lads took off hot under the collar. We had to pull them apart. Hopefully whatever that was is over. This beach is too nice to be fighting."

"That was awful. Luckily no one was hurt."

"If we wouldn't have stopped the fight, I think the guys would have fought until someone was badly hurt. That was weird." The fight caused a discomfort. Evan never thought fights happened in Hawaii. Hawaii was a happy couples, families, and friends sort of place from what Evan was always told. The fight made Evan feel like he was back at home for a minute.

CHAPTER 26

MARSHAWN PALMS WERE SWEATING AND his forehead was damped. Marshawn had to grab a paper towel to wipe the sweat from his forehead. The police officers were parked in an unmarked van listening with the wire Marshawn had tapped to his chest. Marshawn made sure to add a black t-shirt to his blazer so that the wire was not noticed. Marshawn said a few words at the front desk. A message was written down for him. He never heard of anyone being wired for an alleged drug deal gone wrong with an addict. Marshawn didn't understand why the police assumed his business was the place of the transaction without any evidence. Marshawn wandered into his office. The two guys from the photos were waiting for him.

"Maurice, Jess. How is everything going?" Marshawn avoided direct eye contact pretending to look into his desk drawer for something.

The two guys looked at one another not knowing how they wanted to tell Marshawn about the mayor and her friend.

"Everything is good boss. What's going on with you?"

"Nothing much, tons of work and a lot of clients results to look over." Marshawn wiped his seat off.

"Did two women stop by to see you?" Jess asked.

"I get clients in here all the time. Are there any specific clients you guys are asking about Jess?"

"You were not in the office when two women stopped by to talk to you. I believe one of the women is the mayor. You have not talked to her yet?" Maurice looked at Marshawn trying to hide the anger he was feeling that the other woman got away.

"I've been busy. I haven't had time to speak with the mayor. Is there something the mayor wants you guys to tell me?"

"I'm not sure." Jess stayed calm.

"I will let you know when I speak with the ladies. If that is all I need to get back to work gentlemen." Marshawn stood up to walk the men out of his office.

Maurice and Jess reluctantly walked toward the door and opened the door. The men were a few feet away from Marshawn's office when the police approached from the other direction. Jess panicked and grabbed Marshawn by the collar. Maurice pulled out a gun while Jess dragged Marshawn back into his office. Marshawn was pissed off that the police did not give him any warning freaking the guys out. Marshawn was in the middle of a deadly deal gone bad and wanted no parts of the beef.

"What the hell are you doing Jess?! Put that damn gun away Maurice! Are you trying to get us shot by the police! Maurice locked Marshawn's door.

"I'm sorry boss. I can't let you leave. I think those two women called the police on us."

"Why would the mayor call the police on two guys working in my office?" Marshawn didn't want Maurice and Jess fibbing to him.

"I'm not sure. I think the ladies have us confused with someone else." Jess shakily answered.

"Stay calm Jess. Tell me what happened with the two ladies."

"The mayor and another chick came to this office asking questions about drugs and a friend that was given a drug. The mayor claims that the victim said the drug came from this building. Apparently something happened to the person the mayor is asking about."

"Why would the mayor's friend think that the drug came from this building? We have clients here to be educated after rehabilitation. We do not have any drugs in this building. The prescriptions come from the doctors of the clients once we evaluate the client's progress. We offer classes for clients with injuries to heal and teach proper healing techniques. The classes are to make sure the clients do not get hooked on drugs. That is why we offer natural healing to wend them off of prescribed pain medications."

"We know boss." Jess moved away from the door after hearing someone turning the knob.

"Come out with your hands up. If you harm a hair on Marshawn's head you guys will never see the time of day." A police officer on a loud horn yelled into Marshawn's office.

"Why did you guys panic? I could have told the police you worked for me. There was not any reason to pull out a gun Maurice. You have made the matter worse."

"I thought the ladies were with the police. I'm not going to jail."

"How are you going to get out of here if you don't plan on going to jail? You garnished a weapon in plain sight of the authorities and locked me in my office. It is out of my hands now. I will have to see what I can do after you open the door and turn yourselves in."

"Marshawn we are not turning ourselves in. You make the police leave or we have no choice but to shoot you."

"WHAT! What the fuck you going to shoot me for! I didn't call the police."

"Wait a minute Maurice. The boss is right. We can't shoot him. We will really be in big trouble. Let's think about this." Jess sat down on the top of Marshawn's desk with the gun.

"Do you have another way out of this office?" Maurice searched around.

Marshawn had a flashback come to his mind of bullets flying. The two suspects were injured or killed and shook his head at Maurice.

Maurice was not accepting no for an answer and paced around the huge office looking for an escape route. The silver button was a nice size mystery sticking out from the wall. Maurice wondered what the silver button was connected to in the office. Maurice dashed back over to Marshawn asking him about the silver button on the wall. Marshawn closed his eyes in heavy thought knowing this could not end well for the guys.

"Maurice trust me, you don't want to do this. You have a bright future ahead of you. Why would you throw away your life for a misunderstanding? The police do not have anything on you. It is not illegal to carry a firearm."

"Boss I am not trying to hear all that. Where does the silver button on the wall lead? Don't make me shoot you. You know I don't have anything against you." Maurice agitated because he could not leave.

"Boss, listen to Maurice. We do not want to harm you. We are not going to jail for two nosy ass ladies. We did not hurt anyone. Once we are locked up the police will find anything to try to keep us locked up. The ladies that came over here will say we are guilty. We will end up doing time. I cannot do any time. I have a family."

Maurice looked around his office trying to find anything to distract his employees for a minute to get away from the silver button that led to a hideaway in Marshawn's office. Marshawn did not want anyone in the secret room. Marshawn had secrets as well and could not afford to let the police know about the hideout. The guys were causing him more than enough problems that Marshawn did not need. Marshawn did not know how the situation turned to police drawing out guns when the police was supposed to wait for Marshawn to bring the guys out of the building.

"Marshawn I do not have all day! Push the button or I swear I will pull the trigger!" Marshawn jolted out his daze to see the gun at his head.

"Alright, alright stay cool fellas."

"Open the door or we will shoot. I do not want anyone to get hurt.

I have asked you guys to come out with your hands up. Step away from Marshawn!" The police loud horn could be heard outside of the door.

Maurice fired a warning shot in the air blasting a hole in Marshawn's office ceiling. Marshawn ducked. Jess stared at Maurice as if Maurice had lost his mind.

"Have you gone mad fool! The police are going to shoot back. What were you thinking? Put that damn gun down Maurice. You are not thinking clearly. Why are you acting so crazy? You want us to die in here. I am not going down with you." Jess walked toward Maurice signaling to lower the gun.

Maurice put the gun down on the office table. Maurice was distraught. The office felt like a closed in cage. Maurice rubbed his temples. He was not going out without a fight. Maurice rushed toward Marshawn having Marshawn push the silver button on the wall and press in the codes. The hidden door opened up smoothly revealing guns and survival kits of all kinds. Maurice pushed Marshawn back eyeing the display of grenades, rifles, military gear, and endless supplies of food.

"Marshawn what do you do?" Jess whistled walking around the large hidden escape room.

"I don't do anything. I think it is important to always have a hiding spot in your home and office to be prepared for the unknown."

"This must have cost you a fortune. You sitting on racks huh Marshawn." Maurice slapped Marshawn on the back.

"Maurice I have been adding little by little for years and moved some of my equipment to this office. Maurice that does not mean that you get to put me in your conflict, you have to turn yourself in. The police are outside the door."

"Why would I turn myself in when I have all this ammunition that can take out the entire block if I have to escape? Marshawn you better go to the door and tell the police to go away. I don't care how you do it.

You are going to get rid of the police. Tell them we escaped through the window or something."

"The police are not going to believe that."

"The police will believe that if you hurry up before more backup comes. Close the door. Jess and I will be listening from in here. If you open this hiding spot you are facing a lot of time."

Maurice stared at Marshawn with piercing eyes his gun back in his hands. Maurice tramped over to a rifle picking up the rifle. Maurice pulled bullets from the shelves. Jess retrieved two of the rifles filling the rifles with bullets. Marshawn was scandalized. He had no choice but to try to get rid of the police so that he would not do any time himself.

"Okay, okay." Marshawn closed the guys in the hiding room nervously checking for a place to tell the police the guys ran off. Marshawn settled on the back window that was a good escape without the police having access to the outer part of the building from that angle. Marshawn heard a loud boom before he could turn the door knob. The police rushed in guns drawn. Marshawn threw his hands in the air frantic.

"Where did they go?!" The police yelled searching the office. The other two cops bulldozing passed Marshawn checking the open back window.

"Sergeant I believe the suspects got away through this window. Contact all patrol units to be on a lookout for two suspects." The tall police officer spoke into his radio running out the office door giving a description of what the suspects were wearing.

"Marshawn our undercover agent did not give the guys time to exit the building. One of our officers screwed up and entered the building from the side door. He stated he thought he heard some screaming.

Marshawn crumpled down in disbelief. He could have been shot. The manila folder on Marshawn's desk had files of his secret life. Marshawn flipped the folder over and opened his desk drawer tossing the manila folder in the desk drawer.

"I will contact you with the whereabouts of the suspects when we track them down." The lead officer informed Marshawn leaving Marshawn to an untidy office with papers flung all over the floor.

Marshawn touched his chest breathing in slowly and outward. He was shaking and filled with sweat by the time the police left. Marshawn had to figure out how he was going to get rid of the employees without incriminating himself. Marshawn could see Maurice and Jess from his security camera he set up at his desk. The two guys were taken too much interest in his secret hideout infuriating Marshawn. Marshawn grabbed his cell phone to call one of his cullies.

"Jackson we have a sitch." Marshawn spoke into the phone. Marshawn explained in particular to the person on the other end of the phone. Marshawn put the phone back on his desk. Marshawn could live with the plan his main man came up with to get him out of the snake pit. Marshawn bimbled over to his cabinet and pulled out an expensive glass to pour a potent drink, his hands shaking identically to neurological patient with dementia. Marshawn downed the drink and poured another one. Marshawn looked up to see Maurice and Jess pressing their side faces up against the door to see if they could hear what was going down in his office. Marshawn downed the drink. He was going to let the guys stay in the secret hideout until his cleanup crew came.

Maurice's patience was growing thin as he stepped back from the door and turned to Jess.

"You think Marshawn is ratting us out?"

"Do you think we will be here if Marshawn was ratting us out? You tripping Maurice. Marshawn has just as much to lose if he rat on us. We are safe in here for now. Besides we cannot do anything until we know the women are taken care of. They can identify us from those photos. I called my boy for new identities and passports. We are leaving as soon as we can."

"Jess we can't up and leave. I have ties with my people working for me. I have to see my plan all the way through. I have money involved."

"You stay here Maurice. You call me when you ready to leave. As soon as Marshawn opens this door, I'm gone. I am not about to get locked up for no money. I can make money anywhere. I'm not going to jeopardize my freedom staying in this city. The police are not going to stop looking for us until we are behind bars. If we stay in the city we will be behind bars real soon."

"You right Jess. Where are we going to go?"

"We can go anywhere we want. We have enough money. I have connections in the Bahamas. We can lay low until this dies down and resurface."

"We are not going to be able to resurface Jess. We are hot. We need new faces and all. The police out there are not going to let us come back and not recognize us. I have to call Shannon. She is going to have to do some plastic surgeries on our faces. We are not going to be able to see that big deal through if we don't."

I cannot get any plastic surgeries on my face Maurice. Don't you think that is going a bit far?"

"Not if we are talking about coming back. That is the safest way. I have to come back. I have too much to lose if I don't come back." Maurice rubbed his chin in heavy thought.

"I say we lay low and let this blow over. We did not kill anyone. We did not shoot anyone. We are not going to be on the fugitive list for allegations of drugs. We do not even know who the girl is or if she is willing to testify or verify us. The ladies did not bring the snitch with them. We don't know who the snitch is yet." Jess holding off on losing his temper quelled Maurice wrath.

"You right Jess. We have not been identified of a crime. I say we leave later this evening. I have to make one stop."

"That's what we need to do Maurice. I'm telling you we will be good after a month or two months. No one will be worried any more if they think we left the city."

Maurice felt a bit better thinking about the ups and downs of their circumstances.

CHAPTER 27

"**A**STELLE A TOAST IS IN honor of your completed projects generating wealth in the seven figures. Congratulations, my friend." The congressman tribute to Astelle's success was good-natured. The congressman unfailing specifications for rallies and flexible pledges to make a change for the people by Astelle was admirable.

The half-dressed hosts with immaculate figures and art formed features served the guests with precise orders. Marg could not take her eyes off the firmly sculptured manikin waiters excellent services making everyone feel welcomed and special. Marg tugged at her thin wraparound shawl. Matthew gulped his drink flagging the waiter down for more rounds.

"Matthew you better slow down or you are not going to make it to the club old timer." Henry jived talking to Matthew.

"I am full of vitality. I'm not old Henry. I'm primed. I can hang out all night."

"I bet you can." Marg took a piece of fruit from Matthew's plate.

Matthew pulled Marg thin shawl up more on her shoulders.

"My wife gives me such a hard time when I let my guard down and kick my feet up. I have one life. I am going to make the most of my life. I love being out and having fun. It is the only way to live. I bring my wife along. I don't know why she is always making a fuss." Matthew tossed a pineapple in his mouth from his chicken, rice, and vegetable platter.

"I will back you up as long as you are on your best behavior when we get to the club. Do not get in the club thinking you can out dance everybody and start dancing freaky on the women. I want to let my hair done and paint the town red tonight." Marg dug her fork into her own delicious meal and spooned up another bite for Matthew to consume.

Matthew chewed and swallowed the food the flavorful meal sapid. "I would not do that to you honey. I'm a teaser and a respectful guy. That is why people love me. I know my boundaries."

"In all fairness Marg, Matthew is telling the truth." Astelle agreed.

"The jury is out on that one." Henry tapped Matthew.

The congressman and his lady friend ate in silence admiring the couple's closeness. The congressman lady friend excused herself to go the restroom. Marg and Astelle excused themselves to accompany Stephanie.

"Stephanie how do you like the place?" Marg asked.

"The restaurant is the most upscale and highly recommended restaurant in this city. The waiters are gorgeous with the best manners. I enjoy coming here."

"The restaurant is definitely upscale." Astelle admired the restroom.

"I don't mean to pry. Are you and the congressman dating?" Marg didn't hear the congressman introduced Stephanie as his woman.

"We have been friends for years. I have known Michael since we were kids. I am not certain if we are ready to be in a relationship. I will let the friendship take its own course." Stephanie treaded into one of the stalls. Marg washed her hands. Astelle occupied another stall.

The ladies met back at the mirrors of the restroom.

"I think you and Michael make a fine couple indeed. You guys compliment one another. What is it that you do Stephanie?"

"I dab into a few things. I love to sell art. I am into modeling. I have a few books out. I work with Michael on some of his campaigns."

"Super Stephanie, a woman with many skills. Good for you Stephanie. I engage in a few hustles myself. Astelle and I both are hustling Women. It is a great way to meet good people." Marg grabbed a napkin. The ladies left the restroom.

Henry, Matthew, and Michael were in a deep discussion about politics when the ladies walked back to the table and had a seat. The discussion was immediately halted as the men attended to the ladies.

"I want to wait on drinking until we get to the club. I heard the bartender is fierce. I want to try the new desert flame. I heard that drink is fantastic and give a great buzz." Astelle supped her water.

"Water it is." Henry told the waiter and ate another spicy meatball from his plate.

The couples talked for a while before heading over to the club to enjoy the rest of the night.

The club was completely striking. The line was around the corner. Michael ushered the couples to follow him and went into a side door that a Security Guard opened for them. Astelle was impressed. The club was huge with many magnetic gadgets. Astelle raided the bar to test the new drink. The rest of the gang interested to try out new drinks.

"Oh my, this drink is everything described plus more." Astelle handed Henry the desert flame to taste.

"Whoa. That is delicious. I felt a kick instantly." Henry gave the drink back to Astelle ordering him a blue canal.

"I would like a whiskey sour and two dry martinis for the two ladies." Michael knew the bartender.

"Sure Michael, how have you been?"

"I'm doing tremendously. Thank you, how about you?"

"I can't complain."

"I know you are doing well with socialites like these extroverts every weekend." The waiter agreed with Michael handing them their drinks.

Marg took Matthew to the dance floor filled with social butterflies.

Everyone else followed ready to get the night jumping. The crowd was going wild and groups of dancers were showing out on the dance floor. Marg and Matthew were in tune with the party pleasers getting a thrill out of every bit of the party life. The other couples seem to fall in line just as quickly looking very young fitting in the ambience. A guy came over by Astelle asking Henry if it was okay to dance with her. Henry nodded. Astelle was an expert dancer staying on beat in full energy. Marg allowed Matthew to go through the crowd dancing with numerous people as Marg danced with a few people on the dance floor. Stephanie ended up dancing with Henry and Michael was dancing with two women that stepped on the dance floor in similar outfits. The two ladies looked like twins. The DJ blasted out jazzy words on the microphone pumping up the party. The music mixture was blended excellently with different songs by the DJ.

"I need to grab another drink and water." Astelle cat walked off the dance floor.

Henry and Matthew followed. Henry ordered another drink. Marg, Stephanie, and Michael drained a few water bottles.

"I have to say I enjoy this atmosphere." Michael crunched on ice from his water.

"I feel twenty years younger." Astelle's hands moving to the music.

"You dance twenty years younger Astelle." Michael saluted Astelle. Astelle saluted back.

"Astelle don't play on the dance floor. I think my wife use the dance floor as her exercise." Henry deeply in love with Astelle vocalized.

"Let's get back at there and show the hoofers what we working with." Marg led Astelle back on the dance floor.

The DJ slowed the music down and popular slow jams moved the crowd. The couples paired up moving from side to side to the slow music falling back in love. Michael looked at Stephanie wanting to ask her to be his woman. Michael was terrified of what Stephanie would say and allowed

Stephanie to lean her head into his chest as the slow dance took on a new meaning for Michael.

Stephanie could feel Michael heart beating. Stephanie knew Michael well enough to know Michael was falling for her. Michael had something that he wanted to say and was avoiding telling Stephanie. Stephanie would wait until they were alone before she found out what was on Michael's mind.

The moment was disrupted by a change of pace in the slow playing music. The DJ went back to upbeat music.

"I don't want you love birds falling asleep in here." The DJ performed mixing and scratching on the turntables making the party goers rebound to the fast pace beats.

Michael kissed Stephanie unexpectedly. Stephanie returned the kiss. Astelle nudged Henry toward the couple smiling. Marg and Matthew caught Michael and Stephanie kissing jumping for joy for the couple. Stephanie shyly obliged the approval mesmeric with Michael dancing joyously.

"Looks like a love connection tonight." Marg whispered in Matthew's ear.

"Good for her. Michael is a good pick. He told us he was really fond of Stephanie when you guys were in the ladies room. I wish them all the happiness. Love is special when you find true love with the right one."

"Matthew they have known one another for quite some time. I wonder why Michael waited so long."

"You didn't know Marg? Michael was a ladies man. He had all kinds of women on his arm. I won't say he slept with every woman he was seen with. There was a few."

"I didn't know."

"Don't let the innocent smile fool you. That man knows his way around the ladies."

"You should know Matthew."

234

"Here we go Marg. I should have kept my mouth shut. Now you think I am involved. Woman, enjoy the music and stop whining." Matthew hugged Marg.

Marg hugged Matthew back. She couldn't help going in on Matthew. Marg was aware that Matthew knew his way around the ladies. Marg remember days of Matthew flirting like he was single. Marg do not think Matthew ever cheated on her. Matthew was the type that loved to be the center of attention. Matthew had come a long way. Marg gave Matthew another hug. She knew how hard it was for Matthew to not want to seek attention in big crowds.

The couples jammed their way over to the sitting area in the club. Michael ordered another round of drinks. Astelle shook her head asking for more water.

"Party pooper, what happened? You tired Astelle?" Matthew sat next to Astelle.

"I want to get back on the dance floor after a while. You know I don't drink that much when I am out Matthew."

"I'm living it up. Two drinks isn't that much alcohol for me. I have to get back to work. I am not thinking about anything besides having a good time tonight."

"Count me in Matthew." Henry picked up one of the drinks Michael ordered.

"The host gave them glasses that were small and skinny. Two glasses equaled one full glass." Henry clonked glasses with Michael.

"Stephanie you want some more water." Michael passed an ice water toward Stephanie.

Stephanie drank the water inhaling. Her feet were aching. Stephanie wished she had brought another pair of shoes. Michael took off Stephanie's shoe massaging her foot one after the other. Stephanie felled in love with Michael that night. Michael was tentative and very sweet. Stephanie always knew Michael was the one. The fact that he was willing to rub her feet in a crowded club in front so many men stole Stephanie's heart. Stephanie was ready to get back on the dance floor and wrap herself in Michael's arms when the slow song she loved came on at the request of someone at the club.

"Did you see that?" Marg hugged Matthew.

"I told you Michael knows his way around the ladies."

"The gesture was perfect. Michael stole my heart. I think that was the sweetest thing Michael could have done." Astelle kissed Henry.

"You ladies are so emotional. Come on let's get back out there before you two cry a pond."

"I was almost in tears." Marg dabbed the moist in the corner of her eyes.

"Marg you are the biggest cry baby over anything romantic." Astelle hugged her friend going to the dance floor with their husbands following behind them.

"Astelle you are too." Marg exhaled.

The party goers were in groups having competitive dance offs with large crowds edging the dancers on. Astelle, Henry, Marg, and Matthew stood in the audience watching the dancers.

CHAPTER 28

L EILANI AND EVAN'S NEW FRIENDS edged their way along the beach with bags and tents. The beach did not allow tents. The couples snuck the tents to the beach. They all planned to go out farther away and chill for the rest of the night.

"We live here so we know how to get past the beach spies." Leilani new friend Amber sat down all the bags she was carrying. We can go toward the end of the beach that way. That is where Mark and I usually chill when we come to the beach overnight."

"Cool." Evan helped carried the bags and tents.

"Do we have enough food and water?" Mark opened up Amber's bags for an inspection of goodies.

"You brought everything. I knew I could count on you." Mark replied.

Evan and Leilani watched the couple enthused about sleeping on the grandeur beach.

The stars were bright. The weather was warm. The sand felt indestructible. Leilani was in heaven spreading out the tent. Evan set up some of the food. Mark turned on a portable radio. Amber unfolded the blankets. The couples ate and talked about everything they loved about the beach. The night became the morning in a flash. Leilani was disappointed to have to leave. Everything was lovely. Evan packed up most of the belongings handing some of the bags to Mark as the couples headed for their rooms to rest a bit more.

"We have three more days here." Leilani told Amber handing the soft blanket back to Amber when they reached the hotel.

"I know a lot of vivacity things that we can do while you guys are here if you want to hang out more."

"I would really like that Amber. I enjoyed last night."

"I will call you in a few hours. I know you want some alone time with your man." Amber gave Leilani a knowingly haha. The ladies gave one another assurance to hook up later that day.

Evan opened the room door and felled on top of the bed. Leilani went straight for the bathroom turning on the Adam's ale.

Leilani wrapped her hair in a towel returning to the bed and getting under the covers. Evan was knocked out snoring in an outstretched position. Leilani opened her beverage and watched the rest of the movie she started from the prior day. By the time the movie was over Evan sat up rubbing his neck.

"Do you want to meet up with Mark and Amber when I get dressed?" Evan rubbed his sleepy eyes.

"Sounds like a good idea. Do you need me to get your clothes out?

"I would like that."

The hotel phone dinged. Leilani without doubt knowing it had to be Amber.

"Leilani you guys had enough me time? Mark and I were on our way over to take you guys out." Amber was on the other end of the hotel phone with loud background noises.

"Evan should be dressed by the time you two arrive." Leilani remade the bed.

"See you soon." Amber hung up.

Leilani styled her hair and put on light makeup ironing out Evan shirt and placing his pants on the bed. Evan had his toothbrush brushing his teeth picking up his clothes putting clothing on after another meticulously. Leilani walked back into the bathroom to finish getting primed putting her diamond earrings on that complimented her sexy outfit. Evan stood over the bathroom sink rinsing his mouth with mouthwash. Leilani exited the bathroom.

A knock on the door startled Leilani. She opened the door to see two cops at the door.

"How can I help you?" Leilani looked stunned.

"We are asking guests if they saw these two persons of interest yesterday." One of the officers showed Leilani a photo.

Leilani took the photo. The men did not look familiar. Leilani shook her head handing the officer back the photo.

"We have evidence that suggest the guy in the green shirt may be armed and dangerous. Please be careful and call the authorities if you see him on the beach or anywhere in the vicinity."

"I will, thank you officer." Leilani closed the door. A rush of chilled wind tussled her thin beach outfit.

"Who was that Leilani, Mark and Amber? I am coming out shortly. I am putting lotion on." Evan called from the bathroom.

"The police." Leilani answered back applying lip balm to her lips when another knock disrupted her conversation with Evan.

"The police." Evan walked out of the bathroom to see Mark and Amber staring at him.

"The police stopped by our place to tell us about an altercation from yesterday. I'm guessing the police came here." Mark shared his story about the police visit.

"The police left after showing me a photo of a guy in a green shirt. The police said the guy was armed and dangerous. I have never seen the guy before." Leilani pondered.

"Evan have you saw the guy since you been here?" Mark wondered.

"I was in the bathroom. I did not see the photo."

"I think I may have seen him before hanging out. Amber and I see a lot of faces coming and going. He looks familiar. I can't remember where I saw him though." Mark made a face.

"I don't think it was the two fighters we saw earlier Mark. I didn't see anyone brandish a weapon. Did you?"

"That's it. It could possibly be one of the fighters from yesterday. I hope no one gets hurt or killed. The bigger guy was very heated swinging madly. I thought for certain he was going to kill the other dude if we didn't break up the fight." Mark pictured the fight in his head.

"Someone from the beach staff must have reported the fight." Evan grabbed a sweater and the hotel key.

"The fight was intense. I saw the bigger guy pull out something in his tote bag running away after you guys broke up the fight. I cannot say for sure if it was a weapon. Should we report this to the police?"

"NO!" Mark, Amber, and Evan shouted at once.

Leilani looked up at the group. They all started laughing. Mark slapped hands with Evan.

"We are not getting involved in that. Next thing you know we will be held up for days if we report the fight."

"Come on you guys. Someone can get hurt." Leilani was concerned.

"That is not our problem Leilani." Evan pulled Leilani's body toward his and moved her hair away from her face.

"Trust me you do not want to have to go to the police station out here. Evan is right. We will eventually be treated like the suspects if we help out. That happens to everyone that tries to do their part. All of a sudden they are questioned about things that does not have anything to do with the suspects. I am not about to have my life turned upside down for stopping a fight." Mark unlocked the car door for Evan and got in the driver's seat. Leilani and Amber sat in the back.

Mark drove past tall palm trees, small shops, boat equipment shops, fishing shops, and fruit stands. People were milling through the streets buying up products. Mark stopped at a beige building with seafood printed on the front of the building.

"Evan you and Leilani eat salmon, fish, or lobster?"

"We like it all dude." Evan unhooked his seatbelt.

Good. You are going to be addicted to Sam's salmon spread and innovational drinks. He is the man out here. Amber and I frequent this place on a regular. You won't have any complaints." Mark led the two new guests into the seafood joint.

"Sam my pal, I have new visitors. I want the usual and bring out your best for our guests." Mark wrapped his jacket behind his chair.

"Drinks coming right up Mark. Hey Amber you looking good." Sam reached out and gave Amber a kiss on the cheek.

"Thanks Sam."

Amber directed Leilani into the area where her and Mark had sat and ate for years. Amber lived the life of fresh seafood and unsurpassed outlooks. People always packed the seafood joint. Mark and Amber table was always available for them. Thanks to their long-term friend Sam. Sam was a loyal friend that treated Mark and Amber like royalty. The big trips of out of sea fishing and favors to keep Sam's home repaired Mark and Amber did for Sam definitely didn't hurt the friendship.

Leilani slid in the soft cushion seat holding in high regards the festoon atmosphere. She was infatuated by the embellished conglomeration.

Evan visualized Leilani and him living on the island taking in eye catching artistic creations.

"Evan how long does you and Leilani have before you are out of college." Mark peeled the paper off his straw and stuck the straw in his drink.

"I have two years to go. Leilani has a year in a half to graduate. She started college before me. Leilani wants to become a doctor. I am going to be an attorney." Evan dipped chips into the salsa.

"Great career fields for you two." Amber applauded.

"Mark we have new friends that are going to become a doctor and an attorney. We lucked up." Amber rodomontade at Mark.

"I knew you guys were cool. I hate we met breaking up a fight. At least we were not a part of the fight. I would like for you and Leilani to stay in contact with me and Amber. Amber does tours in the area. The pay is decent. I am a builder. I build homes. The money has Amber and I living comfortably. We plan to take a few vacations soon. We may stop off to see you and Leilani."

"Mark you are always welcome. Let me know when you guys want to come where we are. We will make sure you and Amber have a memorable experience." Evan eyed the samples with satisfaction.

CHAPTER 29

ALEXIS LOOKED AT HER WATCH. She had not heard from the chief of police about the suspects that drugged her friend. Alexis was sure the chief would have called her before it was time to leave from work.

Amy had the radio on typing away at a report that needed immediate attention. Amy was addressing the graffiti on the owner's buildings. Amy wanted to post security outside of the buildings. The security officers will offer protection and an end to the graffiti for the business owners. The community will also be providing jobs for families by hiring a few security officers.

"Amy, how is everything coming along?"

"I have everything in order for the business owners. I sent out the emails. I have a few qualified security officers that can start tomorrow once the business owners sign the papers."

"You work fast. Marty got you on your toes."

"Marty is a big help. I love resolving issues you know that Alexis. I am a conflict resolution master that will not rest until a reasonable solution is met." Amy closed her laptop.

"Has anyone called you about Marshawn? I didn't receive any missed phone calls or voice messages." Alexis sat across from Amy.

"I was going to ask you about Marshawn. I didn't receive any word yet. Maybe we should call the chief for an update. I hope Marshawn okay. Those guys look like trouble."

Alexis's cell phone ranged with the chief name flashing across the phone screen.

"Speaking of the chief." Alexis put her phone up toward Amy for Amy to see the chief's name on her phone.

"Hello Alexis. I have bad news. One of the officers sent out to question the two suspects in question ended up in a battle with the two suspects. The suspects locked Marshawn in his office and got away before we could question them. You and Amy have to be very careful. I am sending patrol cars outside your work and homes for a couple of days until we apprehend the suspects."

"Chief you don't have to do that. I have body guards."

"I will not feel right if I did not have the patrol cars outside of your homes and job as a safety precaution for a few days. One of the suspects was armed and sounded very dangerous and angry."

"Oh my God. Was Marshawn harmed?"

"No, no, nothing like that. Marshawn was taken into his office by gun point after the police officer entered the building without my word spooking the suspects. The officer claimed he thought he heard someone scream. I do apologize for this getting out of hand. We did not know one of the suspects was armed."

"Did you get a chance to speak with Marty?" Alexis could not imagine what Marshawn was going through.

Marshawn was shaken up. He made a statement that the two suspects exited out of one of his office windows. His office was in disarray. Marshawn didn't seem too happy about the officer setting his two employees off. Alexis and Amy were going to have to make it up to Marshawn some kind of way.

"Thanks chief for calling me. I will let Amy know. Enjoy the rest of the day." Alexis hung up completely nerved about the outcome.

"Marshawn is going to be livid with us. I knew we should have gone with him." Amy sat up from her seat.

"The suspects can identify us. The suspects probably would have really pulled a gun if they saw us. Amy it is not anyone's fault. Marty's employees are to blame. They are the ones in the wrong. There would not have been anything that we could have done if we went to Marshawn's office today."

"I don't believe that Alexis. We could have made sure the two suspects were apprehended. The suspects are on the loose and can be headed our way. I have to let Marty know so he doesn't get ambushed." Amy sped dial Marty and told him about the confrontation at Marshawn's office. Amy hung up the phone attempting to be brave.

"Don't worry Amy. Everything will work itself out. It is not like we don't have backup. We will catch the guys who did this to my friend's friend and you. We have to be patient."

"Alexis I don't know how dangerous these guys are and what they are capable of. What if they go after Marty? If the suspects pulled a gun out in front of the police that means they are crazy. Marshawn said he never heard a bad word about them." Amy fidgeted.

"Marshawn did not hear anything about his employees because people were afraid to come forward. It does not sound like Marshawn's employees leave witnesses. We know how to protect ourselves. More than likely the suspects are out of this city. I doubt if the guys are going to hang around knowing that the police are looking for them."

"You are right Alexis. I hope they did leave. I don't want to be in the news for a shootout with two crazy nutcases."

"I know the feeling. Let's put that behind us for now. We need to go over the checklist for the complaints we received. I have the majority of the names on the lists forwarded to the right team to assist them. You completed the graffiti concern. I have to contact the court director. We are

almost finished with the complaints. Shall we call it a day and head home."
Alexis wanted to submerge in her bathroom tub then relax in her jacuzzi.

"I can't concentrate after the chief's call. We should resume tomorrow
after taking a break. Hopefully my positive state of mind will come back."
Amy folded her papers and tucked the papers neatly in her desk drawer.

"I agree. You want to come over and get in the jacuzzi? You are tensed
Amy. We are in this together. Nothing is going to happen to you if I can
help it." Alexis took her friend in her arms leaving the building emotional.

CHAPTER 30

Marshawn's friend Ace pulled up with five armed men entering the building. Marshawn welcomed the men in his office and locked the office door shut behind him. Marshwan pointed to the camera showing Ace the guys in full view.

"How do you want me to handle this Marshawn. I brought silencers." Ace opened the gun case.

"How do you think we should handle them Ace. My office is hot because this one pulled out a gun." Marshawn pointed to Maurice on the camera.

"If we shoot them my cleanup crew could have the office cleaned in no less than a couple of hours. It is up to you."

"Maurice is a hot head. Jess knows too much. They are both trying to make me go down with them. That is why they are in my hidden room. I tried to reason with Maurice to let the police question him. Maurice and Jess were not in any real trouble until Maurice pulled out a weapon."

Ace listened adjusting his silencer. The other five guys stood around the office blocking the front entrance of the door prepared to go to war.

"Do they know you called me?" Ace looked at the camera again to see how he was going to get the guys out of the secret room before they could pull a weapon.

"No. I told them to lay low until the police left. We could wait until they fall asleep and rush them. That way Maurice and Jess don't have time to grab a weapon.

"That's the best way to handle this. If you let them leave and they get caught, the police might end up finding out about your secret stash."

"I can move all of my ammunition and guns once we drop them off somewhere. If they tell on me, the police won't have any evidence."

"It is your call Marshawn. I am here to assist you if you want to have my cleaners get rid of Maurice and Jess permanently. I cannot tell you whether or not they are going to tell on you. I don't know the cats. I can say that either way you have to make a decision quick. We don't want the police coming back to find them or the ammunition and weapons. You are going to be looking at a lot of jail time. Harboring suspects, arsenal banned, and we all know the district attorney gets off on adding all kinds of additional charges." Ace walked toward the secret hideout ready to do whatever Marshawn requested.

"Damn I had no idea I would have to deal with something like this from these two. They were my boys. I never heard a peek out of them. I guess I am left without any choice. Ace we are going to have to get rid of them so my business is not closed. I cannot afford to lose my business over two hot heads. I worked too hard."

"I hear you Marshawn. I wouldn't hesitate to fight for mines. Did they bring the police to your office?" Ace placed his silencer next to the chair by the silver button.

"I am not sure how it all went down. Maurice and Jess said two women came in here asking questions. He told me he did not know what they were talking about. Next thing I know the mayor and her colleague was telling me that the police was involved. Somehow, the women believed Maurice and Jess had some affiliations with drugs in my building. I was asked to meet Maurice and Jesse by the chief of police and the mayor at my office to have the police escort Maurice and Jesse out the building for questioning. The mayor stated Maurice and Jesse kidnapped her colleague in the building. Alexis had Amy tell me everything at her office. Amy ended up getting away by a client that came to my building. Un-freaking believable, these guys are going to have me in deep trouble if I don't get rid of them."

"Kidnapping and drugs?"

"Kidnapping and drugs. I haven't heard of Maurice or Jess in kidnapping or any drug dealings in the building until now. My secretary would have let me know."

"Marshawn you might have to go ahead and chalk these two up to the game. The police are going to associate your business with the kidnapping and drugs too. You will never see the light of day if Maurice or Jess talks. I don't know what to tell you. I don't see keeping them alive working out for you."

Marshawn sat at his office desk contemplating the choices. If he killed Maurice and Jess and hid the bodies long enough, the police would think they two men fled the country. If he allowed them to live the police might catch them and the aftermath can fall back on Marshawn. Marshawn rewound his security footage to hear the conversing back and forth between Maurice and Jess. Marshawn turned up the volume so the cleaners could hear what the two employees were saying behind Marshawn's back.

Ace listened quietly nodding his head at Marshawn. After the cleaners heard the two employees talking Marshawn sighed in relief.

"That's what's up Marshawn. Maurice and Jess thinks you are going to rat them out. I don't think you need to worry about them telling on you. Let's drop them off where they need to go. I will drive my vehicle to the back of the building and let you know when to send them out." Ace and the cleaners headed toward the front door office.

"For sho. They will be coming out once you have the car ready to pick them up." Marshawn led the men out the office and walked over to the secret hideout button to let Maurice and Jess out.

"What the hell took you so long?!" Maurice rushed out the secret room impatiently.

"You got me in this situation. I had to make a few phone calls to get you guys out of here without anyone noticing. My patna going to meet ya'll in the back of the building. Do not stop for any reason. Let him know where you both are going. He will drop ya'll off no problem."

"I knew you weren't turning us in Marshawn. We owe you." Jess gave Marshawn a pound and grabbed his bag.

Marshawn received a notification to send the guys out the building. Marshawn shook his head astounded by what had transpired. The mere fact that he was about to have to kill people he knew was taking a toll on him.

"What's good homie?" Maurice jumped in the SUV shaking hands with Ace.

"Nothing to it folks, where do you guys want to go?" Ace put the SUV in drive.

Jess gave Ace the address. Ace floored the chromed out SUV. Ace cleaner's following him in an unmarked car.

Maurice and Jess ran to the hookup without another word to Ace. Jess had a few friends about to leave the city and Maurice and Jess were going to be hidden cargo so no one could identify them.

CHAPTER 31

"I AM BEAT MATTHEW. I AM ready to go back to our rooms and catch some zzzz's. We can liven this party back up tomorrow." Marg gave Matthew the signal.

"We are right behind you Marg. "Astelle, Henry, Michael, and Stephanie gathered their jackets.

"I haven't had that much recreation in a long time. We have to do that again before you guys leave Henry. Call us tomorrow once you all recuperate." Michael and Stephanie said their goodbyes.

Henry was physically restrained holding on to Astelle. Astelle held on to Henry tagging alongside Marg who was in full energy pacing toward the car waiting for them.

"Marg slow down." Astelle took Henry jacket and Henry got in the car first.

"You women got every bone in my body aching. I knew not too try to hang with yoga veterans and old school runners."

Astelle and Marg chuckled at Henry as he tried to scoot over for the ladies.

"Old timer you are going to have to carry muscle relaxers to hang with us. I'm used to the pain." Matthew got in the car feeling alive.

"I have to give you your credit Matthew. You a tough cookie, I haven't danced that much in years. What in the hell was them young folks doing?" Henry hung his head back on the car seat.

"All of the new dances. The younger crowd comes up with new jigs for that social media mess. It's an entertaining extravaganza." Marg answered.

"The guy in the gray and black stripe pants had moves. He was more flexible than me. I do yoga. I didn't feel comfortable doing some of those moves. What are the younger folks on?! He was bouncing and standing on top of his head and twisting his legs. I thought a bone was going to pop." Astelle made a dancing gesture.

"That's the new generation. They are born differently. He was not going to pop anything. He was in top condition not missing a step with his group. They performed with grace and style. I enjoyed the talent." Matthew accompanied dancers kindred to that group during his night life days.

The car felled silent on the ride back to the room. Henry zoned out for a second. Astelle nudged him to stay awake. Marg checked her voice messages. Matthew stared out the car window thinking about how he used to be the life of the party.

"We here folks, get your butts out. Henry, do I need to carry you to your room?" Matthew poked fun at Henry.

"You might." Henry slowly stepped his legs out of the car.

The mosey to the room stretched Henry's bones. He began to unwind on the elevator. Astelle held back tears of sniggering. Henry was going to spend their vacation in the room. Astelle knew she was going to have to leave Henry there for recovery.

"What's so funny Astelle?"

"Don't act like that darling. I told you, you did not have to take the trip with me. You insisted. You know you have a few meetings when we get back. You are not going to be able to attend every meeting."

"I'm fine woman. I'm about to soak in some lukewarm water. The lukewarm water helps my soreness. I will be brand new by the time work rolls around."

"If you say so." Astelle followed her husband to the bathroom to change clothes. Astelle and Henry made out like forbidden lovers with Henry grimacing from dancing all night making Astelle giggle every time he moaned. Astelle directed her husband to the bubbling water.

"Henry we can't fall asleep. Let's get in the bed in about thirty minutes. That's enough time for you to stop aching."

Henry nodded in agreement feeling relaxed after making love to his wife. Astelle knew Henry was going to fall asleep if she did not make sure they were out of the water after thirty minutes. Astelle cell phone buzzed.

"Astelle did you happen to see my necklace in the car? I seem to have misplaced the damn thing." Marg sounded restless.

"We can check the car in the morning. I am sure if it is in the car the necklace is safe. Are you sure that is where you last saw the necklace?"

"I don't recall where I last saw the necklace. I am not sure if I last saw the necklace in the club or in the car. The necklace has sentimental value to me. It was my great grandmother's necklace. I never take the necklace off. I don't know how I lost the necklace. Astelle I am freaking out."

"I understand Marg. I have a few jewelry pieces from my grandmother. I will be livid if I lost the jewelry. If it soothes you I know Michael knows the club owner just in case the necklace was found in the club. I will make sure to ask Michael to look out for the necklace. I know the necklace is going to turn up. Try to get some sleep Marg."

Marg hung up bothered by the thought of not having her grandmother's necklace around her neck. Marg used the necklace as a good luck charm. The night was going to be stricken with grief for Marg. She was completely aghast.

Henry heard his wife conversation feeling badly for Marg. Marg loved that necklace.

"Marg is going to be up all night."

"Henry I don't know what else to do besides to wait until morning to contact Michael. I don't think he is up. If Michael is awake, I'm sure his hands are full with Stephanie."

"Did you see the two of them on the dance floor? The heat was hotter than the young performers. I thought Michael might explode. There are going to be fireworks wherever they are at tonight?" Henry put his towel around him and stepped out of the water.

Astelle landed in the bed falling on top of her pillow.

"The night catching up with you."

Astelle barely nodded closing her eyes and not moving. Henry watched his wife for a second before turning off the night lamp. Henry sat up in the bed thinking about what a great life he had. He was very satisfied with what his marriage meant to him. He wanted to hug Astelle. He decided not to wake her up and settled down next to her.

CHAPTER 32

A MY WOKE UP IN A cold sweat. The nightmare felt so real that Amy walked to the kitchen to get a glass of water to catch her breath. The cool air brushed against Amy hair. Amy rinsed out a glass and guzzled down some faucet water wiping her mouth with the back of her hand. Amy sat down on the kitchen stool thinking about Marty. Marty did not want Amy spending the night outside of their place. Amy had to ensure Marty that she would be fine at least three times before Marty finally agreed.

"Marty are you up?" Amy heard silence on the other end of the phone.

"Are you alright baby?" Marty shot up out of his sleep frantic.

"I didn't mean to jolt you out your sleep. I couldn't sleep. I had a nightmare. It was the worse dream since the incident."

"That is normal after something so unreal. I am having a difficult time breaking down the scenario myself. Do you want me to come pick you up?"

I'm going to go to work with Alexis. I left my car at the job. You can meet me at work around 8:30."

"You want me to bring you breakfast and your favorite frappuccino? I can pick breakfast up on the way to your job."

"I will really appreciate that honey. I do not want Alexis to go through all the trouble of cooking breakfast. I have a lot of complaints to attend to on my desk. I received a few online complaints. I am gong to return some calls to the families that emailed me. I will be booked until the end of the day. I know you have a few things on your plate. If you like you can swing back by the office when you have free time."

"I would love to do that. I will not be able to concentrate without you by my side until we know these fools are off the streets."

"Marty be careful."

"I keep my gun right next to me at all times. I am more alert than usual. I have friends that are my eyes and ears. I'm ready for anything. Don't you worry about me. I wasn't always a business man. I know the streets."

"I'm sorry that I had to drag you into this drama. I know our jobs can be demanding of us. So many people want us to solve their problems. We never have enough time for our own problems."

"This catastrophe will extinguish nothing more than an obstacle that we will pass together. Our jobs come with the territory of calamity."

"My frappuccino is my therapeutic liquid. I have to have a frappuccino at least three days out of the week."

"I will be waiting for you with your liquid drug."

"Thanks Marty. You sure know how to make a woman feel wanted. I miss you so much. I cannot wait to get home tonight to wrap you in my arms."

"When you talk like that. I can get more stuff you like." Marty loved when Amy wrapped him in her arms.

Amy perked up hoping the day sped fast like regular days. Amy needed to be with her man and get some sleep.

Amy hung up the phone exiting the kitchen to do her early morning yoga before work in the guest room.

"I was about to come looking for you. I know it was a rough night. I brought my mat that I have not used for years to do yoga with you." Alexis squeezed Amy.

"Well if I can get you to do yoga with me. I might have to get into some beefs a little more often."

"You better not. Tomorrow I'm back to my own work out." Alexis rolled out her yoga mat.

"Part time friend." Amy tittered getting in her yoga position.

Alexis and Amy exercised simultaneously to the soft beat of Amy's exercising music list. Alexis body was flexible and adjusted to the yoga moves superbly. Amy was swayed by the precision.

"You rocked like a natural Alexis. You covertly do yoga when I am not around."

"I do not." Alexis folded her mat.

"We have to make this a one or two day métier."

"Don't start using those big words on me Amy, breakfast in the kitchen in twenty."

"Marty is going to meet me at the office. I am having a frappuccino moment. My nerves are all over the place."

"Nothing wrong with that, I will be down in a sec. I can feel my abs burning from the stretches." Alexis disappeared up the stairs.

Amy poured another glass of faucet water before getting ready for work. The yoga put her back in a superior state of mind.

The ladies left out the door in high and positive energy to tackle the community obligations.

Marty was munching on a breakfast croissant with a cup of iced orange juice. Amy sashayed over to Marty's car getting in and kissing him seductively on the lips. Marty handed Amy her breakfast and took another bite of the mouthwatering croissant.

"Babe you jazzed up. I know you said you were having a hard time sleeping. It doesn't show. You executed your early morning yoga, huh."

"Yep, I got Alexis to do yoga with me. She completed yoga rigorously with little attempt."

"Way to go under stress. I'm glad you were able to shake that dream and spring into action."

"I have no choice because I have too much on my desk to stay in a rut. You know your woman a soldier."

"I salute you. I will be saluting you tonight." Marty stole a kiss.

"Slow down bad boy. Mama has to get to work. I will see you in a jiffy."

Marty fixedly gawked at Amy in bewilderment. Amy transformed into a warrior before his eyes. Marty thought he was running to rescue a damsel in distress. Amy was fresh faced, glamorously groomed, and taking charge. Marty worries were put on hold. He felt more acceptable to leaving Amy for a while to handle his business. Marty drove off wonderstruck.

Alexis turned on her computer typing up letters and checking the responses to her emails. Alexis had to check on Anthony's politics class to see how the class was working out. Amy stopped by Alexis's office before getting on the phone.

"Amy I was about to call Anthony about the politics class. You are going to be dandy without me."

"Yes ma'am. I will survive." Amy made her way toward her office.

CHAPTER 33

MAURICE AND JESS WAS WRAPPED in some plastic and boxes and placed on an airplane next to cargo with Jess friend's hook up on their way out of the country. Maurice made contact with his homies before their business arrangements. Jess wasn't too happy to be leaving the city but knew it was the best way to stay out of jail. Maurice was more discomposed about The airplane prepared for takeoff.

"How long is the flight Jess?"

"Don't think about the flight Maurice."

Jess closed his eyes fantasizing about his lady where they were going. Jess knew the trip would not be a big disappointment. Jess was not staying out of town for a couple of months though. The vacation was untimely and unplanned.

The turbulence made Maurice greasy. Maurice had to get the two snitches out of his mind and stay focused on the mission at hand. Jess and Maurice were meeting some dangerous homies that Maurice did not trust. Jess and Maurice were close friends for years. Maurice did not trust anyone. Maurice did not have time to get a crew to fly. Jess didn't know if they were being followed or if Marshawn was setting them up. Jess panicked and wanted to leave the minute Maurice was off the call with his boys. Jess had to rearrange his shipment and meet his homies some kind of way without the authorities finding out. Maurice was not too familiar with the routes where Jess was taking him. Maurice had too much to lose. Maurice fretted about in anguish. The air bubbles was itching his nose.

Jess daydreamed the history of him and his ex. They continued the friendship and promised to revisit the relationship in a few years. Jess was working on himself and getting his money together. His ex Marlene was working as an executive producer in movies and was doing well all over the World. Marlene was in Hawaii working on a romantic piece for the movie she was producing. The Bahamas would have to wait. Marlene invited Jess to come spend a few days with her. Jess did not tell Marlene that he was in big trouble. Marlene couldn't wait to rekindle the romance and stayed single. Jess had a lot of making up to do. His finances had triple folded. He could afford to spoil Marlene if he chose. Jess was shocked Marlene was not married or had children. She was a beautiful woman with everything a man desired.

The plane ride finally ended with Jess in a trance, thinking about Marlene's gorgeous smile.

"Jess you alright in there."

Jess's boys met them at the back of the plane unwrapped them and was moving around cargo and plastic as quickly as possible. Maurice leaped out prancing toward the exit like a curious kid. Maurice wanted to check out the island to see if he knew anyone there. Maurice always found someone he knew since he was well known.

"Jess what's the plan?"

"My girl picking us up, she should be in the front."

"I am starving dude. We have to get food. I haven't eaten since yesterday."

"When you are in a rush and in fear of your life you forget to eat."

Marlene flew out of her fancy ride hugging Jess. Jess introduced Marlene to Maurice. They hopped in Marlene's ride and sped off.

"I have someone I know you will like Maurice. She was fussing about being bored out here. Maybe you can occupy her time while I get this movie scene out the way. My girl driving me crazy, you would think she would take full advantage of an island and place this picturesque."

"I don't see why not. I would love to meet your friend. What is her name?" Maurice tilted back taking in the background.

"Mystic. She's a knockout. Guys are nonstop approaching her since we arrived. Mystic hasn't taken interested in anyone so far."

"Do you think I should put my bid in? She's all over the place with her feelings wanting to be left alone. I cannot have my girl not having the time of her life. It will make me feel poorly. I have been ripping and running. We have had to redo scenes. My makeup running and I'm all over the place directing scenes. I am glad you guys touched down. I need a break. My assistant can handle the whole shooting match while I take in the islands."

"Where she at?" Maurice lightened up.

"We on our way to Mystic then we can grab some cocktails. There are so many nice spots out here. I love it. I have a great seafood spot that will not disappoint."

"I'm down." Maurice was in need of female company.

Mystic was fumbling with the phone charger cord and rumbling through her purse for some lipstick. Mystic had been in a bad mood all morning. She was not feeling the islands and wanted to go back home. The movie scene was taking a toll on her and she was tired of people arguing and making a big deal out of every small thing.

Mystic looked up to see Marlene pulling up and dashed toward the car.

"Marlene I'm ready to." In mid sentence, Mystic stopped her complaint peering inside the automobile.

"Hello pretty lady, my name Maurice. Can I take you out for some good food and conversation to make your day better?" Maurice drove right into come-hither manner.

"Who the hell are you?" Mystic eyelashes batted with irritation.

"My bad, my name is Maurice. I am Jess's patna. We were about to grab something to eat. Marlene mentioned you."

Mystic hesitated lugubrious getting in the back seat with Maurice.

"I don't mean to be rude. I'm having one of those days." Mystic extended her hand out to Maurice. "Nice to meet you."

Mystic fastened her seat belt checking out Maurice from head to toe.

"Where are you from?" Mystic sat Maurice glasses to the side.

"Here and there." Maurice checked out Mystic body frame.

"What about you?"

"All over too. I travel a lot. I guess wherever I go is my home temporarily." Mystic popped a mint in her mouth offering Maurice some.

"I like that. A woman that is worldly."

"I guess you can say that." Mystic took her mints back from Maurice.

"Where are we headed Marlene?"

"Seafood spot you adore."

"Good. My mood has been up and down all day. I don't know what is going on with me."

"I can help you with your mood if you want." Maurice offered.

"I doubt that. Don't get too comfortable like you know me." Mystic turned her face toward the window on her side.

Maurice felt stupefy. The ladies always flocked to him. Maurice figured maybe he was losing his touch. Maybe after Mystic ate she would feel better. Maurice expressed an apology.

CHAPTER 34

ANTHONY WAS COMPLETING A FOLLOW up about the shootout at Alexis's favorite café when Alexis phoned in.

"Hey Alexis I was going to shoot you an email about the shooting at the café. The business owner has security set up. I have a full class going strong on politics strategies. The students are sharp. The class filled up to the point I had to buy more chairs. I didn't know I was working with a bunch of nerds. The students explained every detail and resolution for most of the complaints that we received. The students and I have been knocking the complaints out in my class. The students wanted to help resolve the problems and answer some of the emails with me. The complaints were finished two hours ago. I was emailing you the resolutions to get your final say."

"I appreciate you taking care of that long list. The list was going to have Amy and I in the office late tonight if you guys did not help out. I'm sure you and the students did a great job. You can send me over what you guys came up with. I will read through the complaints resolutions after I finish with the courts."

"Was that the reason you were calling me?"

"Yes. I wanted to see if the class was successful or if we needed to do something else."

"The class is a huge achievement Alexis."

"That's what I wanted to hear. We can keep the class going. I think it is very important to teach all the new staff that we hire about what politics is about to stay on top of building the community."

"The students are very interested. The students are reaching out to people in the community to see what else they can do to make sure families are supported."

"I will talk to you at the end of the week." Alexis hung up calling Amy to tell her she could rip up the list. Amy was put at ease and turned her computer off.

"Great. I can look over the resolutions."

"Okay." Alexis forwarded the email to Amy.

Alexis hasten to Charley's office to ask about Leilani well being. Alexis knew the vacation for two weeks would have Evan and Leilani breezy by the time they returned. Evan told Charley he was going to marry Leilani before he graduated college. Leilani was unaware of the marriage proposal that Charley picked out rings for when they returned from vacation.

"Charley where is Evan and Leilani?"

"They have a few more days in Hawaii." Leilani said she would contact me when they are leaving."

"Anthony finished the complaint list. You can scratch off the café. The business owners are hiring security officers. The jobs are helping families with additional incomes."

"Stupendous. I have a few volunteers to clean up the graffiti. Some of the owners are going to hire Artists to paint murals to attract more customers for their business." Charley marked the list checking off all the complaints.

"Murals do attract people. I saw graphic murals on the building of the guy that we had the complaint about with the drug given to my friend. Do you know there ended up being a police stand off? The two suspects fled."

"My gosh, I did not have any idea. Did anyone get hurt?"

"Charley the two suspects held Marshawn at gun point. Marshawn was locked in his office with the suspects for a long period of time before the suspects escaped out of one of the office windows. The suspects are still at large. I do not know why they did not want to be questioned to get it over with. There is an ABP alert out for their arrest."

"Strange. Maybe the suspects are the ones that gave your friend's friend the drug that landed her in the hospital."

"The way the suspects are reacting, they could be guilty. We won't know until the suspects are found."

"I'm glad you told me. I have to make sure to let the other staff know. I am going to call Evan and Leilani and send them the photo. You never know."

"I forgot about that. We should inform the other staff. We wouldn't want anyone else hauled in this impropriety." Alexis forward her email alert to the staff and other people that may know the suspects. Charley added other people to the emails to make sure no one was left out of the loop.

"We are done for the day. A pronto morning." Charley pressed Kimberly's number leaving out of his office with Alexis.

Amy flagged Alexis and Charley down handing them both the resolutions that Anthony emailed over that Amy printed out. They left the building exhilarated.

Marty was bopping his head to music when Alexis, Amy, and Charley reached the parking lot. Marty got out the car to acknowledge Alexis's presence and gave Charley a handshake.

"Long time no see Marty." Charley and Marty dapped.

"Marty you making sure Amy shielded huh?" Alexis smiled at her long time friend.

"You know me. I cannot let anything happen to none of you guys. We are family. Have you heard anything about those two imbeciles?"

"Not yet. I will make sure I let you guys know if I do."

"Where are ya'll about to go?"

"We are out for the day. Anthony and his students handled all the complaints on the list. Alexis and I concluded the security for the owner's building. Charley finished up another complaint we had."

"You all maintain a cool little amalgamate going strong I see. That's what's up. I came right on time. I thought I was going to have to stay for hours. I brought food and everything."

"Food?" Charley peeped in the bag.

Marty smiled broadly. Amy opened up one of the dishes and tasted an egg roll.

"I was going to sit in the car and wait on Kimberly. We should go back in and eat. Don't waste good food, people are starving." Charley helped Marty with one of the bags as Amy broke into a laugh.

"I'm hungry." Alexis strutted back toward the City Hall building.

Marty shook his head at his friends. They could never turn down good food. Amy held the door for everyone as the group piled in the building.

"Marty I heard you were going to open up another girls and boys club in the community with swimming lessons and instruments lessons."

"I am Charley. I am also working with a business partner to open up a basketball team to help high school kids get into the NBA. We have already succeeded in getting a lot of us our own businesses with trustworthy employees."

"Phenomenal. The parents are going to praise your kindness verily. Sports are a magnificent contribution for parents that are fighting to keep their kids out of trouble."

"I aim to please. I used to want all those programs growing up. I was blessed to have people help me. I want to help others. I feel like we can all benefit from helping the communities thrive."

"Charley is going to be helping college kids with the trading school programs." Amy panegyrized Charley.

"My man, Charley you are stepping up in the World."

"I provide a lot of preeminent blessings. The reward is to witness the programs progress throughout the community."

"Same here, I believe we will reap the rewards by watching our youth rise." Marty gave Charley another pound.

The bunch proceeded to Alexis's office plunging into the chairs and desks available.

"Marty the food is palatable. Thank you!" Charley sampled the lobster cake.

CHAPTER 35

A STELLE OPENED HER EYES TO Henry's strong arms draped around her in the sleeping position the way they first were when they fell asleep on their first date. Astelle loved her husband. He was awesome in every way and so overprotective of Astelle. Astelle didn't want to wake Henry so she carefully removed his arm to freshen up and take advantage of the deluxe coffee and tea maker on the table to rejuvenate. Astelle tiptoed in the bathroom and turned on the shower stepping into the shower sprays. Astelle let the waterfall drenched her for a few minutes. The water woke Astelle up instantly with the steaming morning tea brewing. Astelle retrieved a towel sauntering back in the room where Henry was esconced changing positions awaken from Astelle's movements.

"Hey sweetness. You left me. I wanted to grind on you." Henry made a sad face at his wife.

"I wouldn't dare wake up an old soul." Astelle enjoyed getting Henry fired up.

"You know you are wrong. I am not that old. You have to admit I did hang the entire time and stayed on the dance floor until we left the club."

"You did. I give you credit for not falling asleep in the club."

"Thank you. Can I have some of that steaming hot mixture I smell?"

"You can my dear."

"What are you watching?"

"I haven't seen much that caught my attention. You want to see what's good on? I revived myself under the cascade."

Astelle flicked through the networks pausing when she saw two male suspect's faces. The broadcast claimed the two men held their boss at gunpoint in his office. The police had to bust into the office. The suspects were at large for getting away through an office window.

Astelle left the TV on and went to join her husband in the shower. Henry was whistling and singing a tune when Astelle slipped off her towel and hugged her husband from behind taking the soap to wash him down. Henry body welcomed Astelle and the two made love under the water.

"Henry I think your buddies were on the news." Astelle dried her husband off.

"What do you mean honey?"

"Two suspects images captured in the office of a building that looks very familiar. I think the story has something to do with the mayor's office where Charley works if I am not mistaken. When you get some time and we are back home call Charley and make sure everything is okay."

"I will. You think the news will run the story again?"

"I left the news on the same channel. We can see."

Henry and Astelle dressed waiting to hear the story again. The hotel room phone lit up. Henry answered his face never leaving the TV screen.

"What are you two up there doing? Ya'll better not be being freaky." Matthew's silliness making him chuckle some.

"Man what do you want?" Henry playfully poked fun at Matthew.

"Marg and I were coming to your room. Is the fine couple appropriately covered?"

"Yes we are."

"I would inform the Mrs." Matthew advised Henry ending the conversation.

Astelle and Henry lotion one another putting on comfortable clothes that reflected appealing taste.

"Babe did you pack my brown shoes?"

"Your brown shoes are in my carry on bag Astelle. I forgot to put them in the suitcase when we were leaving."

Astelle brown glam heels sparkled when she slipped them on. Henry was rubbing his head with moisturizer when Matthew knocked on the door. Astelle embraced her friends at the door moving to the side to let Marg and Matthew in.

"Matthew and I had hot coffee. We can use one more cup." Marg poured coffee for her and Matthew.

"Drink as much coffee, and tea as you want. I have a little something something in the refrigerator if you want some." Henry pointed Matthew to the refrigerator.

Matthew walked over to the refrigerator. Matthew poured a little of the brown liquid in his coffee.

"What's on the agenda for today?" Marg helped Astelle with her hair.

"Wherever you guys want to go I'm down." Astelle added some holding spray to her front curls.

Michael and Stephanie were all over one another in the room. Michael couldn't keep his hands off Stephanie. Finally Stephanie and Michael cooled down. Michael dialed Henry number.

Henry answered telling Michael to come to their room so they could figure out where they were going. Michael and Stephanie tidied up to meet their friends.

Matthew played card games at the table with Astelle waiting for Michael and Stephanie to arrive. The newly wed behaving duo floated into the room rapturously in a heavenly aura. Stephanie kissed Astelle on the cheek taking a seat to get in the card game. Michael pounded fists with Henry and Matthew.

"We all stayed in later than usual. Stephanie and I had to rehydrate our bodies after that long night of dancing. Let's try something less physical today. How about we go on a boat ride and check out the city." Michael suggested.

"Yes we should take a boat ride." Marg was onboard.

The gang agreed to go boat riding after a few games of cards. Astelle was whooping Matthew behind. Matthew desperately tried to catch up but to no avail was Matthew able to pull the right cards. The card game ended with Astelle leaving Matthew behind by two hundred and some points. The winner had to get to five hundred points to win.

"Pure luck Astelle. A rematch before we leave this room." Matthew moved to the seat over for Stephanie and Astelle to start a new game. Marg made a face at Matthew being a sore loser. Henry patted Astelle's shoulder proudly as Astelle shuffled the cards. Stephanie made herself comfortable and counted her cards once Astelle dealt the cards out to Stephanie. Michael and Henry sparked a conversation about the two suspects at large.

"Astelle was flipping through the channels when the story went live. I'm going to get in touch with my folks Charley once we are back in town. I hope the suspects are caught by then."

"Stephanie and I heard the very last of the news on the suspects as we were leaving out the door. We saw their faces brought up on the screen before turning off the TV. Those guys are dangerous. I wonder how they were able to get a job working in an office with patients being taught rehabilitation." Michael was confused.

"There are companies that hire people with past records or if the applicants qualify without much questions unless the applicants do something wrong on the job. People have been getting second chances to help their parents, and other family members and friends with bills and wipe their past records clean. I support the second chance programs. It has been a big success rate. There will be a few employees that go back to their old ways. We cannot fault the ones who done well for themselves through the second chance programs. I have a few guys working for me that had records early on in their lives. The brothers are dedicated and have managed to do a great job in my business. I am glad I gave the men a second chance." Henry knew he was doing a good deed.

"Michael it is a risk. I know you take chances. I feel like people do learn from their mistakes and do better when they are not in the same toxic environment. I was able to survive in a very negative environment. It depends on the person." Matthew remembered being judged throughout his success negatively by people who did not know him.

"If you are determined to be someone in your life you can beat all odds. There are so many people hoping that the ones that were secretly voted to not succeed do not make it in life. I hate that there are people like that out there." Stephanie was picked on in school by mean girls saying she was going to marry rich so that she did not have to work.

"Michael I want you to get involved with me and my mixed family that works with Henry. We are demanding that the courts staff that allowed all of the people that were not represented to be taxed and garnished or held liable. We have to stand firm on no representation no taxation. We cannot let that slide through the system. There are thousands of people that have back taxes coming back during tax season and unlawful garnishments from people that they worked for or received a loan. The victims were promised jobs after schooling and other promises that the debt collectors did not fulfilled. The victims should not have to pay for a lie and a waste of time taking years of their lives away from their families. The state and federal government has never been forced to accept that reality of the victims being promised jobs and other promises. The state and the federal government are garnishing the victim's checks." Astelle was reading her cards as she spoke to Michael.

"We have a bunch of robotic companies with employers that comes up with any excuse not to use their resources to protect their own employees. The employees that works long hours for the companies in question compensation should not be withheld for accusations that are not the employees fault. The employees earned the employers to fight with them and their families instead of excuses after excuses. We have to fight against the companies being set up in our communities taken advantage of employees and taking so much money out of their checks." Michael tone disappointed at the constant harassment.

"Henry and I used our legal team to give back to numerous employees that was not being represented by their union representatives solely on race. The racists groups have to be removed from most of the companies. They are providing too many hardships when the business owners allow other races to be treated unfairly and take away the jobs from decent workers. We are demanding that the union representatives are removed from their positions when they only represent specific people. The chosen employees not having any experience in communication to take jobs away from people that are more qualified is absurd. Most people know training is completed no matter if you went to school or not. We have to balance out the families that want to work. We do not force people to not speak English to work in our communities." Michael research findings were upsetting.

"There are too many long-term idiots destroying the reputation of unions. We have to make sure all races of families have the representation in the workforce against cocky groups that take advantage of other people. People working without unions are being sexually harassed. It is best we nip their companies in the bud with large amounts of damages. We cannot keep allowing arrogant abusers to attack the families that are working to do right." Stephanie added slapping a card on the table.

"Astelle I am all in with a few contacts when you get back to town. I have a strong legal team that can go up against any company stopping this form of discrimination from happening over and over again." Michael welcomed the challenge.

"I will be ready on Monday. I have written down all of the companies that took advantage of employees. The cultures practiced on the work sites are discriminatory. We have to draw the line on the culture beliefs gaining

273

access to businesses to wipe out a lot of people based on culture beliefs that disrespect women." Astelle knew she would defeat the overbearing men.

Henry and Michael cheered Astelle on. Matthew kept an eye on the card game for his turn again.

"I have to say I am disheartened how we come so far to witness abusers try to make a come back every time we wipe the abusers out. All of the different nationalities engender a lot of egotistical warfare in the workplace. I am repulsed by their macho ignorance that keeps us having to fight so much. We cannot rest because of their reckless and minatory actions to protest when they are overstepping their extremities. Every time we resolve a conflict fairly. We have to fight another deceptive and prejudice group that wants trouble for being called out for their dissimulation." Matthew picked up his phone to check the time accidentally leaving his watch in his room.

"I am tired of selfish pricks getting into business in our communities. If people know that they do not have what it takes to operate a business maturely why waste everyone's time embarking on a business in the community affecting the community's growth." Henry hated having to address irritating topics.

"The ones committing the crimes against women and certain races are people with money that do not know what to do with themselves. They have been a problem in everything. That is why we have so many protesters. The arrogant ones need to learn how to conduct themselves when it comes to business. It will make our jobs so much easier."

"Matthew, I have piles and piles of complaints on my desk about bosses who have committed something sadistic to an employee. What a disgrace to have to tell grown men how to conduct themselves in the work place. I have hundreds of sexual violations on employers. Some of the men are truly jerks and need some guidance."

"Marg I hate that you have to deal with that. The women are pushed in the workplace. It is not fair to their families to waste their time fighting off perverted men. We all have so much that we have to do than to stop what we have been achieving to address this kind of sick behavior." Astelle won a book adding to her other books collected.

"It takes a team like ours to keep up the fight. If we do not protect the people in our communities going through the tragedies, no one else will." Michael was fully aware of the long-term abuse of power by some of the men who Michael despised in the work place.

Astelle, Henry, Matthew, Marg, Michael, and Stephanie played cards for a couple of hours. The pack ended the card game when Astelle won again beating Matthew by almost two hundred and fifty points. Matthew bowed down gracefully. Astelle was the best card player in the group.

CHAPTER 36

LEILANI AND EVAN HAD A penchant for Amber and Mark's entourage. The family environment at the restaurant made Leilani miss her family back home. Evan ordered extra oysters. Leilani and Amber talked about what it was liked where Leilani and Evan lived.

"I grew up here on the islands. People tell me how fortunate I am to been raised in such a tropical and magical place. I am tired of being here. Mark and I have outgrown this place. We want to have a family in a regular city with city folks and big schools. I want my children to experience the city college life."

"Amber I am the opposite of what you vision as a mom. I would have enjoyed growing up here. It is so homey. The population is not overpopulated. You guys heal one another. There are so many attractions and everyone knows one another. I would want my children in this kind of habitat."

"I don't like that everyone knows everyone. I would love some privacy. In crowded cities Mark and I can have some privacy and not have to worry about everyone trying to tell us what to do."

"That happens no matter where you go. Once you meet people they love to give advice whether you ask for advice or not. That's just how people are."

"Mark and I are well known around here. We feel claustrophobic. It is not a secret that the people that work at the beach know that Mark and I sleep over at the beach from time to time." Amber smirked.

"The beach is so clean and spectacular. I could sleep at the beach every night. I don't think I could ever get tired of sleeping at the beach."

"You say that now. You will get used to the affinity after a while. I will be visiting you and Evan to see where Mark and I are going to move. Mark and I plan to get out of here as soon as we can. We have saved enough money to purchase a home and find suitable jobs. Mark wants his own business. He feels like he will earn more money in the city."

"You two have it all figured out. As long as that is what you guys want I do not know why there would be any katzenjammer. You and Mark are grown. No one can stop either of you."

"Thanks for listening Leilani. Mark and I have had to listen to so many people try to convince us to stay to launch our business here. I think some of the people on the island do not believe in us. It makes Mark and I really want to leave."

"You and Mark do not have to prove anything to anyone."

"I'm ready to leave all this behind us and work on our future." Amber caught sight of a popular figure that visits the island frequently.

"Hey Marlene. How are you doing?" Amber beckoned Marlene and her friends.

Marlene wended her way over to the table given Amber some love.

"I am doing fittingly. I was chopping it up with my home girl Leilani. I'm thinking about moving to the city."

"Amber you are not going anywhere. Every time I see you and Mark you say that." Marlene responded back.

"Hey Mr. Big I want the quotidian. I have three ravenous friends with me. Can you bring out a pitcher of your fruity potion?"

"Whatever you want Marlene coming up."

Marlene motioned her friends over to where Leilani, Evan, and Mark were sitting.

"Sit down wherever you like. I ordered the food. Amber this is Jess and Maurice. You met Mystic."

Everyone acquainted themselves settling back down in their seats after the introductions. Evan and Mark explored the ups and downs of Mark leaving his homeland to venture off into another World completely different from his upbringing. Mark wanted to leave with Leilani and Evan. Mark was telling Evan about his plans. Evan gave Mark some pointers.

The restaurant door opened again. A guy with a mean look on his face approached the counter. After he ordered he seated himself down behind Evan and the rest of the couples. Mark tapped Evan.

"Don't look back yet but I think that is the guy that the police came to our room about sitting at the back table."

Evan waited a few minutes before he turned toward the guy to not make anything noticeable.

"Is that the guy we stopped in that fight on the beach?"

"He looks like the guy."

"What is he doing in here?" Evan body tensed a bit.

"I don't know. He looks upset."

The door to the restaurant opened again and three guys strolled in. The men looking guy straightened up immediately and pulled out a weapon. Evan and Mark saw the gun first.

"Oh shit. This guy is crazy." Mark turned toward the commotion.

"Put down the gun and fight me like a man." One of the guys yelled.

"You are the one that brought your buddies with you coward." The guy with the gun pointed.

"Man, we didn't come in here for you. We came here to eat."

The mean looking guy cocked the gun and shot up in the air.

"If you are not out of here when I count to three, these bullets are going in your chest."

The three guys tailed out the door in a jiffy not to catch a bullet.

The mean looking guy flopped back down, the shooting of the gun in the air not fazing him. The restaurant felled silent.

Maurice and Jess mugged the guy up and down. Maurice felt for his gun on his side. Jess reached for his gun on his backside. Both of the guys were ready to shoot the mean looking guy if he made any sudden movements.

Evan held Leilani and Mark scooted next to Amber.

"I think it is time for us to go." Mark whispered to Amber.

"How are we going to get out of here with this lunatic right by the door?"

"He is not going to say anything to us. We don't have anything to do with his beef with the three guys."

"I say we wait a few minutes and let everything cool down." Leilani felt uncomfortable.

Maurice and Jess kept their cool shooting the breeze with Marlene and Mystic not to set the mean guy off. Maurice was ready to shoot if the guy turned toward them with any deportment. The host came out with trays of food. Three waiters set food down at Mark and Evan's table and then on Marlene and her friend's table.

One of the waiters was hesitant to ask the mean guy for his order. He walked toward the guy slowly. The guy seemed to have forgotten what he was upset about and ordered his food.

"This guy is totally insane." Mark side eyed the mean guy after the host took his order.

"Ready to go?" Amber wrapped up their food.

"I am ready." Leilani helped Amber with the food.

Amber was about to stand up when the three guys rushed back in the restaurant rushing the mean guy before he could pull his weapon back out.

The three guys dragged him out of the seat and was kicking and hitting the guy as he felled to the ground.

Maurice and Jess pulled out their guns screaming for the three guys to stop. The three guys halted and stood looking at the mean guy covering his face.

"Ya'll cannot be doing all that in here! This is a family establishment." Mystic outraged attitude adamant.

"Sorry that you guys had to witness that but this guy keeps starting fights with my patna. He behaves like something is wrong with him. We couldn't let him get away. He hit my boy in the back of the head earlier. We did not know he was going to be in here."

"Your boy keeps popping his jaws thinking he's hard core. I told him to stop coming at me like that. He started the fight at the beach. I was playing volleyball with a few people. Your boy came over and ripped our net for no reason."

"I told you that's my girl, you kept flirting knowing that I was standing there."

"She said ya'll was not together. You mad at the wrong person."

"I don't care what she said. I told you man to man that she was my woman and we were arguing. You were trying to play me in front of her and sucka punched me."

"I asked you not to step in my space."

Maurice and Jess listened to the beef standing in between the guys.

Leilani and Evan received emails from Alexis of photos of two suspects.

"What the hell is going on?"

"You read your email Leilani." Evan exchanged the email with Leilani looking at Maurice and Jess.

"We need to get out of here."

"Those are the two guys that held Marshawn at gun point."

"Who is Marshawn?"

"Some guy Alexis and Amy were questioning about their friend's friend being drugged."

Maurice and Jess overheard Evan talking and turned toward Leilani.

"Do you guys have a problem?" Maurice pointed the gun towards Amber and Mark table.

"What are you talking about dude?" Mark on the defense stood up.

"I am not talking to you. I am talking to him and her." Maurice looked at Evan and Leilani.

Evan pushed Leilani behind him ready to fight in her honor.

"I don't know what you are talking about. I will appreciate it if you lower your gun. You are making my girl uncomfortable."

"Let me see your phone?" Maurice barked at Evan.

"I am not letting you see nothing. I suggest you walk away." Evan anger was getting the best of him.

Maurice and Jess stood in the middle of the three guys and the mean guy. The three guys eased out of the door. One of the guys was opening the door to leave. Someone else was on the outside of the door turning the doorknob.

Numerous police officers raided the restaurant grabbing the three guys, the mean guy, Maurice, and Jess. The police snatched the guns and placed handcuffs on all the guys.

Evan and Leilani read their emails from Alexis saying that the two suspects were armed and dangerous and to be careful.

Evan walked over to the police showing him the email. The police read the email and grabbed Maurice and Jess quickly marching them out of the restaurant.

Leilani emailed Alexis back telling her that the two suspects were apprehended.

Alexis dialed Leilani's phone number hurriedly concerned.

"Are you guys with the suspects?" Alexis's voice trembled. Amy was next to Alexis worried.

"We were. The police took the suspects into custody. Evan gave the police your email."

"Thank God you guys were not hurt."

"They pulled guns on us when they overheard Evan and I reading your email."

"I'm so sorry Leilani. I don't know what I would have done if you two were hurt."

"We are fine. I will tell you all about it when I get back." Leilani assured Alexis she was okay once again before hanging up.

Mark and Amber made their decision to leave the island with Leilani and Evan when it was time for Leilani and Evan to board the airplane.

Printed in the United States
by Baker & Taylor Publisher Services